mixing up mayhem

heather nix

Paperback: 978-1-922936-55-4

First paperback edition October 2023.

Editing by Priscilla Rose

Cover art and Chapter Headings by Malu Bayona

Cover Layout by Eternal Geekery

Internal Formatting by Amber Palmer

Printed in the USA.

www.booksbynix.com

content warnings

This book is sweet and cozy, but does feature some kink. Please visit www.booksbynix.com/contentwarnings for a comprehensive list of potential triggers

contents

1
jackie

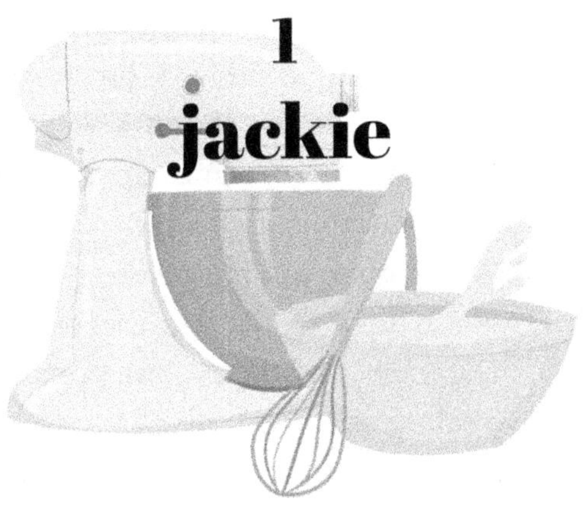

JACKIE MILLER HATED THE FERRY.

After a long night at the Bainbridge Alehouse, she stumbled up the ramp and slumped into a window seat. Her head ached. Celebrating her new job had sounded like a great idea at 6:00 p.m. on a Sunday, but now, at 7:30 a.m. on Monday morning, she had some regrets. Her girlfriend, Camille, was visiting family in San Francisco, so she had gone out with a small group from the kitchen at Saint Marte. Nearly every sous chef and prep cook at St. Marte was a twenty-something guy, and as a thirty-five year old woman, Jackie felt like she had to go twice as hard to keep up. She swallowed, pushing down the rising flood of last night's tequila and god knows what else. *You can't puke on the ferry, Jackie,* she told herself. Thankfully, the ride was fairly smooth, and as the ferry docked in Seattle, she pulled her sherpa-lined denim jacket tight and pulled her hood over her short, bright pink, hair—*suck it up, buttercup. It's time for work.*

Jackie never wanted to leave the staff of St. Marte, but opportunity came knocking and refusing its call would have been idiocy. Martin Valardi was a household name. When she had opened the email from Martin@CanidKitchen.com she had been absolutely sure that it was a prank.

"Jacqueline," the email had read, "I recently had the pleasure of presenting at the Northwest Culinary Association's annual summit in Fremont." *Yeah*, she thought, *I'm aware. I was there.* "The meal left much to be desired, but I was remarkably impressed by the dessert course. When I enquired as to the name of the chef, your name came up. I'll admit, I was surprised to discover that you are an older woman—" *Older?* "—but your skill is undeniable. I am aware of your employ at St. Marte, but I would love to discuss the possibility of you joining Canid as our new pâtissier. I am prepared to offer a highly competitive salary, and the type of exposure and experience that can only be found at a restaurant such as Canid. I await your reply."

She had stared at her laptop screen without moving for close to ten minutes. Sure, Martin was a notoriously pretentious douchebag, but he was also the most acclaimed chef and restaurateur on the West Coast. He was basically royalty—it was like getting an email from the fucking Queen of England.

He had won a well-known reality TV program a few years back, shocking everyone by beating out chefs with far more experience. Then, he had been barely twenty, and somehow managed to trounce the competition, taking home the half-million dollar cash prize, and a full year of mentorship. After he somehow managed to poach a master sommelier from an internationally acclaimed restaurant in Paris, he hired one of the most famous interior designers in the nation to bring his vision to life, and found a location capable of being converted from a hundred-year-old factory into a sixty-table dining room and impressively modern kitchen. A big-name investor saw Chef Martin's blueprints, backed the project, and Canid was born.

Jackie had immediately clicked out of her mail app and opened up Canid's website. She had never been, and her bank account would sooner finance a new Clydesdale than a trip to Canid. As she scrolled through the pages detailing the staff and inspiration, even she was impressed. It was a gorgeous restaurant. The dining room was airy and bright, despite being lined with rich, dark wood paneling. The light fixtures were brushed brass, supporting large glass globes which held cool-toned bulbs that gave the illusion of natural light, even in Seattle's gloom. Or, it could have been good photo editing. There were three long planters which ran the length of the dining room, overflowing with lush foliage that looked to be a combination of plants native to the Pacific Northwest, herbs, and some large-leafed tropicals to give height to the arrangements. The tables had apparently been made from locally-sourced reclaimed wood, and the art which adorned the walls had been painted by a local mixed-media artist. Jackie had spent a few minutes looking through her instagram before turning back to the laptop. Even the fucking chairs looked luxurious—mid-century modern Scandinavian style chairs that the website bragged were modeled after Ib Kofod-Larsen designs, but made from sustainably-harvested wood and handwoven textiles. It was annoyingly stunning, somehow feeling classic and timeless while also giving a vibe of effortless modern chic.

Is this some sort of fever dream? Jackie thought. *Or am I really going to work here?*

Canid had defied all the odds and risen to fame within its first year. Much to the astonishment of the Seattle culinary scene, Canid garnered the attention of the mysterious Michelin star inspectors shortly thereafter, becoming the only Michelin guide acknowledged restaurant in the state. Then, two years ago, Canid received its first star, fully cementing Martin Valardi as both the most envied and most hated chef in the Pacific Northwest. Martin fucking Valardi had taken his place at the top of the Seattle food chain, and of all the pastry chefs in the country, he had set his sights on Jackie.

Her interview and stage had taken two days. In a move which surprised nobody, Chef Martin had given zero direction on how to prepare for her first day. She had arrived in her best fitting black chef coat and a new pair of non-slip Doc Martens, and was greeted by a station filled with fresh produce, unique flours, and the most upscale equipment she had ever encountered in a restaurant kitchen. He asked her to "impress him," and so she had done her best. The plated dessert she had prepared had been fucking inspired, if she said so herself. A fluffy nest of spun sugar sat atop a caramelized bed of pandan-scented banana. Tucked within the delicate nest was a trio of miniscule white-chocolate-encased coconut sponge spheres. Quenelles of thai tea infused gelato, crisped ube rice and the tiniest leaves of micro thai basil had surrounded the adorable little nest, and a molded chocolate sparrow filled with layers of pandan-coconut sticky rice and mango mousse sat beside it, like a darling, edible mama bird watching over her sweet, little eggs. It was the most detailed thing Jackie had ever made, and she was still petrified that it wouldn't be good enough.

Chef Martin had tasted each element in silence, thoughtfully chewing each mouthful before moving onto the next. Jackie thought she would have a fucking heart attack, standing with her hands clasped behind her back, watching his thin frame take tiny spoonful after tiny spoonful. He hadn't spoken for what seemed like an hour, but finally had looked her way and simply clapped.

"Asian-fusion is clearly not the vibe of Canid, and I trust you will incorporate our vision of local sustainability into your future offerings, but this is superb. If you are interested, the position is yours," he had said, looking smarmy as all hell. And she was—interested, that is. He had offered her a starting salary of six figures. It took every ounce of her high school theatre training to resist jumping up and down and clapping like a schoolgirl. Six figures? She could finally move out of her shitty little apartment in Capitol Hill. Hell, she could finally ask Camille to marry her. This was a once in a lifetime opportunity, and it had landed squarely in her lap, on her skill alone. Things were finally looking up for Jackie Miller, and her love for the staff at St. Marte was not going to hold her back.

But today, as she nearly stumbled into the doors of Canid for her first official day of employment, she thought that maybe, just maybe, she might puke on Chef Martin's shiny little shoes.

MARTIN VALARDI IS A FUCKING ASSHOLE.

Jackie had been at work for three hours of her ten-hour day, and she already wanted to hang him by his toenails. Despite the gleaming kitchen and spectacular team he had assembled for her, it was clear that Chef Martin felt some sort of way about having a woman ten years his senior as his pastry chef. Generally, Jackie didn't have to deal with male fuckery. She was very obviously a lesbian, and men seemed to see her as less of a threat, but Chef Martin apparently considered her to be on par with one of his little boy lackeys, or, worse, to be invisible. He made condescending comments within her earshot about the female servers, any women who walked by the floor to ceiling plate-glass windows, and even the poor girl who had the misfortune to deliver the farm order. The boys in the kitchen ate it up, elbowing one another and sniggering. Chef Martin would never be crass, but he facilitated an environment where toxic masculinity was the norm. The only female employees at Canid were waitstaff, and it was very apparent that Jackie had not been what anyone had been expecting.

She felt intensely uncomfortable in the open, airy kitchen, huddling close to her station and speaking only when absolutely necessary. The kid who had been hired as her assistant was a quiet, gangly little wisp with a tidy mustache named Everest. He had come from another well-known restaurant in Seattle, and had started a few weeks ago, training to work under Jackie and temporarily taking the place of the previous pastry team. He was clearly nobody's favorite, was visibly queer, and his relationship with the other guys seemed strained at best. She'd done what she could to make him feel welcome, but she was also a little fish in a big pond, and the boys' club mentality wasn't doing either of them any favors.

When it was time to break for lunch, the chef de cuisine, Andrew, called everyone over to help themselves to a plate of the current day's entrée special. Jackie was late to the table, busy making certain her station was spotless, so she missed the full rundown of what it contained. She grabbed a plate of some sort of braised meat atop what looked like tostones, and shoveled it into her mouth quickly, not wanting to spend any more time than was absolutely necessary among the neckbeard squad. Goddamnit. She *hated* how good it was. Martin might be a world-class prick, but he was undeniably talented. It was spicy and savory, layers of flavor built upon one another with the perfect balance of salty, sweet and umami. Her big, blue eyes darted to the table to see if she could grab seconds, but it had already been cleared. Everest stood to the side, picking at a plate that appeared to just hold plantain.

"Not hungry?" she ventured, sidling up next to him, noticing that they were roughly the same height, which wasn't much.

Everest sighed before poking at one of the yellow disks with his fork. "I'm vegan. Andrew of course made sure that he put meat in every fucking component of the meal. He even cooked the vegetables in duck fat. God, they're all such assholes."

Jackie snorted, hiding her amusement beneath a hand. "You're not wrong," she replied, watching Andrew's head tip back in laughter, surrounded by a gaggle of young men who were obviously vying for his attention. "He seems like an asshole." Jackie considered making a comment about Chef Martin, and how far up his ass everyone seemed to be, but she didn't know Everest well yet, and she needed this job. And as much as she hated to admit it, he was brilliant. If anyone deserved the right to be kind of a dick, it was Martin Valardi.

Everest sighed, pushing his mousy brown hair back from his forehead. "I'm really glad they hired you. If I had to spend one more day alone in this cis-het hellscape I'd probably have hurled myself overboard from the ferry. I may be a guy, but goddamn, I'm so tired of hearing about tits and ass."

"Oh! You're a ferry rat?" Jackie said with a smile. "Where-abouts do you live?"

Everest rubbed the back of his neck. "Bremerton. I'm a navy brat. What a life."

"Ooof," Jackie let out a low whistle as she tried to dislodge something from between her teeth. "How the hell did you end up across the sound?"

"I went to school at Seattle Central," he replied. "Growing up in Kitsap was not the most welcoming for a baby gay, so I ran off to—" he made air quotes with the hand not currently holding his plate "—that dirty commie city. I'm still too broke to move out, but at least I can escape to Seattle most days. My partner lives in Fremont, and told me to apply here a few months back."

"That's cool," Jackie said, reaching for her stainless steel water bottle and chugging a few mouthfuls of too-cold water. "You wouldn't happen to have any Advil, would you?"

Everest laughed. "Actually, I do. Long night?" He reached into his coat pocket and pulled out a small bottle, shaking a few pills loose and passing them to Jackie.

"Had my goodbye party last night out on Bainbridge. My old boss may have been trying to sabotage me and keep me there, now that I think about it." She gave Everest a rueful smile as she swallowed the capsules. "I don't have any other explanation for the amount of tequila she bought me."

Three sharp claps rang out across the kitchen and everyone snapped to attention. "Four hours til service!" Martin drawled in his weaselly voice. "Let's make 'em count."

The guys all replied, "Yes, Chef," with such absolute brown-nosing enthusiasm that Jackie almost threw up again. She had tons of respect for the guy. He had made a name for himself in one of the most difficult culinary scenes in the US, and his food and following were undeniably impressive. But she was thirty-five years old and wasn't about to start groveling at the toes of a twenty-five-year-old's feet—no matter how fucking famous he was.

"A word?" Chef Martin said, gesturing towards Jackie.

She straightened her shoulders and walked over briskly. "Yes, Chef?"

"You look tired. If you can't give this job the respect it deserves, there are plenty of people chomping at the bit to take your place."

It's champing at the bit, you twat, she thought silently. But instead, she replied, "Yes, Chef. I am one-hundred percent in, and you won't be disappointed."

"Carry on," he said, waving a hand. "I look forward to seeing your work this evening."

"Yes, Chef," she responded in a carefully restrained tone. "It's an honor to be on the team."

She lifted her chin towards Everest as she turned to head back to her station. "I need that flat of strawberries hulled and sliced, and when you're finished, if you could get them macer-ating in that bourbon & bitters, I'd appreciate it!"

He nodded, tossing a towel over his shoulder and walking to the hand-washing sink. "No problem, Chef!" he replied with what sounded like genuine enthusiasm. *See,* she thought. *Speak to people like they're people and they're happier to do what you ask.*

Jackie could get used to this, she thought as she lit a burner to start tempering chocolate. Martin Valardi wasn't ever going to be her buddy, but she could get used to this.

2
jackie

THE CRACKED screen of Jackie's outdated phone flashed in time with its screeching alarm. The sound was so goddamn loud, she nearly fell out of bed. Bed? No, she apparently fell asleep on the couch. Her head pounded, and as she sat up in preparation to head to the cramped bathroom, she knocked over a wine glass with her still-booted foot. *Goddamnit.*

She reached down to right the glass, but the tip of her index finger found a sharp edge, and she cursed, pulling her hand back and popping the finger into her mouth. She shook her head, annoyed at every facet of this too-early fuckery. She didn't recall pouring a glass of wine, or sitting down on the couch, but the menu screen of her favorite comfort sitcom was still playing. The jaunty sax of the theme song played over and over, *way* too loud, and she spied the neck of an open bottle of merlot on the kitchen counter. Jackie flopped back onto the couch, messy pink head sinking into the velvet cushions, and prayed to whatever god was listening. *Please let there be coffee.*

Twenty minutes later, glass swept into the trash can, hair stuffed into a Canid baseball cap, and stainless steel tumbler full of coffee in-hand—Jackie and her newly bandaged finger made their way down the stairs of her apartment complex two at a time. Two days in a row, waking up hungover and almost late to the most important job she's ever landed? *What the fuck, Jax?* Without Camille here to act like the adultier adult, Jackie sucked ass at pretending to be a functional thirty-five year old.

Thank fuck they had found an apartment in Capitol Hill, much to Camille's dismay, and moved in after two years of dating. Their mutual friends had been shocked. Two years? That's basically a decade in lesbian years. They should have already had a dog and a pair of matching Subarus in the driveway. Instead, they had a grumpy old rescue cat named Mimolette, and Camille had a vintage Peugeot bicycle. Jackie rolled her eyes thinking about it as she ducked into her fifteen-year-old hatchback. Of course, Camille, with her blonde waves and tanned ballerina legs and annoying performative environmental activism, rode a bike. Which, naturally, meant that Jackie drove her everywhere, because for the most part Cam said it was too rainy to be safely biking anywhere. "It's one of the top ten most bike friendly cities in America!" Camille had exclaimed when she asked Jackie to move with her, and Jackie, of course, had smiled and patted her knee and thought about what type of donuts she would get in the morning. That was two years ago, and she still took Camille to work or picked her up at least twice a week. Camille was a brilliant woman, fun in bed, and a very kind person—but she was a bike-riding, carabiner and Tevas lesbian, and Jackie was craft cocktails and Docs. In so many ways they were wonderful together, but when the topic shifted to chlamydia ravaged koalas or the 5 counties with the greatest soil for recumbent oxygen farming or some shit, Jackie's interest was a runaway train, speeding far, far away from the topic at hand.

It took three tries to get her car started, and she glanced at the oil change reminder sticker on the windshield. *Only a year late*, she thought. She told herself she'd do it this weekend, but she knew that was bullshit the instant the thought crossed her mind. She winced as her car stereo began blasting KEXP. Turning down the radio, she chuckled thinking that she probably wouldn't do it until her dad called and yelled at her about it. He had taken impeccable care of the car before letting her buy it from him. She, on the other hand, was a fucking disaster.

She pulled into the underground parking at Canid with seven minutes to spare. The sky had begun to leak a misty, grey semblance of rain, and she thanked twenty-minutes-ago Jackie for having thrown on the hat. She grabbed her coat from where it hung in the backseat, the purple plastic hanger dangling precariously from the "oh shit, she's turning too fast" handle over the window. It was the grey, wet part of spring, but the trees in the distance were a lush emerald against the cement-colored sky. For all her bitching about the rain, Jackie loved Seattle. She loved the orcas that popped up in the sound, the stunning magnitude of Mt. Rainier in the distance, the way the cascades and the water seemed to frame this little metropolitan area in the midst of nature's majesty. She took a deep breath of air that was still cold enough to hide the urine scent of the city, and walked into Canid, ready for her second day.

SHE WAS NOT ready for her second day. Chef Martin was in a terrible mood, Everest seemed sad, Andrew was mansplaining how cornstarch worked, and the restaurant was fully booked for the 6:00 p.m., 8:00 p.m., and 10:00 p.m. seatings. Jackie had a to-do list as long as a drugstore receipt, and nowhere near enough hours or hands to get it all done. Fortunately, if there was one thing Jackie Miller was very, very good at, it was task management. She planned out the most efficient way to get through the absolutely necessary things on her list. She gave Everest very precise directions for the basic prep she needed. She conscripted another little kitchen boy who had been mindlessly cracking eggs—*too slowly*, she thought. And then she shut out the rest of the hustle and bustle of Canid, falling into a strange sort of meditative state.

Jackie was so focused on the work directly in front of her, that it took her a solid minute to realize that Chef Martin had been calling her name. She whirled, finding him tapping his little toe, arms crossed, exuding the thoroughly un-intimidating aura of a macaroni penguin. She brushed the flour from her apron and walked to him on quick feet. "Yes, Chef! Sorry, I was really in the zone, there."

"Your *zone*," he said, voice dripping with condescension, "is where I need you. Right now, I need you to get the Panmarino in the oven."

"Yes, Chef," she began. "I've got the afternoon plotted out so that everything is done at the exact time it needs to be! As soon as I get this custard divided and into the blast chiller, the Panmarino will be done proofing and will be ready to bake!" Honestly, she was proud to show off her meticulously planned tasks. She wanted Chef Martin to realize he had made a good choice in hiring her. But the second his thin upper lip curled, she knew she had fucked up.

"That," he said, "is not what I asked. I want the bread in the oven now. You can fuck around with custard later." He didn't give a rat's ass about efficiency. His focus was making sure she knew that he, Martin Valardi, was the executive chef of this restaurant. And she, Jackie Miller, was a washed up old spinster who should be lucky he had bestowed his great and thoroughly superior culinary mind upon her.

But Jackie hadn't risen from a bagel shop assistant in San Jose to head pastry chef at the most renowned restaurant in Seattle to be cowed that easily by a man fifty pounds smaller than her. So she reined in her expression, set her mouth in a determined and outwardly respectful smile, and nodded once. "Yes, Chef. I'll get it done."

It was not an easy day. Jackie limped out of Canid two hours later than she should have. She peeled the hat from her head, choosing to not look at the sweat-soaked pink mop beneath. The t-shirt under her chef coat was stuck to the small of her back and her fingers were stained on one hand, and pruny on the other from wearing a glove over her wineglass-sliced finger. So when her phone flashed Camille's face and started playing their song through its barely functional speakers, she considered letting it go to voicemail.

She loved Camille, even planned to propose once she got settled into her new salary at Canid, but currently she looked like hell, smelled like a barn, and needed a shower more than words could convey. However, picturing Camille's pale pink lips all twisted up in annoyance if she didn't answer, she stuck the phone in her car mount and swiped it open.

"Hey baby!" Jackie tried to sound chipper, despite her bone-weary exhaustion.

"Hello," Camille sounded pissed, and Jackie flinched at the icy greeting. "Do you have time to talk?"

"Um…." Jackie ran through her mental calendar, trying to sort out if she had missed some sort of important date or anniversary or if Mercury was in gatorade or something. "I'm driving home right now, but I can give you a call after I shower?" Camille didn't immediately respond, and Jackie's heart jumped into her throat. "Is everything okay, baby?"

"Yeah, uh… we just need to talk about some stuff," she replied. "That's fine, just don't be too late, I've got plans with Stella tonight."

Stella was her older sister, and the president and sole member of the "We hate Jackie" association. "Okay, I'll be quick," Jackie replied. "I'm fucking gross from work and I just really need to clean off before I touch any of the furniture."

She expected a laugh, a chuckle, even a little snort out of Camille's nose, but all she received was a flat, "Okay." And then, the call ended.

Jackie's brow furrowed in confusion. *What had she done?* She used one finger to flip through the online calendar she and Camille shared, but there was nothing. Camille had been in San Francisco for nearly a week, and other than the occasional photo or goodnight text, she pretty much hadn't heard from her. It wasn't terribly out of character; Camille wasn't a "technology person" outside of work, and unlike Jackie, who thrived on fighting with bigots in comments sections, Camille preferred to either talk on the phone, or simply wait until they saw one another to talk.

Her family lived in San Fran, and she visited them a couple times a year. Her mom, Yvette, was a pretty, nice lady. She worked as an art professor at SFSU and had once said that Jackie's career was "creative yet practical." Not exactly what she wanted for her daughter, but tolerable. The girls had all inherited her blonde hair and honey-colored eyes, and Yvette looked young enough to be mistaken for one of the sisters, rather than the matriarch. However, the Archer girls had all also inherited their father's olive skin which tanned into a burnished bronze in the sun, as well as his sharp, angular jaw and severe looking brows. Cam's sisters, Stella and Dominique, owned an upscale resale shop called "Once Bought, Twice Loved" in the Castro. They bought and sold designer clothes and handbags, and honestly, they did really well. They had quite a few celebrity clients, and had a very well-known online presence where they auctioned off some of the more expensive garments consigned to them. Yvette, Stella and Dom lived in a massive house in Telegraph Hill, paid off with the life insurance settlement that the late Mr. Archer had left behind when he passed. He was some sort of genius Silicon Valley developer, and died from a completely unexpected brain aneurysm ten years ago, shortly before Camille had graduated college. She had never come out to him, and Jackie knew it still hurt. So she spent a few months each year with her remaining family, making sure she soaked up all the family love she could.

Jackie pulled into her parking spot still lost in thought, replaying the short conversation in her mind. She thought about the fights she and Camille had gone through before, the argument they'd had when she dropped her off at the airport last week. Camille was mad that Jackie hadn't asked her opinion on taking the job at Canid. She thought it was "single woman behavior" and that Jackie should run "life changing decisions" by her. Jackie, on the other hand, thought that she was a fucking adult and if she wanted to take a way better job that paid her nearly twice as much, that was her decision to make. But she regretted arguing about it, and as she plodded up the stairs to her apartment, she rehearsed what she would say when she called Camille back.

Baby, I'm sorry. I know you just want us to be a team. I'm shitty at it, and I'll do better. I love you, and I can't wait for you to get home.

Yeah, she thought, *that'll be good.* Mimolette yowled at her as she opened the door, and she paused to shake some kibble into his bowl before kicking off her boots, pants, and repulsively moist socks, pulling her t-shirt over her head, and stepping into a shower that would have made a lobster scream.

Twenty minutes later, freshly scrubbed and dressed in her comfiest sweatpants, Jackie flopped onto the green velvet sofa and pulled up Camille's contact. The phone rang twice, and when Camille answered, Jackie was disappointed to hear the same chilly tone to her voice as before.

"Hey baby," she began. "I'm so—"

"Jackie," Camille interrupted. "Let me say what I need to say first. It's better for me to just get it all out in one go."

Jackie tried in vain to swallow the anxiety wrapping its arms around her throat. "Okay."

"We've been together for four years," she began. "And I feel like I've been really accommodating. I didn't care when you started at St. Marte, or stayed out til dawn drinking with your boss. I didn't get mad when you brought home a ten-year-old cat without asking me. And I didn't get mad when you bought your dad's car instead of fixing the Jeep. But I feel like it's always *me* making accommodations for *you*. You took this job without even asking me how I felt. And, like, I was annoyed, but Stella really got me thinking about all of it, and it's not one thing with you, Jackie, it's just you as a whole. You act impulsively and you don't care how it affects anyone else."

She paused for what felt like her first breath, and Jackie interjected, "I know baby, and I'm sorry. I know you wante—"

"I'm not done," Camille cut in. "I'm moving home."

Jackie sputtered, but she kept going.

"Mom is retiring next year, and she wants to spend more time with all of us. Once Bought is doing really well, and Stella and Dominique need a full-time social media manager. You can afford the apartment on your new salary, and I'm not going to take anything except my bedroom set and my clothes."

"Are you," Jackie choked out, "Dumping me over the fucking phone?"

"I guess. I know it's not ideal, and I'd have liked to have this discussion in person, but I'm not coming back to get my stuff. Cassie is going to pick it up and drive it down later this month."

"Cassie? The fucking barista?" Jackie's face heated and she sat up straight, bracing her forearms on her thighs. She'd asked Camille about her when she had started doing advertising for the coffee shop downtown. She *knew* that Camille had been attracted to her. She was Jackie, just younger and hotter and thinner. Camille certainly had a type.

"She's not a barista, Jackie. Don't be an asshole. She owns BeanBar, and they're thinking of opening a location in San Francisco, so she's going to help me out."

"Are you fucking her?" Jackie bit out. "Don't lie to me, Cam. Just tell me the truth. Are you fucking her?"

Camille's long pause and deep breath were all the confirmation Jackie needed.

"Go fuck yourself, Cam," she said. "Nice try, trying to put this shit on me, but this isn't about me, is it? It's about that barista's hot little ass and your inability to commit to anything in your goddamn life. I was going to fucking propose to you, and here you were on your back in a knockoff Starbucks. How very Seattleite of you."

Camille laughed, and the sound was cruel, devoid of any kindness whatsoever. "Actually," she said with a sneer Jackie could hear through the phone, "Cassie is the one on her back most of the time. You can keep the fucking cat. At least he can't leave you."

And then she hung up.

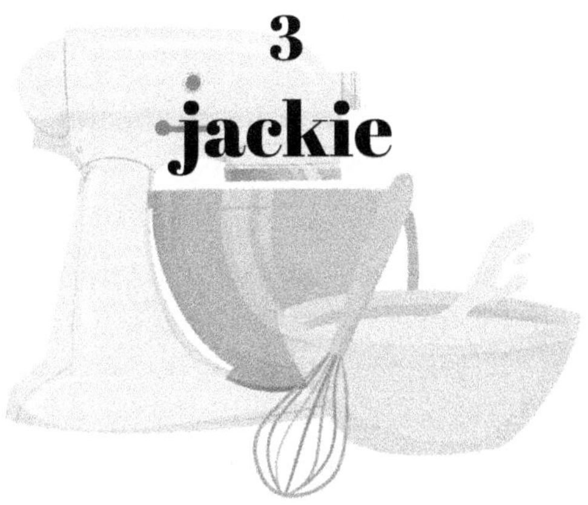

3
jackie

IT TOOK Jackie roughly forty-five seconds to go from angry to sobbing.

Mimolette jumped up on the sofa, butting his patchy orange head against her thigh as she cried. At some point she ventured to the kitchen to retrieve the open merlot from last night, not bothering with a glass, and simply taking swigs from the bottle like a goddamn pirate. Once her puffy eyes had run dry, and the wine had loosened the sadness clutching her heart, Jackie decided she was going to make herself feel better.

Camille hated chocolate, said it smelled like dirt, and so Jackie never wanted to bake her favorite cake in her own apartment. *Well, fuck her.* After tossing the empty wine bottle in the recycling, she rummaged around the sparsely stocked fridge, finding a bottle of pre-mixed margaritas, three eggs that were still within their date, a nearly empty carton of heavy cream, and half a stick of butter. Luckily, she had a pantry full of vacuum-sealed containers filled with everything she could possibly need for baking, so with her margarita in one hand, she set to gathering what she needed. Soon, the counters and floor were covered in a fine dusting of flour, an accidental spill of Dutch cocoa, a measuring cup dripping with the remnants of olive oil and melted butter, and way more bowls than were necessary. Her cut finger had soaked through its band-aid, and she grumbled as she teetered to the bathroom to find another.

The face that stared back at her from the smudgy mirror looked like a stranger. Her aqua eyes were red-rimmed and bloodshot and a smear of chocolate spread across her cheek, partially obscuring her freckles. She opened the medicine cabinet, and was glad to peer into the chaos of her pill bottles and single tube of mascara. She didn't want to look at that pink-haired woman anymore. She looked down at herself and sighed. *Maybe this is why she fucked a twenty-five year old barista.*

Jackie was confident. She knew she was hot, and made no apologies for it. But she also knew that she wasn't "conventionally" attractive. It had never really bothered her; she had no trouble dating gorgeous women. Camille had looked like a model, and every woman before Cam had been equally stunning, in different ways. They all loved her thick thighs and round ass, liked her tattoos and big, blue-green eyes, fawned over her plush lips and long eyelashes. But Jackie was thirty-five. Her tits weren't where they were ten years ago, she had a permanent line between her dark brows from making "what the fuck" faces at kitchen boys for fifteen years. Her pants fit tighter and her stomach felt rounder with each season that passed, and for the first time since she cut her hair and told her classmates she was gay, she felt self conscious.

No, she told herself. *Camille didn't cheat and then dump you because you're chubby. She's just a piece of shit with long legs and long hair and a mouth that's shaped like a heart and a pussy that tastes like...* She shook her head. *Nope, nope, nope.* She ripped open the band-aid wrapper with her teeth and spat the tiny bit of paper on the floor. *First, band-aid. Then, margaritas.* Thinking about Camille right now was not going to help anyone or anything.

The cake timer went off and Jackie jerked upright from where she had been just resting her eyes and definitely not sleeping at the kitchen table. The kitchen smelled delicious, all rich chocolate and quality butter. She pulled the cake pan from the oven and set it on the stove. With a shrug of her shoulders, she grabbed a fork and took a bite. If she didn't have to share, who gave a fuck if she ate it before it cooled? But just as quickly as her lips closed around the tines of the fork, she spit the cake out directly back in the pan. *Sugar*, Jackie thought. *You forgot the goddamn sugar.* She grabbed a towel and picked up the cake pan by the edge, slamming it against the rim of the trash can. The still-hot cake immediately melted a cake-sized hole through the bag and settled itself smugly in the bottom of the can. Jackie stood and stared at it for a few moments, blinking, and then lifted her foot from the little pedal, let the lid slowly fall shut, and walked right out of the kitchen. This was a problem for the Jackie of tomorrow.

It was only 8:30 p.m., and though her head swam with sugary tequila, Jackie wasn't wholly drunk. She sat in silence in the living room for a few minutes, thinking, and then made a decision. *Camille is not going to ruin my life*, she thought. *I will be the best goddamn pastry chef Martin Valardi has ever seen.* And with that thought, she dropped the half-full bottle of margaritas into the sink, turned off the lights, double-checked the oven, and set her alarm for 8:30 a.m. before falling face first into her bed, still covered in chocolate.

SHE WAS thirty-three minutes early for work. Jackie smiled as she looked at her phone screen, leaning her seat back a few inches so she could comfortably listen to music while she waited to walk in. She had doggedly refused to be sad this morning. Finding some scarily old concealer in the bottom of a drawer and smearing it under her eyes like war paint, she had looked into her own red-tinged eyes and told herself, *you're going to bake your fat ass off today, and not even Chef Martin is going to dull your shine.*

She kept that energy throughout her shift, whistling slightly as she worked, losing herself in the comfortable ease of the job. When they broke for lunch she made conversation with everyone, even Andrew, and then wandered over to Everest to eat.

"You're peppy today," he said as she stepped next to him, shoving a bite of chicken into her mouth.

"I got dumped last night," she replied.

"Fuck! Are you okay?" he asked, genuine concern lighting his eyes.

"I mean, I've been better, but I'm not going to let her ruin this for me. This job could be the most important move of my career, and losing her just means I have more energy to devote to work." She shrugged. "Plus, she cheated on me, so she can eat glass."

Everest nearly choked on his couscous. "Damn, well, my partner and I are headed out to a bar on the peninsula with live music tonight, you wanna come?"

Jackie thought about it for a moment, twisting a carrot around her fork. Did she want to be a third wheel? No. But she also didn't want to get drunk at home with Mimolette. She needed to get her booze habit under control, and she needed some friends that weren't Camille's. "Sure," she said after swallowing the really fucking tasty carrot. "I'm down."

"Awesome. Do you need to go home after work? Or do you want to just catch the ferry with me?"

She did a quick mental inventory of the clothes that littered her backseat. She'd make it work. "I'll ride with you! I just have to grab clothes from my car and change first."

Everest smiled. "Hell yes," he said. "I'm excited for you to meet Seven."

"Seven?"

"My partner," he replied. "Chosen names, you know." He winced, and she chuckled at his scrunched-up face.

Chef Martin clapped twice and their conversation was over. Jackie tied her apron back on and gathered with the rest of the staff. She found herself genuinely listening to Martin, interested in his briefing and not even thinking about Cam. When they all broke to head to their stations, Everest looked at the clock before turning her way. "Five hours!"

"Well, let's fucking go," Jackie replied. "Time flies when you're having fun, or whatever."

EVEREST STOOD OUT BACK, smoking a cigarette when Jackie emerged from the building, freshly changed into a pair of cuffed Levi's and a black tee with a leather jacket slung over her shoulders.

"You're going to freeze on the ferry," Everest said, flicking ash onto the damp pavement and straightening his dark green sweater. Jackie thought it looked like a vintage Pendleton. She hated that she knew that because of Cam's sister's shop.

"Nah," she replied. "Plus, I'm going to sit inside."

Everest shook his head. "No thanks. Not only does it smell like old coffee and armpit in there, but nighttime is my favorite time to ride the ferry."

"Why?" Jackie asked. "You can't even see the water."

"But I can see the stars," he replied. "Seattle is so bright, the only time I really get to enjoy the night sky is while I'm on the ferry."

"Cam, my ex, used to make me go camping. One summer we camped in the middle of the desert in California. There were no buildings for miles in any direction. The sky seemed so large," Jackie said, sounding a little wistful.

"I would love to do that," Everest sighed. "I've only been to California once, and we just went to the zoo. Maybe someday when I move out."

"It *sounds* nice," Jackie said, shuddering. "But did you know that scorpions glow under blacklight? We brought a blacklight to check our sleeping bag for scorpions, and I ended up spending the entire night shining it all around the tent. I counted twenty of them by morning."

"Okay, well, I take it back," Everest said, wide-eyed. "I'll skip that. Thanks for the nightmares."

They walked to the ferry terminal, boarding together and finding a spot to sit up top. Everest was right, Jackie was fucking freezing, but he was also right about the stars. She didn't remember the last time she just sat and looked at the sky. So much of her time was spent working or drinking that she had forgotten how it felt to just be still and sober. How many fuzzy-memory nights did she spend in a bar because Camille was in SF? Was she drinking because she wanted to, or because she *could*?

Camille and Jackie were very different people. Cam spent her free time picketing animal mistreatment or camping or calling bureaucrats to demand harsher restrictions on waste-water. It always bugged her, because in the same breath Cam shopped at fast fashion retailers and threw glass bottles in the garbage can. But Jackie never started shit over it, she never argued about wanting to see her friends when they visited instead of waking up early to drive Cam to and from work. She never complained when Cam demanded, suddenly, that Jackie was also not allowed to eat meat in her apartment anymore. (She put her boot down when it came to eggs and butter, but she went along with the meat.) She had always tried her best to do whatever made Camille happy, so it rankled that Cam had tried to pin this breakup on her. Yeah, she had gotten a cat and bought her dad's car, but neither of those things compared to the isolation that Jackie had felt when Camille had asked her to move to Seattle.

The ferry docked in Bremerton and Jackie had the strange sensation of having traveled in time, realizing she had thought about Camille for nearly the entire hour-long ride.

"You good?" Everest asked as she stood, stretching her tight shoulders and pushing her fingers through her hair.

"Yeah, just in my head a little," she replied, following him off the ferry.

An extremely tall and remarkably broad man with black hair and dark eyes stood in the parking lot beside a very, very small car. Jackie thought it would have looked ridiculous if Everest hadn't burst into a wide, radiant smile. He wore indigo jeans with yellow stitching, cowboy boots and a white tee with rolled up sleeves. He looked like an ad for a big and tall store in Texas. "Hello, handsome," Everest said as he wrapped his arms around the man's middle.

Seven kissed the top of Everest's head. "I sure did miss you," he said in a rich baritone.

Everest giggled. "It was ten hours. You didn't miss me that badly."

"Ten hours too many. Y'all ready?" He stuck out his hand toward Jackie. "Forgive him, his manners are shit. I'm Seven. It's nice to meet you, Everest has told me you're the best part of this job."

Jackie felt her cheeks go hot, and she shook his hand, grasping it firmly in hers. "I mean, working at a place like Canid is pretty fucking cool, if you ask me."

It was Everest's turn to blush. "You're right," he said, looking at Jackie sheepishly. "I am really honored to have been hired, and I love the job. It's just hard to be the little queer trans kid in the fine dining world."

Jackie's head tilted and her eyebrows shot up. Seven laughed, placing a hand on his round stomach. "See?" He pointed at Everest, a wide grin spreading over his round face. "You owe me five bucks." He looked back at Jackie. "He doesn't talk about it at work, safety, you know."

Jackie's brows drew together, but she fought back a smile. Seven's grin was contagious.

Everest and Seven shared a secret little grin. "He said you probably had no idea, and I said you had to know. Guess he won," Everest replied.

Jackie looked between them. "Good to know you were talking about me." She pantomimed flipping her hair over her shoulder.

Seven's arm draped across Everest's shoulder. "Let's get some beers."

THE BAR WAS as divey as they come, and Jackie absolutely loved it. The band playing in the corner was somewhere between alternative and bluegrass, and the lead singer was a thick redhead in a fringe-trimmed leather jacket. Seven and Everest made goo-goo eyes at each other over the small tabletop while Jackie sipped her beer and bobbed her head to the music. *Sipped.* She'd been here for two hours and still had the same drink; she couldn't remember the last time that happened. It felt good, she thought, to sit and laugh with other queer people and be sober enough to remember it. In-between songs they chatted and shared stories about growing up gay.

Seven was lucky, Jackie thought. He was massive, and despite spending his childhood in rural Montana, he was never bullied solely for the fact that he could beat the shit out of anyone who tried.

Jackie and Everest had a lot in common, they found. They both moved around a lot as kids, Everest's mom was in the Navy and Jackie's mom was a "free spirit" who didn't do well with commitment (or employment.) They both had a hard time fitting in, and were labeled "tomboys" from an early age. They both came out in middle school. But Everest had begun his transition on his eighteenth birthday, and had been on T for six years, whereas Jackie had cut her hair and declared her intentions to never touch a man. They both had ended up precisely where they wanted to be.

"So, you really had no idea?" Everest laughed, his words a little louder and a little more slurred together than they were four beers ago.

"Nope," Jackie replied between bites of mozzarella sticks. "I mean, it's also not something I really think about. You're clearly a dude."

Everest beamed. "You have no idea how validating that is to hear, even after all this time." He swiped a buffalo cauliflower "wing" from the appetizer platter sitting between them. "I've been living as a man for a quarter of my life now, but there are still days where I wake up and see childhood pictures and wonder which person people see when they look at me."

"That's fair," she replied. "But I hope you know that it doesn't matter in the slightest what other people think. It took me a long fucking time to really believe that, but it's incredibly freeing. Being a fat lesbian with colored hair has not always been easy." She laughed. "I'm a white cis woman, so it's not like I'm being wildly oppressed or anything, but I understand what it feels like to not fit in. You've just gotta find your people and say fuck the rest."

"I'll toast to that!" Seven said, raising his pint glass. His black hair fell into his eyes and Everest reached up and pushed it back, looking into his deep brown eyes with something akin to wonder.

"You two are disgusting," Jackie said, clinking her glass against theirs and setting it back down without drinking. "You're so in love it makes me sick." She laughed. "Didn't Everest tell you I got dumped last night?"

Seven's eves went wide for a second, and he sputtered. "I... I'm so so—"

"Kidding, kidding," Jackie said, holding up a hand. "I definitely got dumped, but I'm looking on the bright side. I'm beginning to realize that maybe my life will be better off this way."

Everest patted her hand, leaving a smear of buffalo sauce behind. "Speaking of, I'd better catch the ferry. I don't want to get stuck over here, and it's past 11:00 p.m."

"Do you need us to walk you back?" Seven asked. "It's dark, and this isn't exactly the safest area."

"You forget I live in Seattle," she said with a grin. "This is nothing. Plus, I've got pepper spray on my keychain." She held up her keys and jiggled them. "See? Safe."

"Thanks for coming out," Everest said, standing.

He hugged her, his sweater scratchy against her chest. Seven hugged her too, and she barely reached his armpits. As she walked out of the bar, sober, full and happy, she looked back at her new friends. The small man with a well-trimmed mustache and a green Pendleton, and the massive guy dressed like a cowboy were people she never would have been able to hang out with if Cam was here, and she couldn't help but feel a little tinge of guilt at the thought. She should be sad, but she was relieved. As she stepped out into the cold night, she took a deep breath. *This is what I've been missing.*

4
jackie

SATURDAY MORNING, Jackie woke up clear-headed and in a fantastic mood. She didn't have to be at Canid until 3:00 p.m., so she decided to do something she had never done in her two years living in Seattle. She threw on a hoodie and jeans, and walked to catch the light rail. After a short ride and a relaxed stroll, she turned a corner and smiled. "Public Market" in big red letters stood above the entrance to Pike Place market, already full of people and teeming with sounds and smells. She had been here a couple times, but she had never been by herself, and she had never had the luxury of wandering the market without Camille demanding they get what they needed and leave.

She didn't think she'd ever really feel like she belonged here, but she did love the city. Jackie had grown up in Southern California, moving north to San Jose after culinary school. She met Camille a few years later, and they got a small apartment in South Bay. She had worked at a bagel shop while she applied to decent restaurants, and had worked in a few nice kitchens scattered across the city, but San Fran hadn't felt like home either.

Here, the sky was grey most days, just like it had been there, but the people were a different breed. She shouldered past an eclectic assemblage of tourists and natives, watching the fish fly with a small laugh and checking out indie art and fresh produce. She had fried chicken and an enormous biscuit for an early lunch and then walked around aimlessly.

She smelled the shop before she spotted it. Strong incense and the warring scents of herbs caught her attention, and she turned in a slow circle, trying to find the source. The herb shop had an aged-looking photograph above the door, and when she walked in, row upon row of bottles stared back at her. The shop was surprisingly quiet, and it was disconcerting after the noise of the rest of Pike Place. It felt like someone had tossed a blanket over her ears. The woman behind the counter smiled at her in greeting and Jackie gave an awkward little wave. Oils and herbs and resins and tinctures of every kind filled the small space, and a sign advertised readings of various kinds. She must have looked lost, because the employee walked over to her, asking if she needed any help,

"I don't know," Jackie replied honestly. "I'm just wandering."

"You look like someone who has a lot on their mind," the woman replied.

"I guess you could say that," Jackie said with a shake of her head. "Any magical herbs or potions to get through a breakup?"

The woman put her hand on her chin thoughtfully. "Are you happy or sad? Want to get rid of bad energy or bring them back?"

A laugh burst out of Jackie before she could stop it. "I'm sorry," she said, pulling herself back together. "I don't want her back. Definitely some bad energy. Maybe opening some new horizons?"

The woman's eyes narrowed, and her mouth went to the

side. After a moment, she nodded, and walked behind the counter, gathering bottles and jars as she went. After a few minutes of shaking things into bags and pouring stuff into smaller bottles, she dropped a handful of items into a paper bag and grabbed a notepad from beside the cash register. She scribbled onto the yellow paper, folding it in half and dropping it into the bag when she was finished. "I wrote down some ideas and labeled the herbs and oils," she said. "Definitely do some googling before you start throwing things together, I don't want you to accidentally banish your dog to another dimension or something."

Jackie chuckled. "No dog, thankfully, but I'll let the cat know you were lookin' out for him." The woman didn't laugh, and Jackie cleared her throat. She held out her debit card and tried not to react when the total flashed on the screen. "Thanks for your help," she told the employee as she gathered her bag and slid her wallet back into her pocket.

"Of course," she replied. "Be careful."

And with that, Jackie and her sack of herbs walked out the door and back into the din of the market.

THE ABSOLUTE LAST thing Jackie Miller expected to see walking back to catch the light rail was the entire cast of a well-known anime. Even stranger, still, was the group of six-foot-tall men following behind dressed as rainbow colored ponies. She stood, flabbergasted, and watched them clip-cop all the way across the street, linking arms and laughing loudly as they walked into Pike Place. It took her a solid forty-five seconds to realize that it was March, and this meant Emerald City Comic-Con was in full swing. She had spent so much time at work lately, and had only gone out across the sound, so she hadn't seen any of the con-chaos until now.

It was midday, so it made sense that some of the attendees would be taking a break from panels and booths to see the city or grab a quick lunch. When they had moved here, Jackie had told Camille she wanted to go. Cam had wrinkled her nose and called it "a capitalist nightmare," and that was that. Jackie wouldn't call herself a "nerd" per-se, but she liked pop culture, and she *loved* people watching, so she had been looking forward to checking it out. *Holy shit,* Jackie thought. *Now I can.*

The light rail trip was another exercise in self reflection. Realizing all the things she had been blind to over the last four years had Jackie feeling unmoored. When she walked into Canid at 2:45 p.m., she felt like she was walking in a dream. Chef Martin was hunched over a notebook in the back, and when he noticed her, he waved her over with a flick of his wrist.

"Jackie," he said, "I'm glad you're early. I have a concept I think you may be able to execute."

She leaned down, looking at the notebook, and narrowed her eyes as she peered at the scribbles and doodles that covered the page. "Is that a bubble?" she asked.

"Of sorts. Do you have practice with sugar work? Blown sugar specifically?"

"Not since culinary school," she said, rubbing the back of her neck. "Which was a long time ago."

"Okay, well, I'm going to need you to figure it out," he replied. "I have reason to believe that someone from the Times is coming in next week, and I need him to be impressed."

Jackie reminded herself of her new commitment to being the best pastry chef that Martin Valardi had ever seen, and she straightened her shoulders. "What do you have in mind?"

At the end of the conversation, Jackie had packed a box of equipment on loan from Chef to practice his concept at home.

She had her own scribbled sketches, and she spent the small moments of free time throughout her shift pondering ways to make it work. She had to change her glove three times thanks to her sweaty hand and sliced finger. She wondered a few times if she should have gone to urgent care, but it hadn't seemed like a particularly deep cut. *This is why we aren't drinking anymore,* she thought. By the time she closed her front door behind her, she was grinning with excitement and nervous anticipation. It was close to midnight, but she felt like she had just drunk ten shots of espresso. She unpacked her box of scientific-looking equipment, tied on her apron, and got to work.

5
jackie

JACKIE FELL into bed at 2:30 a.m. with sticky fingers, smoky hair and a plan.

When she opened bleary eyes on Sunday morning, it took her only a few minutes to shake the sleep from her mind. It had taken her a long time to fall asleep, her thoughts had been racing more quickly than she could file them. She had tested out all the stuff she brought home, learning how everything worked, and re-familiarizing herself with tools she hadn't used since college. But she felt confident today, knowing she had a seriously plausible plan for making Chef Martin's frazzled sketches into something real and delicious. She set up her kitchen with all the gadgets she had brought home. Her kitchen looked like a laboratory and she chuckled at the dichotomy of her retro, pastel kitchen alongside all the stainless steel high-tech tools. She preheated her vintage oven, pulled out her mixer and got to work.

Her original plan had been to bake her cakes first, so when the rest was finished she could assemble it immediately, but she realized that she was doing something she had almost zero experience with, for the first time in a decade, so she decided to practice the tricky bits first. She switched on the tabletop heat lamp she borrowed from Canid, and pulled out a bag of isomalt. She melted it down, dumped it onto a silpat and made herself a cup of coffee while it cooled.

Her bandage was bloody again and she couldn't help but mutter, "What the fuck?" as she drank her coffee and changed the band-aid. The cut wasn't large, or deep, but it was in a high-movement spot on her finger, right beside the knuckle, so it kept splitting open instead of healing. If she could leave it uncovered, it would probably scab in a day, but working at Canid, she had to keep it covered, and that meant it was always sweaty and damp. She wrapped it in gauze and threw some medical tape over it, maybe the dry gauze would help. She put on a few pairs of gloves, not wanting to burn herself, and picked up the little puddle of isomalt.

Why hadn't she done this since school? Kneading the little ball of sweet goo was shockingly pleasant. It was like play-doh, but more fun. She set the ball beneath the heat lamp and reached for a little hand pump. It only took a few minutes to blow the isomalt into a sphere. It looked like a balloon, and she sliced it from the pump with one hand as she grabbed the smoke gun. She had loaded it with rosemary and a couple herbs she had picked up from the herb shop that had smelled good. It took a couple minutes, but she got the tube from the gun inside the sphere, and filled it with smoke. *Fucking sweet!* She thought when the smoke swirled inside the clear globe. She unceremoniously plopped it onto a plate and waited. Grabbing a small stainless steel mallet, she rapped the top once, and the isomalt shattered, leaving a jagged half dome and a rising, twirling plume of fragrant smoke. Jackie giggled maniacally.

Chef's concept had been an edible terrarium. Canid had a decidedly botanical vibe, and the image of a lush jungle beneath an edible dome had been brilliant. However, it was

Jackie's idea to use smoke that would elevate it to something truly special: a fully edible jungle scene, smoke curling amidst the leaves, atop a rich chocolate cake base, enrobed in luscious dark chocolate. She looked at her notebook, reaching into her fridge for the rest of what she needed, and started putting together the other elements. This time, she remembered sugar, and before long she was cutting discs from her sheet of cake, shaving curls of chocolate, painting edible chocolate rocks and setting sugar-dusted mint leaves to dry.

The cake was not her usual chocolate cake. She had, on a whim, used more of the herbs from the shop. She was pretty sure they were all edible—the ideas given to her by the cashier had included teas, but she didn't put too much thought into what she grabbed. If it smelled good, it went in. She had infused the butter for the cake rather than putting the herbs right into the batter, and it smelled fresh and green and luxurious. A hint of rosemary and a touch of cool mint rounded out the flavor, and she stole a nibble, groaning with pleasure as she let the taste spread across her tongue.

She gently placed a dark chocolate collar around the cake discs, sandwiching creamy frosting between them. It made a perfectly smooth little column, and as she carefully assembled the dark cookie crumble, sandy grains of crystallized dark chocolate, chocolate rocks and candied leaves, it began to come together. She added small purple amaranth greens and basil blooms for some color, and a few micro fennel sprigs. Goddamn, this was pretty. She *really* hoped the sugar dome was going to work. She did exactly the same thing she had done earlier, blowing the isomalt, but melted the sphere's base on a hot plate left beneath the heat lamp. She cheered aloud when she lifted a perfect dome from the plate, praying silently that she had gotten the diameter right.

Jackie paced the kitchen while the isomalt dome cooled. Sure, it was early in the day, and she could keep practicing, but she wanted this to work so badly. Her finger stung, and she pulled off the layers of gloves with a scowl. She tossed them in the trash, along with the gauze, and shook her hand back and forth as she walked, trying to make the sharp sting fade. Her phone buzzed on the counter, and her brow furrowed as she walked to grab it from the terrazzo tile. Cam's face stared up at her, and she dropped her hand to her side as she froze, suddenly unsure of everything.

WHEN JACKIE HAD MET CAMILLE, she was thirty, with blue hair and a lip ring. Camille was everything she wasn't: tall, graceful, dripping with confidence, with blonde hair that fell down her back and sharp honey-colored eyes that caught the light and looked like molten gold. Cam had been working as an intern at an ad agency and was interviewing some schmuck at a coffee shop. Jackie had been grabbing a latte before work, and had stopped dead in her tracks when she saw Camille. When her long, manicured fingers had tucked her hair behind her ear, Jackie had been done for. She waited for the guy to leave, watching them out of the corner of her eye from where she sat on a worn sofa, and when Camille had begun to pack up her laptop and looked around, she caught Jackie's eye and smiled. It was the one time where Jackie had felt truly nervous. She ran her hand through her hair and walked over to the little table, looking down at the empty chair across from Cam expectantly. Camille's laugh had sounded like music, and she had simply said, "I have twenty minutes before my next appointment." Jackie sat down.

Cam had been late to that appointment, losing nearly an hour in conversation with Jackie. They had talked about everything and nothing, and Jackie had been absolutely smitten by the way Camille moved, the timbre of her voice, the confidence with which she spoke about her job. Jackie had been the one to ask for her number, not even stammering when she finally got the nerve to ask. They had gone on their first real date three days later, and by the end of the next week, they were officially dating. Jackie was head over heels for this golden princess, and Cam seemed to feel the same. Moving in together two years later had felt only natural, but Cam had lost the spark of affection that had fueled Jackie's flame for the entirety of their relationship. Jackie needed love. *Loud* love. She needed to be told she was wanted, to hold hands in the kitchen and get kisses in the grocery store. Camille was practical and steady, and fell easily into routine.

Sometimes Jackie wondered if Cam just wasn't attracted to her anymore. She'd gained weight, was five years older than Camille, and worked long, hot days in a kitchen. She came home looking messy, and Camille was the tidiest person she had ever met. But still, she loved her, and until Cam had dropped the ball that she was leaving Jackie for a barista, Jackie had planned on proposing. She still loved her, despite it all.

But now, seeing Cam's pink lips on her phone screen, stretched into a smile she had given to Jackie alone for four years, Jackie just felt angry. Angry that Cam had abused her trust, angry that she hadn't spoken up about needing more, angry that she had been dumped over the goddamn phone like a high schooler instead of a grown-ass woman. She slid the phone open and pushed the button for speaker, not wanting to hold the phone in her now-sweaty palms.

"What?" she asked with a blunt tone that left nothing to the imagination.

"Can we talk?" Camille replied, her voice sounding vulnerable even through the tinny sound of her outdated phone's speaker.

"What's there to talk about? Is your new girlfriend on her way to get your bed?"

Camille sighed. "She's not my girlfriend."

"Oh, sorry, sorry," Jackie laughed. "I apologize for not knowing the right term for the person you clearly cheated on me with when I thought you were at work."

Cam was quiet for a moment and then took an audible breath. "She's married."

Jackie's eyes narrowed. "So? Cam, you'll forgive me if I don't really give a fuck. What do you want?"

She heard tears in Camille's voice when she answered. "I messed up. I don't know what I was thinking. I felt stagnant and unloved, and I did something stupid. I didn't mean to, Jax, and I have spent days wishing I could take back what I said."

"Take back what, exactly?" Jackie asked incredulously. "Dumping me? Telling me you were fucking a barista?"

"All of it. I do want to move home, and I do think we need some time apart. But I want to figure it out. I don't want to lose you Jax. I don't want to lose the life we've built, I think I just need some time to sort myself out. I messed up, and I know I can't ask for forgiveness, but I am so sorry."

Jackie laughed, a manic, cold sounding thing that was foreign even to her own ears. "You want forgiveness? You cheated on me, Camille. I was going to fucking propose to you. I loved you. I spent four years of my life doing every-thing I could to make you happy, and you lied to me, betrayed my trust, and then dumped me over the phone. Why the fuck would I forgive you? You've been a bitch to me since we moved to Washington. You're controlling and snooty and your family can't stand me. Why would I want to go back to that?"

Cam didn't answer for such a long time that Jackie looked at her phone to see if the call had dropped. Finally, her voice came over the speaker, sounding tired, sad, and entirely too young.

"You're right, Jackie. I messed up something I should have treasured. I'm sorry."

"I don't have time for this," Jackie replied. "I'm busy with work, and the last few days have actually felt really good. Maybe we can talk about this another time, but I really don't know. I gotta go."

"Okay," Camille said softly. "If you ever want to talk, you know where to find me."

Jackie hung up the phone without another word.

IN CULINARY SCHOOL, Jackie's favorite instructor had given them advice that had stuck with her all these years. "Never cook angry." Generally, cooking brought Jackie joy, and so she never really did. She had been frustrated before, but not ever really mad, but today she was pissed. She was pissed at Cam for trying to walk back their breakup. She was pissed at herself for feeling guilty. She was pissed at the universe for manifesting her dream woman and then making her a cheating asshole who had fucked a barista while she had been supposedly working an ad campaign. So right now, Jackie was sloppy.

She nearly broke her carefully crafted isomalt dome, and cursed at herself in the process. *Breathe, Jax,* she scolded herself. *Cam isn't even in the state. Focus on work.* She walked to her fridge, opening the door to the aqua Smeg that had cost her nearly a month's salary at St. Marte. She removed her cake carefully, placing it on the speckled terrazzo counter and taking a few deep breaths before continuing. She loaded the smoke gun with wood chips, rosemary and a few pinches of herbs. With infinite care, she lifted the isomalt dome with her bare fingers, feeling its smooth surface against her fingertips. She placed it atop the chocolate-collared cake, and held up the edge of the dome just enough to insert the tube of the smoke gun. As smoke began to curl into the dome she giggled, overcome by just how fucking *cool* this was looking.

Finally, it was the moment of truth. She stepped back, looking at the gorgeous dessert before her. Sparkling leaves, soil and rocks sat inside the clear "glass." Smoke curled around the little details, looking like a dense jungle filled with the mist of morning. The entire thing could fit in the palm of her hand, and it looked like something from that fancy French guy she followed on social media. She couldn't believe that she, Jackie Miller, had made this with her own hands. She grabbed the small stainless mallet and lifted it above the dome. If she could crack it and release the smoke without smashing the cake, this would be a success. She kept her arm steady, hinging only at the wrist and rapped the top of the dome. She squealed and stomped her feet in unrestrained glee as the smoke curled out, scenting the air with rosemary and cherry wood, but as though watching it happen in slow motion, she couldn't move as she saw the drop of blood run down her fingertip. Her eyes widened and her mouth dropped open into a perfect 'O' as the tiny, crimson droplet fell through the smoke, directly into the center of the cracked dome, hitting the top of the cake.

There was an intense flash, and thunderclap of sound, and the floor of the kitchen fell away. The stink of sulfur filled the room as smoke curled in the air and an angry orange light was cast upon the entire room. As Hell seemed to open up in her kitchen, Jackie Miller passed out cold.

6

vexx

VEXXANTHE DESMODEUS HEKATE MARIE MORNINGSTAR awoke to the cheery sound of birds singing. She rolled over in bed, pulling a black silk pillowcase over her head, and snapped her fingers twice. A feral growl tore through the air. There was the sharp clatter of shattering glass, a terrible cacophony of squealing and squeaking and then nothing but the sound of gnashing teeth and whistling wind. With a contented sigh, she snuggled back into her blankets and fell back asleep.

Three hours later, a loud rapping on an iron door woke her once again. This time, she had no choice but to rise, stretching with her thin arms above her head and yawning widely before standing. She was nude, but grabbed a floor-length black velvet robe from a nearby chair and put it on, tying the belt loosely as she walked. She lifted the massive iron door bar with one hand, looking at her red-manicured fingernails with the other, and as she pushed the fifteen-foot-high door open, she narrowed her eyes at the watery red light that landed upon her face. A serpent the length of a limousine was coiled before the door, looking as annoyed as a serpent was able. "Vexxssssssth," it hissed. "It'ssssth midday."

Vexx rolled her eyes and placed a hand on her hip. She opened her mouth to speak, but paused, cocking her head. "Wait," she replied in a low, silken voice. "How did you knock, Astie?"

The serpent hissed out a long, very annoyed sigh. "I've asssthked you not to call me that." She blinked at it, and it flung its head back, grumbling. "Your father has sssthummoned you. Pleassthe get ready. I really do not withhhhh to return."

She giggled, showing a peek of sharp canine teeth between her deep ruby lips. With an outstretched hand, she patted the terrifying creature on its cheek as though it were an annoying cousin. "Okay, *Astaroth*," she said, putting emphasis on the name. "Tell my *dear father* that I will grace him with my presence momentarily. I just need to shower and get dressed. And do my hair. And my makeup. And maybe have some coffee." With each activity she listed, she extended a finger. When he hissed in annoyance, she flipped her hand around, leaving only the middle finger up. "I'll get there when I get there." She turned, pushing the colossal door shut with her foot, and strode back into her bedroom.

Vexx stepped into black fur slippers and walked to her closet. She pulled a gold chain which hung from the ceiling and a light clicked on, illuminating the sprawling space in fluorescent light. She reached for a long gown of black brocade, but dropped it, walking further into the closet until she reached a line of much shorter dresses. A smirk lifted the corners of her lips, and she plucked a very, very short black organza a-line dress from its hanger. She tugged the chain once more on her way out, leaving the room cast in darkness once again. Somewhere in the darkness, a massive creature panted like a dog.

The coffeepot gurgled as Vexx showered. The water was so hot that every mirror in the room was soon frosted over with steam, and there were a *lot* of mirrors. When she stepped out into the still dark room, she walked naked to the kitchen with ease, stepping back into her slippers and pouring herself a large mug of coffee. She padded to the fridge and opened it, making a sound of displeasure at the bright light, and grabbing a bottle of hazelnut creamer. After pouring a hefty stream into her mug, she replaced the bottle and kicked the fridge closed. She drank, taking swallow after swallow of the near-boiling liquid until the mug was empty, and she let out a surprisingly dainty burp as she set it in the sink.

She took a seat in an ornately carved black chair with a burgundy satin cushion, and reached for the lamp on her vanity. When the light clicked on, she could see herself at last. Vexxanthe Desmodeus Hekate Marie Morningstar, Princess of Infernius, The Second Kingdom of Hell.

Vexx walked out of her room nearly two hours later, silver hair hanging down her back in perfect soft waves. The heels of her black boots clicked against the black marquina marble floor of the hallway as she walked, her reflection mirrored up at her by its glassy finish. She glanced down at it briefly, nodding appreciatively at her smooth, unblemished, pale grey skin and her precisely executed eyeliner. At least she looked good.

Eventually, she reached an ornamented door, surrounded by black filigree and a cathedral-arched doorway. She blinked up at the archway and rolled her eyes from beneath blunt-cut bangs. *Such dramatics.* When she rose on tiptoe to reach the heavy iron door knocker, she was well over six feet tall. And, thanks to the length of the high-necked dress she had chosen, half her ass was currently exposed. A lesser demon walked by, using its arms to propel it and swinging its legs behind. It let out a low whistle and stopped behind her, but when Vexx turned around and it recognized her, it trembled violently. She said nothing, only stared at it, and it cowered, curling its shoulder inward as though it could disappear.

The door creaked open and smoke curled out from the hot darkness of the room. Two glowing red eyes looked out into the hallway before flicking to Vexx. "It looked at my butt," Vexx said with a shrug. Before she had taken another breath, the creature burst into flames, screaming for only a second before it was entirely incinerated.

"Well, Vexxanthe, if you dressed appropriately, we would not have this issue," boomed an imposing voice at an impressively low register.

Vexx flipped her hair over her shoulder. "I've said it before, and I'll say it again. I am not responsible for the gaze of others. It's 214° down here, and if I want to wear a short dress, I will."

"You're asking for attention, Vexxanthe," the voice replied. "I do not wish to continuously smite my subjects for gazing upon you."

"Then teach them some respect." She shrugged her shoulders. "I didn't tell you to burn it, I was just telling you why it peed on the floor." The door swung open a bit further, the iron making a terrible grating sound. "Father, you're the ruler of a kingdom of Hell. Can you not pay for someone to grease these doors?" she said as she stepped inside.

The figure standing before her was over fifteen feet tall, with shoulders nearly five feet wide and clawed hands the size of hubcaps. One of which was currently sliding down an inhuman, black face—the universal sign of "I'm so fucking sick of this." The eyes that appeared from behind said hand glowed like embers, casting faint illumination on the heavy brows and immense curling horns above. "I do not wish to argue, my darling child," echoed the foreboding voice. "In fact, I would like to have a *nice* lunch with my only daughter. Could you please manage to get through one meal without lecturing me on the injustices you face?"

Vexx scoffed. "They aren't *my* injustices, Father. They're the male condition. It's exhausting existing in a female body."

"Yes, yes. So you have said. Forgive me, for not keeping a tight moral tether on—" he took a deep breath "—THE CITIZENS OF HELL." The words were spoken at such a powerful volume that the walls vibrated and someone in the distance screamed.

Vexx rolled her eyes. "You don't have to shout. I'm here. I came as summoned. Are we eating or not?" With another flip of her hair, she walked past the colossal demon as though he were nothing more than a golden retriever. Vexx's father, Bozuran, was the king of one of the kingdoms of Hell, Infernius. But to Vexx, he was simply her father who quite often overextended his jurisdiction.

She took a seat at a stone table, the legs of which were crafted with the bones of both humans and demons. He ducked his great horned head and sat across from her rather than at the head of the table. "How are your studies?" he asked, tone intentionally light.

A small, emaciated demon with long, stringy hair poured two chalices of dark wine, and Vexx sipped hers before replying. "Well, I suppose? Humanology is just so boring. I regret declaring it as my minor."

"But communications is going well? Do you still plan on pursuing journalism after graduation?"

Vexx nodded her head in thanks to the demon server as a plate was placed before her. "I guess," she replied. "Though, I'm not sure what the point is if you aren't going to allow me journalistic integrity."

Bozuran exhaled slowly and lifted what, in his goliath hand, appeared to be a comically small fork to his mouth. When he had finished chewing and swallowed, he spoke. "I never said I would deny you full agency over what you write. All I said is that I could not allow you to run exposés on the other rulers and their families."

"Precisely," Vexx replied. "I can write whatever I wish

unless it's a piece about powerful individuals. I *became* a communications major in order to speak out against the things that occur behind throne room doors."

"Vexxanthe, you speak of these things as though you are not a part of the Hellistocracy. Every one of us is a ruler in Hell, and you, my dear, are royalty, whether you would like to embrace that or not. Wearing unsuitable attire and listening to human music is not going to change that."

"It's not as though I'm in line for the throne," she replied. "Lucky for you, you have thirteen sons who precede me. It would take some sort of act of god to take them all out." She chuckled, and Bozuran's mouth tightened into a grim scowl.

"Not funny," he said sternly.

"Come on, that was a good one," she said, smiling sweetly. "Anyway, I have plans this evening. Did you need something, or did you just want to have lunch?"

"No," he answered, setting his chin in his hand. "I simply wished to share a meal with my progeny."

"Well, this has been great," she replied. "Don't wait up!" And with that, Vexxanthe Desmodeus Hekate Marie Morningstar tossed her satin napkin onto her plate and left her father's chambers.

HELL HAD QUITE a few bars and nightclubs, but this one was Vexx's favorite. It was styled after an old human music venue. Thousands of stickers were haphazardly slapped across the walls, a short stage stood in the corner, and a bar ran along the side. Vexx's favorite bartender was working, and she slid onto a barstool, calling him over with the wave of a hand. The band playing was loud, and she had to shout over the warring sounds of electric guitar, bass, and the rapid staccato of drums.

The singer screamed out an old human tune, and Vexx sang along as she waited for the bartender to make his way to her. *Total… demon control… C-O-N…*

Sounds familiar, Vexx thought. As the bartender finally stepped in front of her, she smiled. "Sid!" she exclaimed. "It's been awhile."

The skinny bartender shrugged his shoulders from beneath his oversized leather jacket and pointed to the empty glass in his hand.

"Yeah," Vexx answered. "The usual is fine."

The bartender nodded and smiled back before turning to mix her whiskey and soda. Vexx went back to bobbing her head to the music, another song playing now. It was, of course, another she recognized. Vexx had a special interest in human music, particularly 1970s-1990s punk rock. Most of the old punk rockers who ended up down below frequented this bar, some even working here. Unfortunately, humans who ended up in Hell were cursed with an eternity of silence, punishment for having lied and cheated in their lifetimes. They were still better company, Vexx thought, than the demons who never shut the fuck up. Everyone was always brown-nosing, trying to get on her father's good side. What no one seemed to realize yet was that Vexx was not the one to kiss up to. In fact, she was far more likely to use your flattery against you.

Vexx drank her cocktail in a few sips and then stood, walking toward the stage. The demon singer was a pretty standard lesser demon: no horns, elongated ears, and hooves peeking out from his torn plaid pants. The band itself was comprised entirely of humans (except for the singer,) all of which Vexx knew from their lives in the human punk scene. The guitarist raised his chin in greeting before continuing his assault on the strings, and the demon singer's voice faltered slightly when he saw her. She wished at times that she could be incognito, but her black horns and long red tail gave her away as one of Bozuran's children. She had tried to hide them both in the past, teasing her hair up or wearing a hat, trying to tuck her tail into jeans, but her tail began to cramp after only a few minutes, and her hair refused to stay big enough to hide the curling horns. She looked like her mother, for which she was grateful, but she had all the marks of her father's kids.

Vexx's mother had been a succubus. From the painting in her father's throne room, Vexx knew she had been stunningly beautiful. She had possessed the same smooth grey skin and big, bright eyes that Vexx had now. Her wings had been delicate and fearsome, charcoal-colored skin stretched along the long bones, and her tail was just like Vexx's own, except it was a deep plum color instead of the red Vexx had somehow ended up with. Succubi could only bear children of high demons, and only thirteen. Vexx had been an accident, but rather than terminating her pregnancy, her mother had chosen self-sacrifice. So now, her mother, Raeleth, thanks to an archaic rule, was in heaven.

It had been quite the scandal, and had broken her father's heart. As a small child Vexx had worried her father resented her for being the thing that took his Rae away, but she was so much like her mother in both appearance and spirit, that she had become the Eden's apple of her father's eye, and she grew up with a loving parent who nurtured her every need. Except, Vexx thought, for the need she felt to dismantle oppressive systems. Sure, she was Hell's princess, but she had applied to schools anonymously, as many children born of angel/demon parents did. She got accepted on merit alone, and that meant something to her. She had also worked for many years as a legal assistant to Lilith, Queen of the Fifth Kingdom of Hell. She saved every obol she earned, and purchased all of her clothes, as well as paying for the adoption of her pet Hellhound, Cupcakes. However, Vexx knew that until she moved out to another kingdom of Hell, or even to another dimension, her efforts to make Hell more equitable would go unnoticed and disregarded. Sure, the humans needed to be punished for all of eternity, but Hell had an entire population of demons who had done nothing, save for be born. There was no reason they, too, had to be punished and treated like servants to the Hellistocracy.

That's why Vexx loved this bar so much. Generally, nobody here gave a flying fuck who she was, or that she could buy the bar in an instant. They were mostly people like her, who wanted to upend the status quo and make life more livable for the average demon. Vexx joined the fray in the pit, towering over more than half of the lesser demons who currently elbowed and kicked at their fellows. She had to restrain herself—possessing the strength of a high demon could end badly if she struck out too hard, but she was gentle and only gave black eyes and bruises. After a few songs, she was feeling relaxed, less uptight and grouchy about her situation. She knew, logically, that her feelings were fucking stupid. She had more privilege than literally anyone else in Hell, and it was honestly her duty to help those who came from less privileged means. Her pedigree didn't mean shit to a lesser demon, and their designation didn't make them "lesser" in anything but title and arcane abilities. She stopped by the bar for one more drink before leaving, twisting her sweaty hair up into a messy chignon. She probably smelled like brimstone, but she felt alive, and that was all she had wanted. She tipped Sid well and walked out of the bar into the sweltering night air. The "sky" above was the color of blood, and flecked with luminous patches of blue-burning fire, and the swirling orange glow of the infernal flames.

Vexx had read about "the sky" in school. She knew about the world above, but the concept of a wide blue expanse was so far removed from her reality that she couldn't even imagine it. In Infernius, the infernal flames were the only source of natural light, and they never went dark. Bozuran's kingdom was constantly cast in an orange light. Vexx walked along the bank of the river of the dead, watching human souls flow by beneath the glassy surface. Walking was calm, it was quiet. She snapped her fingers three times, pausing to wait, and in a few short moments a Hellhound bounded from between the nearby buildings, running right for her. She didn't flinch, he was hers, after all. The shaggy black creature was nearly her height, and his eyes glowed from beneath his long coat. His tail thumped against the ground happily, and she scratched his ears. When he opened his mouth, a long, forked tongue lolled out and his six-inch long, razor-sharp teeth were visible.

"How is my little Cupcakes?" Vexx asked, taking the beast's head in her palms and kissing him on his wet nose. "You want walkies?" The Hellhound let out what might have been its equivalent to a yip—a loud, low sound like the tolling of a bell. Vexx reached down and pulled a femur from the riverbank, throwing it as far as she could. Cupcakes tore after it, leaping over obstacles with ease, and returned with the femur, sloppily panting as he dropped it. Vexx had adopted Cupcakes from a Hellhound rescue three years ago and he'd been her furry best friend ever since. She liked days like this, when nobody needed anything from her and she could spend time playing with Cupcakes and going out dancing. She was twenty-eight years old, damnit. She deserved to enjoy life sometimes.

As she walked along the river with Cupcakes, she tried to think of a future she would be proud of. She wanted to do something with impact, to be known for more than her father's title. She had considered an externship to the world above when she was younger, but Bozuran had quickly crushed that idea, telling her that the surface was no place for royalty. The only demons who lived on the surface were minions sent to acquire more wealth or to seed chaos and corrupt more humans. Hell was a business, after all. Bozuran and the other rulers relied upon a constant influx of souls to staff all of Hell's businesses, to tend to the river and the deeper pits, and to supply the Hellistocracy with adequate sustenance. Though the royal families all ate food like the rest of Hell, they also relied upon the energy of particularly corrupt souls. Without it, their own powers would wane and maybe eventually be lost altogether. A bird flew by and Cupcakes leapt up, snapping it between his jaws and crunching loudly.

"The birds this morning weren't enough for you?" Vexx asked, scolding. "You know we don't get many of them down here. That was a treat. Bad boy."

Cupcakes hung his head, but his tail kept thumping the ground, and when Vexx rolled her eyes and scratched him under his chin, he straightened back up and licked her cheek. A strange sound caught both of their attention, a loud crack that sounded almost like lightning. Vexx peered up, looking for the source, but found no sulfur clouds, not a storm then. Again, the sound rang out, so loud that the ground shook beneath their feet. The river rippled as though a stone had been dropped into it. Cupcakes whined, tucking his shaggy tail between his legs, and when an even louder crack sounded, he bolted, running back toward the palace.

Vexx opened her mouth to admonish him, but the words died in her throat as the infernal flames parted, rock and debris raining down and smashing into the river and the surrounding buildings. She threw her arms over her head and ducked down, hoping to avoid being splattered onto the street, but it was over in an instant and something far more terrifying greeted her when she rose back up.

Daylight, streaming down through a swirling portal in the "sky."

Vexx gaped, not knowing how to respond. The light was so *bright*. A lesser demon screamed as the rays fell upon it, sizzling and turning flesh to smoke. The demon was incinerated before Vexx could move. Dumbfounded, she walked toward the light.

She was, after all, a greater demon. The light may be unpleasant to her sensitive red eyes, but it wouldn't kill her like it did the others. She looked up at the swirling hole amidst the flames, how the edges seemed to blur and the infernal flames pulled back from it as though deprived of air. As she stepped into the light, everything happened simultaneously—Vexx was pulled upward at an indescribable speed, the light grew painfully bright, and the swirling portal began to wink closed like a terrible eye. She spared one glance down at the second kingdom of Hell, and then she had been pulled through, and the doorway closed behind her.

Vexxanthe Desmodeus Hekate Marie Morningstar was not in Hell anymore.

7
jackie

I MUST HAVE HIT *my head. This is a concussion. I am hallucinating.* Jackie Miller thought as she opened her eyes and saw the state of her kitchen. Her table was destroyed, cracked right down the center and laying on the floor in two perfect halves. Chocolate was everywhere, the floor had taken the most damage, her painstakingly crafted dessert looking more like a stomped on cow pattie than anything else at this point. But as she turned to survey the rest of the room, Jackie's breath caught in her throat.

There was a grey woman in her kitchen.

She was pretty in a goth devil cosplay sort of way. Her skin had all been painted grey and she wore black horns. There was even some kind of motorized tail sticking out from beneath a *very* short skirt, Jackie noticed with a little flip of her stomach. She was tall, taller even than Cam, and her eyes were as big as saucers, red contacts on full display. When she looked down and saw Jackie, she screamed. So Jackie screamed. They both screamed until they ran out of breath. Then, the woman took another breath and opened her mouth as though to scream again, but Jackie raised both hands in the air.

"Please, don't hurt me. I don't know what you want, but take whatever it is and please just let me go," Jackie pleaded. She hoped the intruder had heard the explosion and come to help, but she figured it could be a potential looting situation, so she should cover all her bases. *Oh yeah,* she thought, *the explosion.* She remembered the loud crack and the floor opening up beneath her. It must have been some sort of hallucination from those herbs, maybe the shop has slipped her some kind of psychedelic. Maybe she wasn't supposed to burn the herbs. Who knew? But she was glad to see that it had all been in her head and that the kitchen floor was intact, just chocolatey. She really didn't want to lose her deposit.

The grey woman hadn't moved. Her distractingly luscious mouth remained open, and she stared at Jackie without blinking. Was she on drugs too? "Hey," Jackie ventured. "Are you okay?"

At last, the woman seemed to blink away her astonished expression. She swallowed. Her long, thin throat bobbed, and she spoke in a voice like smoke and whiskey. "Is this… Earth?"

Jackie realized two things at the same time. This woman was without a doubt the most beautiful woman she had ever seen, and she was batshit crazy. Jackie got to her feet slowly, brushing cookie crumble and chunks of candied mint from her pants. "Where do you think you are right now?" Jackie said in a careful tone, making sure not to get too close in case the woman turned violent.

She spoke again, that raspy voice making Jackie's whole body tingle. "This is Earth. I am on Earth. Hells fucking shit."

"Yes," Jackie said. "Good, this is Earth. Do you know how you got here? Were you in a hospital or facility of some kind?"

The woman's head snapped to Jackie, brows pulling together. "What? No. I wasn't in a hospital. I was in Hell."

"Okay, so you're from Hell," Jackie said, moving slowly toward her. "And where is Hell?"

The woman looked at her as though she was the stupidest person ever to live. "It's beneath the surface," she said, as though talking to a child. She pointed at her feet. "Down there."

"How did you get up here?" Jackie asked, matching the sarcastic tone and gesturing to the room around her.

"How the fuck would I know?" the woman answered. "I was minding my own business, walking my dog, and a big ass hole in the sky opened up and I was sucked up here like some old alien movie. *You* should be telling *me* how I got up here."

Jackie stopped, eyes shifting to the chaos in the kitchen once more. *Was that real? Was there really a smoking orange portal in my kitchen?* "A hole in the sky?" she said. "Hell has a sky?"

"I mean, sort of? It's the infernal flames, so it's not a sky in a traditional sense." as she said sky, she made air quotes with red-tipped nails. "But it's our version of a sky I suppose."

"What the fuck?" Jackie muttered under her breath, walking to one of the toppled chairs and righting it before sitting down. "Why are you grey?"

The woman just blinked at her, opening and closing her mouth. At last she answered. "There's a demon in your kitchen and you want to know why I'm grey?"

"Of course," Jackie said. "You're a demon. Makes sense. This all makes perfect sense. I've had some sort of psychotic break from some sort of hallucinogen or something, and when all this passes, I'll realize I destroyed my kitchen and hallucinated a pretty girl in my kitchen."

The woman walked toward her, black boots at the end of very, very long legs. "Lady, I'm not a hallucination. I'm a demon. My name is Vexxanthe Desmodeus Hekate Marie Morningstar, but you can call me Vexx. And I'm going to need to know what the fuck you were doing to summon a high level portal without any sort of guidance on this side."

Jackie sat dumbfounded, her eyes raking over this unexpectedly gorgeous woman. Upon a closer look, the grey seemed too perfect to be makeup. Her silver hair was radiant, but had bits of rock and dirt in it. When she blinked, the red didn't move. Those weren't contacts. And her tail? It moved back and forth far too naturally to be mechanical. Jackie Miller's eyes slowly moved up the woman's fashion model body, and met her gaze.

And then she passed out. Again.

WHEN JACKIE'S eyelids fluttered open, a pair of sparkling red eyes were looking into hers. She flinched back instinctually before remembering the absolute fuckery of this evening. Wait, was it still evening?

"How long was I out?" she asked the grey woman seated beside her. Vexx?

Vexx shrugged. "Maybe five minutes? I don't know, I wasn't timing it."

Jackie pushed up onto her elbows, and then slowly sat up. "I really need to clean up."

"Yeah, it's kind of gross in here," Vexx added, looking around.

Jackie's eyes narrowed. "Alright, well, have a good night I guess," she said and gestured toward the door.

Vexx looked at her like she had six eyes. "Where do you expect me to go?" Jackie got to her feet, but when she didn't reply, Vexx went on. "I was just yanked out of my home and brought to another dimension by a human with no clue how it happened. I sure as shit don't plan on staying up here on the surface. I need to know what you used, and what you did, so I can try to figure out what happened. I know how to open a communication portal, but I have no clue if it's the same up here, and I have no idea how the fuck to open a portal to get me home."

The bag from the herb shop still sat atop the kitchen counter and Jackie walked over to it, wincing at the pain in her head. Her entire body hurt. Her ass hurt from hitting the floor. Twice. Her head was pounding, the lights felt too bright, and she felt like she was going to puke. Was this a concussion? All she knew about concussions she had learned from doctor shows, so there was no telling how accurate that information was. She reached out a hand to steady herself, but missed the edge of the counter, stumbling. In an instant, warm hands were beneath her arms, steadying her. No, not warm, HOT. She pulled back. "Holy shit you're hot," Jackie said, a little out of breath.

Vexx laughed and winked as she replied, "Thanks!"

Jackie stammered. "No, I mean, yes, but no... I meant, you're... I... ah, fuck—"

Vexx pulled a chair over with the tip of her tail and pushed Jackie into it. The breath wheezed out of her lungs as her ass made contact with the seat. Vexx smiled, more genuinely this time. "I know what you meant," she said. "Demon, remember? I'm literally from Hell. It's over 200° down there at any given time. I'm sure my skin will adjust to the air up here. But for now, do you have a jacket I could borrow?"

Jackie pointed to her bedroom door. "There's a closet in there, take whatever you need. It'll all be way too big for you, but should at least keep you cozy."

"Thank you."

Vexx patted Jackie's knee, and she could feel the heat of the touch even beneath her thick pants. Jackie watched her walk toward the bedroom door, unable to tear her eyes from the sight of those long legs walking, that very, very short dress, or the sway of her hips. *I must have a concussion,* she thought. *I'm checking out a demon.*

When Vexx emerged from her bedroom, Jackie's mouth went dry at the sight of Vexx wearing her jacket. It was her favorite: hunter green plaid wool lined with thick sherpa. It buttoned up the front, but Vexx held it wrapped tightly around her, silver hair spilling down over the raised collar. "Thank you," she said. "I feel much better. Do you have anything to eat?"

Jackie looked at the destruction surrounding them and back at Vexx's tiny skirt peeking out from beneath her jacket. *Demon. She's a demon,* she reminded herself. And then she took out her phone. "Let's order delivery."

While they waited for their curry, Jackie handed Vexx the herb shop bag. "Honestly, I can't tell you the exact things I used, or how much. I was just sort of grabbing pinches of stuff and sniffing it. If it smelled good, it went in. The other ingredients are here—" she passed her the notebook with her plan and recipe, smeared with chocolate and smelling strongly of smoke "—I used cherry wood, rosemary and some of the herbs in the smoke gun."

"That's not enough to have opened a portal," Vexx replied. "You need more than vervain, sorrel and whatever else is in here." She sniffed the bag. "This—" she pulled out a tiny bag "—smells like witchcraft."

Jackie took the tiny bag and brought it to her nose. "Yeah, I think I used this. It smells like sugar and anise. What is it?"

Vexx shook her head. "I don't know. But it was grown in a witch garden. Is there anything else that happened? Anything you might be forgetting?"

Jackie thought about the moments leading up to the blast. Glancing down, her eyes caught on the thin, red line on her finger. She held it up. "I'm pretty sure I got blood in it."

Vexx stared, blinking silently for what felt like an hour. Then, she spoke in her rich, silken voice. "Yep. That'll do it."

LIGHT WAS BEGINNING to leak through the blinds in lines of pale, slate blue. It was dawn, and Jackie hadn't slept. *Thank god it's my day off*, she thought. Vexx sat in the middle of the kitchen floor, the grey laminate only a few shades darker than her skin. Her eyebrows were drawn together in concentration, and she was surrounded by a mismatched collection of Cam's half-burned candles and empty takeout boxes with a few bites of abandoned Indian food. She had been trying to open a portal for hours, to no avail. A little while ago, she had taken off Jackie's jacket, and much more of her flawless skin was on display. Jackie had never been so interested in someone's arms before, but she found herself watching the way they moved as Vexx tried once more to cast the portal. She moved so gracefully. Even her hands moved with femininity. As she sat, looking over the back of the sofa, Jackie felt suddenly very aware of her own body and the ways she moved. Cam had always said she was attracted to Jackie's mannerisms, but Cam was also a fucking liar, so.

"Fuck!" Vexx shouted. She balled her hands into fists and brought them down hard on her thighs. "Why won't this work?!"

Jackie felt bad. She was useless in this situation, unable to do anything but watch and try not to fall asleep. She got up off the couch. "You want coffee?" she asked.

Vexx replied without looking up. "I always want coffee."

"Perfect," Jackie replied, giving Vexx a wide berth as she passed. She switched on the kettle, pulling her Chemex from a cabinet and setting it on the counter. Jackie was particular about her coffee; she weighed out and ground the beans, a single origin Harrar from Ethiopia, and poured the finely ground beans into the filter. The scent of dark coffee began to replace the scents of smoke, curry, and random scented candles, and Jackie's mouth watered. She poured a mug for Vexx and walked it over, bending to hand the steaming cup to the demon.

"Do you have any creamer? I really like hazelnut," she asked, still studying the floor.

Jackie inhaled, aghast. "You're a demon, and you want sugary trash in your coffee?"

Vexx finally looked up. "Demons aren't allowed to like sweet coffee?" She tilted her head at an adorable angle.

"This isn't that kind of coffee," Jackie replied. "Try it. If you *need* creamer, I can get you some milk and sugar. I probably have some hazelnut extract in my pastry cupboard."

Vexx looked doubtful, but she took a tentative sip of the coffee, and then drank deeply, making a soft noise as she did. Her expression made Jackie's toes curl. "Okay, this is really good. What is this?"

"It's *good* coffee," Jackie replied, a little smug. "It's a locally roasted Ethiopian varietal. One thing about Seattle, we have really good coffee."

"Well, at least there's that." Vexx took another sip. "Fuck, I have been drinking the wrong thing." She set the mug beside her. "I hate to ask this, but do you think you could spare a drop of blood? Typically, I don't need any sort of sacrifice to open a communication portal, but apparently things work differently up here. I really need to tell my father where I am."

"Your father?" Jackie asked. "What is he, the devil?"

Vexx chuckled. "Sort of? There are seven kingdoms of Hell. My father is the King of one of them. It's the fire one, in case you were wondering. Not all of Hell is hot and stereotypical. Some kingdoms are actually cold as fuck."

"So… you're a princess?"

Cringing, Vexx replied. "Yeah, I am."

Jackie bent into a low bow and Vexx feigned irritation. With a playful smile Jackie held out her injured finger. "As you command, m'lady."

Vexx took Jackie's finger in her very warm hand. A lightning bolt of thrill went through her, shooting straight between her legs. Jackie blushed furiously, knowing there was no way Vexx could *tell*, but being embarrassed of her body's reaction to the touch, regardless. "Ow!" she yelped as Vexx squeezed her cut fingertip, jerked out of her thoughts by the sudden sharp pain.

Vexx didn't apologize, just pulled Jackie's hand closer, letting the blood roll down Jackie's fingertip. It seemed to pause, hesitant to drop, but then it fell from her finger, the crimson droplet landing on the laminate. When the droplet burrowed through the floor, opening first a miniscule hole which opened like a camera aperture into one the size of a manhole cover, Jackie let out a garbled sound and scrabbled out of the kitchen to hide behind the sofa.

The kitchen took on a burnt orange glow, and smoke rose through the swirling portal. The stink of sulfur replaced the comforting smell of coffee, and Jackie heard distant screaming and the whistling of wind. The voice that resonated through her apartment filled Jackie with dread, making her limbs tremble, and she felt like she was going to piss her pants. "Vexxanthe," it thundered, drawing the name out. "Where are you? Are you safe?" Jackie had a fleeting thought that it was sweet that even the devil loved his daughter, but the unbearable terror quickly returned, and *she* returned to shaking like a chihuahua.

"I'm on the surface. In Seattle," Vexx replied. "I'm safe, but I don't know how to get back. Can you open a portal for me?"

The voice replied, rattling the kitchen cabinets. "To open a portal to a specific location requires the veil between the surface and below to be very thin, and it is not currently. Right now, if I were to do so, it would likely annihilate the entire city. I can do it, but it will take me a few moments to prepare for the influx of souls. There are over 700,000 people there, and we are not equipped to handle hundreds of thousands of souls right now. Can you wait an hour or two?"

Jackie managed to let out a strangled sound, and Vexx looked over at her quaking behind the velvet couch.

"Wait," Vexx said. "The entire city would be destroyed? No, father, I don't want you to kill a million people to get me home.

"700,000," he replied. "Not a million."

"No. Please do not cause a global catastrophe to get me home." She summoned a small flame in her palm, twirling it around absentmindedly. "When is the veil at its thinnest?"

"There is a total lunar eclipse in twenty-one days," he intoned. "But Vexxanthe, that would put you on the surface, with *humans,* for three weeks. I will not allow this."

"I will be fine," she answered, snuffing the small flame. "Think of it as a crash course in human studies. Maybe Professor Azael will give me extra credit."

"This is not funny, Vexxanthe. It is not safe. You have no glamour, you cannot possibly pass as one of them."

"Humans are weird, father." Vexx replied. "They'll probably just assume I'm very committed to goth culture."

Jackie thought she could hear the powerful demon rolling his eyes, even from another dimension. "Daughter—"

"I'll be fine," she answered. "Just open the portal for me in three weeks."

"Will you remain at this location?" he asked. "How shall I locate you?"

Vexx looked to Jackie, and she found herself nodding. *Did I just agree to let a demon be my houseguest for three weeks?*

"Yeah, I'll stay here."

"Very well." The booming voice took on a lethal note. "If you are harmed, I will raze the city to the ground."

Vexx sighed loudly and pushed her silver hair behind an ear. "Yeah, yeah, yeah. Boil the seas and whatever. I'll be fine."

At that moment, every smoke detector in Jackie's apartment went off at once. Vexx's eyes shot away from the portal, seeking the source of the shrill screech. Jackie heard the voice begin to speak but Vexx interrupted. "Gotta go, father. Talk soon. Feed Cupcakes for me, okay?" and then she waved a hand over the floor and the laminate swirled back together with a strange, loud grinding noise. The beeping alarms quieted, leaving the apartment uncomfortably silent.

"So…" Vexx said. "Where can I sleep?"

# 8
jackie

WHAT THE FUCK *am I going to do with a demon?* Jackie thought to herself the next morning, waking up stiff and still tired on the couch. She had stayed up far too late cleaning the kitchen and hauling the broken table pieces down to the dumpster. Sometimes it paid off to be strong, and she was able to manage it on her own. She picked up her phone and realized, after trying for a solid minute to get it to unlock, that it was dead. She had been so tired and overwhelmed by the day that she had skipped her nighttime routine entirely and forgotten to plug it in. She scrubbed a hand through her hair. *I need to shower.* Yawning, she found her charger and turned on the kettle while she waited for the phone to turn on. Humming to herself, she got lost in the meditative routine of making her morning coffee. Her phone buzzed on the side table as it powered back on, and she sat back down on the couch while the coffee finished dripping through the filter. She had thirteen notifications. *Jesus,* she thought. *What's the fucking emergency?*

Three of them were texts from Everest, inviting her out to dinner after work on Tuesday. *Nope.* The other eleven were from Cam. She tried to ignore them, but her thumb was a traitor, and opened the message thread with a single tap. Jackie's eyes betrayed her as well, and they slid over the words, lingering on a few choice phrases. *I love you. Please. Another chance. I want to come home.* Jackie shook her head and turned the screen off. Mimolette bumped his head against her shin. She was glad he wasn't too traumatized from the night prior.

It was way too early to deal with Cam. But, no, she was not going to let her come back. In fact, she was going to install a door chain today. She poured herself a mug of coffee, and placed the Chemex on her electric mug warmer to keep hot for Vexx if she woke up soon, or for herself if she didn't.

Jackie made up a plausible, and innocent, lie for Everest, and then contemplated how to respond to Camille. On one hand, Jackie wanted to be the bigger person. She didn't want to seem petty or petulant, despite feeling both very strongly. Cam had cheated. She had admitted it, and been cruel when she could have led with apologetic. Jackie wondered if maybe the barista had dumped Cam, and if that was why she came crawling back on penitent knee. She opened up her messages again, looking for some inkling of subtext in the messages, but all she found was Camille being far more vulnerable than Jackie was accustomed to. She felt a pang of guilt and regret. Maybe this is what she had wanted this whole time: a girlfriend who was emotionally available, who was forthcoming with her mistakes and her feelings, who *wanted* Jackie's love and forgiveness.

But then she thought about the fact that Cam had slept with this woman, undoubtedly while Jackie was at work making money to try and save for their future together. She didn't know how long the relationship had been inappropriate, but Camille had worked with her for months. Had Camille gotten into their bed at night, thinking about this other woman? Did she think of Cassie while Jackie's tongue moved between her legs? The anger returned, blazing hot, feeling like Vexx's portal had opened up within Jackie's chest. She set her mug down too hard and coffee sloshed out onto the side table. She jumped up to grab a paper towel, and as she stepped into the kitchen, she heard her bedroom door open.

"I made coffee!" Jackie said, trying to effuse as much cheerfulness into her voice as she could. Paper towels in hand, she turned, taking one step toward the living room. The paper towel fluttered to the floor.

Vexx stood just outside the bedroom door, arms raised above her head, stretching.

Stretching *nude*.

Jackie tried to say something, anything, but her entire body had seized up in some sort of gay panic induced rigor. God, Vexx was perfect. Her skin looked like a swath of pale grey satin, silky and lusciously shaped. Beneath the graceful curve of her collarbone sat high, round breasts with dark nipples that Jackie desperately wanted to run her hands over. She was slim, but not skinny. Her stomach had the tiniest little pooch, and looked so soft that she wanted to press her mouth against it. Her hips were wide, leading to thick thighs that looked strong and capable. Her eyes traveled down, and she was powerless to stop herself from looking at *all* of Vexx. Every single part of her was perfectly smooth, as though she had been carved from marble. Jackie's heart raced, muscles tightened, mouth watered. She was overcome by straight-up lust that washed over her in a heated wave. She felt the throb of her own pulse between her thighs, and with a small measure of self-consciousness, the way her boyshorts suddenly felt damp. Vexx picked that moment to lower her arms and look at Jackie, her radiant red eyes glittering beneath the hall light. "Hey," Vexx said, yawning and rubbing her eyes. "You said coffee?"

Jackie stammered, but couldn't make her mouth cooperate.

The series of flustered sounds she managed sounded more like a skipping record than any sort of human speech.

Vexx gave her a quizzical look, one perfectly angled eyebrow lifting. "Are you… okay?"

"Naked." Jackie blushed a furious shade of red. *Yes, Jax. She knows she's naked. Use your fucking words.* "Sorry, you're naked? I was just, uh, surprised?" She didn't know why the sentence ended in a question. Actually, she did. Because she hadn't just been surprised. She had been drooling. Jackie chided herself. *She is stranded here, completely alone, and has never been on Earth. And here you are, checking her out like a creep. Great job. Very welcoming.*

"Oh," Vexx said, looking down at herself. "Is that an issue?"

"Well, uh, people don't normally let strangers, or acquaintances, see them without clothes on," Jackie replied.

"That seems silly. You're female, I've spent enough time around humans to know we have essentially the same physiology. If you know what's under my clothes, why do I have to wear them indoors? Outside, I get. Infernius is home to everyone found guilty of lust, so I know how a lot of humans can be. But, do you care?"

"Gay," Jackie blurted before catching herself and starting over. "I'm gay, so, I guess it's a little different than if I was straight. I don't want you to feel uncomfortable. I don't want to be uncomfortable."

"Are you uncomfortable?" Vexx asked, sounding genuine.

Jackie quickly weighed the options. She pushed down the voice that whispered in her head, *no, tell her no—let her stay naked.* "I mean… a little? I feel weird checking you out, but I also can't completely ignore you since you're in my apartment."

Realization seemed to hit Vexx after a breath. "You're attracted to me."

It wasn't a question, so Jackie didn't quite know how to

respond. If she said yes, she was pretty much admitting to staring at a naked stranger. If she said no, she was lying. She decided to take her chances. "Yes," she answered truthfully. "So I'd feel more comfortable if you put something on."

Vexx's eyes narrowed, and she lifted her hands in frustration. "That makes no sense. If you're attracted to me, wouldn't you *want* to see me naked?"

Jackie rubbed at her forehead. "It's too early for this, Vexx. Could you just go grab a t-shirt and some boxers from my dresser? Please?"

"If that's what you want." Vexx shrugged, turning and opening the door.

That is precisely the opposite of what I want, Jackie thought as she watched Vexx's perfectly round ass disappear into her bedroom. *I do not want that at all.*

* * *

IT WAS NOT EASIER, Jackie found, to look at Vexx's long legs wearing her oversized t-shirt. Vexx had emerged in an extra large band tee from college, smiling and telling Jackie that she loved the band. Jackie had nodded, trying to look normal, and shoved a mug of coffee into her hand.

An hour later, they sat side by side on the velvet sofa, talking about life on Earth, while Vexx's tail swished back and forth and Mimolette did his very best to eat it. Vexx had looked equal parts excited and impressed when Jackie told her about working at Canid. "You bake? I *love* chocolate," she had said with an almost childlike enthusiasm.

"Me too!" Jackie replied. "Devil's food cake is my favorite." She paused, looking directly at Vexx. "Is that a thing in Hell? Like, do you guys have devil's food cake? Because, you know, the devil?"

Vexx was deadpan when she answered, "Obviously. It's my father's favorite. We get it for him every year."

"Really?!" Jackie exclaimed before noticing Vexx's flat expression. She collapsed back onto the couch, shaking with laughter. At least, she thought, she met her gullibility with humor rather than embarrassment.

Vexx was smiling too, and Jackie noticed that her lips appeared to just naturally be that delicious shade of red. "No, silly," she said. "We have a lot of the same foods as you do on the surface, but many things we can't get below. There are demons whose careers are essentially just smuggling goods from plane to plane. That's how I get my coffee creamer. If I wasn't literally a princess, I could never afford it. Chocolate, however, is a rare treat. Surprisingly, a thing that melts really easily doesn't import well to a 200° climate."

"It's a pity the dessert I made that summoned you ended up exploding. You'd have liked it."

"Are you going to make it again? But like, without the demon-summoning herbs and blood?"

Jackie barked out an embarrassingly loud laugh. "Actually, I need to. It's a project for work, and I need to be sure I have all the kinks worked out before I present it to my chef."

Vexx sat up, unfolding her legs from beneath her and shifting forward on the sofa. "Can I watch?"

Jackie grinned. "Absolutely."

The second time, the entire process was much easier, Jackie thought. She assembled all the components while Vexx watched in what Jackie hoped was stunned silence. When it was finished, save for the smoke, Jackie retrieved Cam's ring light from her bedroom and set it up, snapping photos on her phone from a few different angles. Then she pumped in the smoke and took a few more. She set up her phone on the ring light's tripod and began recording in slow motion, capturing the moment the mallet broke the isomalt dome in a perfect cinematic video.

When she looked over at Vexx, the woman's eyes were wide, lips slightly parted, her chin resting in her hand, and Jackie had never been more attracted to a person. Demon. Whatever.

"So…" she said. "Do you want to help me eat this?"

If Jackie thought that Vexx *looking* at the dessert was attractive, she wasn't sure there was an adequate descriptor for how she looked while eating it. From the moment the fork crossed her lips, Vexx looked like she was experiencing true pleasure for the first time in her life. She took her time with the bite, moving it around in her mouth and closing her eyes. She made a sound halfway between a moan and a purr, and Jackie almost dropped her own fork. When her eyes at last fluttered open, they were heavy-lidded, looking nearly lustful as she met Jackie's hopeful gaze.

"Did you like it?" Jackie asked hesitantly, all of a sudden very aware of the queasy fluttering of unease that had taken root in her stomach.

"I thought I liked chocolate—" Vexx began.

Jackie's heart plummeted.

"—but I had never dreamed of anything tasting like that. How am I supposed to just go on with the rest of my life, knowing that there are things that taste that good and I can't have them?"

The unease melted into flowing warmth, spreading through Jackie until it had reached her cheeks, making them go Barbie-pink. She couldn't even look at Vexx for a minute, trying to compose herself so she didn't sound like a blubbering idiot. When she did raise her head to look at Vexx once again, she grinned as brightly as the sun. "I'm glad," she replied. It wasn't enough, but it would do.

They ate forkfuls of the rich, chocolatey cake and all its beautiful embellishments. When it was gone, Vexx swiped her manicured finger over the plate to snag the last smear of frosting. Jackie watched as that finger disappeared into her mouth, how her tongue lingered, savoring the final taste. *Wait*, Jackie thought. "Is your tongue… forked?"

Vexx let out a peal of laughter, sticking her tongue out and wiggling it at Jackie. Sure enough, it split about halfway down, the two sides moving independently. "I have excellent control of both sides."

Without thinking of the implication, Jackie asked, "Why would you want to move your tongue two different ways at once?"

Vexx smirked, and Jackie coughed, looking up at the ceiling for some totally innocent reason not at all related to the mental image *that* brought up.

"We will need to get you some clothes," Jackie said, changing the subject. "Camille… my ex… some of her clothes would probably fit, but I don't really want you walking around in her stuff. She will probably want them back at some point. Plus, they're not really your style." The mental image of Vexx wearing Camille's clothes made Jackie huff out a stifled snort of laughter. She said a silent thanks to Chef Martin for hiring her; she wouldn't have been able to randomly clothe a demon a couple months ago.

"I know my measurements if you'd like to send them off!" Vexx replied.

Jackie sat quietly for a minute, trying to figure out what Vexx meant. *Oh yeah*, she thought, *princess*. "Actually," she said, "I thought we could go shopping."

Vexx clapped her hands with pure excitement. "I would love that! Most of my clothes back home were custom-made. I'm really into retro human fashion, and they don't sell much of it in Infernius."

Jackie looked at her phone, checking the time and ignoring the text notifications from Cam. *How was it already 5:00 p.m.?* "Well, we'd better get going then. I have work tomorrow so I have to actually sleep a little tonight." She realized Vexx was still dressed in her oversized t-shirt and boxers, so she went to Cam's dresser and pulled out a pair of black leggings. Handing them to Vexx, she said, "Not the most fashionable, but you're a lot taller than Camille, so I'm not sure how her jeans would fit."

Vexx began to change right there in the living room, so Jackie hustled into the kitchen, stacking bowls in the sink and trying not to glance into the living room at Vexx. She thought about what she should wear today, picturing cuffed levis, docs, and a black henley. She had the fleeting thought that they would look good together. That is, before she saw the hole Vexx's tail had poked in the leggings, and the way it hiked up the back of her shirt, moving behind her like a cat's. "Oh, um. Your tail."

Vexx glanced behind her. "What about it?"

"It's, well, it's not something humans have. Is there any way to, I don't know, tuck it into your shirt? Just while we go shopping."

"I can try for a little bit, but it's kind of uncomfortable. It starts to hurt if it is restrained for too long."

"That's fine!" Jackie said. "We don't have to be out long, and we can figure something out. I need to take a shower, I'll be back out in a few!"

Vexx nodded, and Jackie headed to her bathroom. When she closed and locked the door, she let out a deep sigh. This was a lot. Like, a lot a lot. A new job, a breakup, new friends, and now a demon appears in her house inexplicably and she is *staying* for three weeks? Jackie leaned her elbows on the sink, staring at her reflection in the water-speckled mirror. She had dark circles beneath her eyes and her hair was a disaster. Her mind was all over the place, and she didn't quite know where to begin. *One thing at a time, Jax,* she thought. She tossed her clothes into the hamper and started the shower. She liked the water hot enough to sting. By the time she stepped in, the mirror only showed the foggy, blurred image of a thick body and a shock of bright pink hair.

Jackie couldn't get the image of Vexx in the nude out of her mind. She wasn't going to cross a boundary; Vexx was not only a stranger, but a demon, and the last things she wanted to do would be to violate the trust of another woman or to anger the literal ruler of Hell. She stuck her face beneath the stream of near-scalding water, pushing her hair back and out of her eyes and letting the sound of the shower drown out the volume of her thoughts. *What am I doing?* She asked herself. *This is all too much.* Once again, her thoughts slipped to Vexx's long legs, the curve of her waist. *She looks like a vintage movie,* she thought. The grey tone of her skin and her silver hair made her seem as though she was a black and white character trapped in a technicolor film world. *She kind of is. This has to be hard for her, too.* Thinking of Vexx's hair reminded Jackie of how it curled slightly at the bottom, settling over the top of her (perfect) breasts in little swirls of silver. Jackie shook her head as though she could physically dislodge the thought. But it stayed, and with another shake of her head at herself for being so taken by someone she didn't even know, her fingers slid down her body.

Jackie was embarrassed. If anyone would have peeked into the shower, they would have seen a woman trying her hardest not to let base instinct dictate her actions. The stress of the last few days was heavy, and as Jackie's hand moved past her round stomach and found the slick skin between her thighs, she thought that maybe she just needed to let herself relax. She was so fucking wet. She hated that she had allowed herself to think so much about Vexx's shameless nudity, but she couldn't help the way her body responded. She and Cam hadn't had sex in well over a month, maybe two. Her vibrator had been on double duty, but right now, she thought, she didn't even need the mechanical assistance. Her fingers moved against herself in small circles, sending waves of tingling down her legs and up her chest. She was fucking throbbing with want, and even just the light touch of her own hand was almost enough to make her come right then. She picked up the pace, letting the tip of her middle finger find her clit directly, moving back and forth with increasing pressure and chasing the growing sensation building at the base of her spine. When was the last time she had done this? Her mouth fell open slightly as her breaths quickened. She braced herself against the blue tile of the shower with her other hand, leaning forward and moving her legs further apart to give herself more access. She slid two fingers into herself. Her body tensed around her. The feeling of being fucked, even by her own hand, was something she felt like she'd forgotten. She was so often the one taking care of Cam's needs, she'd neglected her own. She moved deeper, going faster until the rest of her hand was making little wet noises as it collided with her. The angle of her hand meant the base of her thumb was coming in contact with her clit each time her fingers slid all the way in. She was edging herself, letting the tapping of her thumb bring her almost to orgasm before moving it away and letting the building climax taper off. She moved her fingers back and forth, feeling how tight she was around her own hand.

She almost moaned, but caught herself, remembering Vexx was close enough to hear. Vexx. God, she was the reason for this in the first place. Jackie let herself think of just how luscious she had looked, how that bare skin between her thighs had pretty much begged for Jackie's tongue. She wished those perfectly manicured fingers were the ones plunging in and out of her right now instead of her own. She wanted to taste her, see if her pussy was as hot as the rest of her skin. She probably tasted like smoke, like the smoky sugar of that fucking dessert. Jackie dropped her hand from the wall, moving her slippery fingers against her clit and pushing two fingers from her left hand into herself instead.

Her head fell back as she gave over to the fantasy in her mind. Vexx, lying back against the blue and green pillows of Jackie's bed, her silver hair all around her as she panted Jackie's name. The way she would slowly drag her tongue through the wet heat of her, pushing those perfect thighs apart, lifting an ankle to her shoulder so she had more space to move her hands and mouth. She'd curl her fingers up, pressing into her at just the right angle. She'd always been good at making women come, and occasionally had pushed them to places they didn't know they could go. The image of Vexx spread bare, every inch of her trembling as Jackie's hand fucked her mercilessly, set the pressure building in her own body aflame. She wanted to make Vexx come, to watch her back arch as she lost control, to feel her pussy clench against Jackie's hand, to see her sheets get soaked as Vexx screamed with each ragged breath. And with that, Jackie came—shuddering and shaking and gasping for breath as her body tensed and quaked with orgasm. *Fuck*, she thought, *how the hell am I supposed to look at her now?*

Jackie soaped up and rinsed her slick thighs clean, washing her hair quickly and hoping she hadn't spent that much time in the shower. She really didn't want Vexx asking questions. Her cheeks got hot thinking about it. She *really* didn't want Vexx to feel uncomfortable around her. She'd already flat-out admitted that she was attracted to her, and that she was gay. Sure, Vexx was a demon, but she hadn't given any indication that she wasn't a straight demon. Women sometimes got weird about it, thinking that she must be undressing them all with her eyes just because she was gay. It was irritating. Being a lesbian didn't mean she was attracted to every woman, far from it, actually. She had a very specific type, and outside of that, she rarely gave people a second glance. She stepped out of the shower and wrapped herself in a towel, wiping the mirror enough to see herself clearly. She rubbed at her hair, trying to dry it the best she could, and pulled some styling wax through the neon strands, arranging it in its signature swooping curls. She swiped some concealer under her eyes with her thumb, and brushed her teeth. This was as good as it was gonna get.

When she was dressed in a cozy hoodie and her favorite pair of Levi's, she walked out of her room to find Vexx sitting cross-legged on the sofa, intently watching cartoons. She chuckled, and Vexx turned to look at her. Jackie didn't miss the way her red eyes moved up and down her body. *She's just looking at your outfit*, Jackie admonished. "Ready?" she asked.

Vexx blinked a couple of times and then smiled. "Sure!" she clicked off the TV and stood. "Let's do this. I've always wanted to go to a human mall."

Jackie took a deep breath. "Well, let's see what kind of trouble we can get into."

9

vexx

VEXX HAD NEVER BEEN in a car before, and was torn between absolute terror and elation. She stared out the window in rapt attention, watching other cars, buildings, and the picturesque Seattle scenery whip by. Jackie had seemed on edge after her shower, and as Vexx contemplated how many of the people she saw would end up in Hell, she wondered if she should tell Jackie that she knew precisely why. Vexx hadn't told Jackie much yet. She'd shared about her father, a bit about her life, and trivial things like food she liked and clothes she enjoyed wearing—but she hadn't gone into what being a princess of Hell entailed. Sure, she wasn't really in line for the throne, she had plenty of brothers who would ascend long before she ever could, but she did have some innate abilities.

Infernius was where the most lustful went to receive their eternity of damnation, and thus, she had a very comprehensive understanding of human wants, needs, desires and sexuality. She was very sensitive to human pheromones, and could sniff out sexual interest from a mile away. At times, when demons returned from a visit to the surface, she could still scent desire on them, and she'd be lying if she said she wasn't at least slightly interested why. Vexx herself didn't have much experience. She'd had a summer fling with an incubus, but her father had incinerated him. She'd gone on a few dates with a gorgon, but her father had incinerated her. She'd had a one night stand with a lamia, which had been *very* interesting, but her father had incinerated them as well. In retrospect, that painted a pretty specific picture, and explained why nobody had expressed interest in a few years. *Thanks, father,* she thought. She had never been able to see what the fuss was about when it came to humans. Those in Hell were unable to speak, and if one had touched her… she didn't even want to imagine what her father would do. Now, here on the surface, she understood some of the appeal.

Jackie was hot. Vexx truly hadn't understood why Jackie had been so flustered by her nudity. Jackie hadn't denied being attracted to her, and Vexx had realized pretty quickly that the sugary scent that seemed to trail Jackie wherever she went was not, in fact, sugar. It was desire. Vexx's hearing was much, much better than that of humans. She heard Jackie's quickening breaths, smelled the intense sweetness carried on the hot steam. Her own stomach had flipped in an exciting rush of adrenaline when she heard Jackie's breathing go shaky and rough. She was glad Jackie had taken her time getting dressed; her tail had been flicking back and forth with wild abandon. Her pulse sped up, pounding in her chest, and she had nearly punctured her lip with a canine from biting it so hard.

Vexxanthe Desmodeus Hekate Marie Morningstar was very, very attracted to this human woman. She really, really didn't want her father to burn Seattle to the ground.

They pulled into a parking lot and Vexx stepped out of the car into cool drizzle and grey skies. The air felt amazing on her skin, and she tipped her head back to feel the tiny droplets of water on her face. Vexx felt eyes on her back and turned to see

Jackie watching her with a smile. In the cloud-filtered daylight she could see freckles spangled across Jackie's cheeks. She wanted to kiss the bridge of her nose.

"You ready?" Jackie asked, still smiling.

Vexx stared up at the massive building before her, at the humans bustling in and out with bags on their arms and expressions that ran the gamut of emotions. She had a million things to say, but instead just nodded, trying not to look as overwhelmed as she felt.

The mall was so much more intimidating than Vexx could have ever anticipated. She realized quickly just how different Hell was. Sure, there were a lot of humans, but they were all silent. The demons all groveled before her, and at least in Infernius, there were not many options for places to go outside the palace. There were bars and nightclubs, but the only stores and restaurants were in Lilith's domain. She had never seen something like this. The sprawling mall was two stories high, with moving staircases and stores stretching as far as Vexx could see. There were eateries with bright lights and steaming pans of Hells know what. There were *so many people.* Everywhere she looked, someone was walking. They were talking on phones, eating handheld foods, chasing children, carrying their purchases. She didn't know where to look or what to do. A gentle touch at the small of her back drew her attention back to Jackie, who was looking up at her with what felt like fond amusement.

"It's a big mall," she said. "You okay?"

"Yeah," Vexx replied, once again looking around with wide eyes. Her tail flicked back and forth beneath the large t-shirt she wore. She wished she could let it out, but she understood why she couldn't. And then, her mouth dropped open. There were *demons* here.

Without thinking, she ran up to the pair of succubi. They looked a little strange, but their large wings and curling horns were a dead giveaway. "Hi!" she said, excited. "I didn't expect to see any infernals here!"

The two gaped at her, so she continued. "Which kingdom are you from? I haven't seen you before? Are you visiting or do you live up here? Do you have on a glamour?"

She felt a tug at her elbow and turned to see Jackie with a puzzled expression. "Vexx…" she shifted to face the succubi. "Sorry, my friend thought you were someone else!" She dragged Vexx away with a firm hand on her arm.

"Jackie," she started, "I was just—"

"They're not demons, Vexx," Jackie said. "Look."

Vexx looked back at the pair, now walking quickly in the opposite direction. She saw, now that their backs were to her, that their tails were rigid and unmoving, their wings looked to be made of fabric and wire.

"What…" she began, confused.

"There's an event going on this weekend," Jackie said. "It's called a comic convention. People dress up as characters from popular TV shows, movies, comics… lots of stuff. They're dressed as characters from a video game."

Vexx twirled a piece of her silver hair in her fingers. "I wasn't paying attention. I was just really excited to see someone who looked familiar."

"I'm sorry." Jackie looked crestfallen. "I didn't think this through. I should have considered how you might feel. This is a huge mall, and there's a million people here. I wasn't thinking."

"No!" Vexx interjected. "I'm excited. Can we still go shopping? My tail is starting to feel crampy."

"Absolutely," Jackie answered, forcing a smile back onto her face. "And you know what? Fuck it. Let your tail out. Let people think you're in costume. It's not like it will be the weirdest thing at a Seattle mall."

Vexx felt a trickle of warmth spread through her, and let her tail snake around until its tip had found the small hole in her leggings. The instant it pushed free of the fabric, she breathed a sigh of relief. It felt much better, and Jackie's seemingly unbothered attitude about it felt pretty good too.

She followed Jackie through the mall, went up her first escalator (which was terrifying) and walked into a clothing store with mannequins in the window clad in what Vexx could only assume were trendy seasonal outfits. The clothes here had an edgy vibe, and as Vexx glanced at Jackie, she realized the crease between Jackie's brows was from hopeful anticipation. She wanted Vexx to like this place; she had considered what she knew about Vexx's style and brought her to a store she thought Vexx would like. Once again, that trickle of warmth made its way through her body, this time finding its way to her cheeks. *Damn,* she thought. *I didn't expect humans to be so kind.*

Her human studies classes had focused on a culture of aggression: wars, mass shootings, rape, racism, homophobia… most of what she had been taught about the surface were all the facts of humanity which led people to Hell. Sure, she figured, the syllabus in a university in Hell was not likely to center around good deeds, but since arriving on the surface, Vexx had seen nothing but nice, busy people. People in the mall had smiled at her, the woman working at the store had greeted her happily when they walked in, and Jackie? Jackie had welcomed her into her home, given her a place to sleep, fed her, even let her wear her ex-girlfriend's clothes. Jackie was *kind,* and Vexx didn't quite know how to respond. Kindness was not exactly a desirable trait in Infernius.

Vexx browsed racks of clothes, asking Jackie's opinion on things, and draping hangers across her arm as she went. Before long, her elbow was sore from carrying her pile of potential purchases, and Jackie flagged down someone to let them into the fitting room. Vexx tugged off the t-shirt and pulled off the leggings, careful to free her tail first. She opened the door with a grin. "Can you hand me the first few outfits?"

Jackie made a sort of choking sound and yanked the door shut. "Vexx! You're naked."

"Um, yeah? I'm trying on clothes," Vexx answered in the same tone she'd have used with a young child.

Jackie flopped a couple dresses and pairs of pants over the door unceremoniously. "Just pass what you don't like back over the door," she said.

Vexx rolled her eyes and let out a huff of annoyance. Grumbling to herself, she pulled a pair of leather pants off a hanger and slid them on. "What is vegan leather?" she asked Jackie. "I thought leather was an animal product?"

"Plastic," Jackie replied. "Probably worse for the environment than just wearing the dead cow. But oh well, at least it's less expensive."

Vexx unlatched the door and stepped out. Jackie's mouth opened, but closed quickly, and she swallowed before speaking. "Wow." Her voice came out lower than Vexx had heard it before. "Put that in the 'yes' pile."

Vexx turned and looked at herself over her shoulder. Her tail was uncomfortably pressed against her back, but otherwise, she could see why Jackie had liked the outfit. The pants stopped just above her ankles, and went up to just below her ribcage. They were skin-tight, black, and hugged every curve she possessed. She had chosen to pair the pants with an emerald green silk blouse, and she had to admit that the color looked good on her. She had never worn anything other than black and red; her father didn't want her looking "too human," so she had never seen her skin tone against such a rich color. With her long, silver hair draped over a shoulder, she looked like a model. She felt a giddy little wave of excitement wash over her, making her skin tingle in its wake. She *liked* that Jackie liked the outfit, and she didn't quite know what that meant for her.

She tried on three more outfits, dropping a few items into

her 'yes' pile, and discarding the rest. With each article she passed over the door to Jackie, Jackie passed a new one back. After what seemed like hours, Jackie finally said, "This is it!" after handing her two dresses and a sweater. Vexx hung the dresses next to the mirror and began unbuttoning the first dress.

"I don't want you to feel weird about this," she said, "but I know what happened this morning."

Jackie was quiet for a long time, but finally took an audible, long breath. "What do you mean?"

"In the shower. I'm the Princess of the Kingdom of Lustful Sins, if I were to try and simplify it. So I'm a bit more perceptive than most when it comes to stuff like that."

Jackie didn't reply, so Vexx went on.

"It's not like I was snooping or anything. I just can... oh Hells, this sounds bad." She chewed her lip, realizing she had to finish the sentence. "I can smell when someone feels desire. And I have very, *very* good hearing."

Vexx would have wondered if Jackie was still outside the door, if it weren't for the sweet scent of sugar still lingering in the air. She buttoned the dress and opened the door to find Jackie looking both stricken and mortified, eyes wide and cheeks flushed a deep crimson. She didn't meet Vexx's eyes, staring at the floor slightly to the left of her feet, her fingers tangling and shifting in her lap as she fidgeted.

Vexx stepped closer, and Jackie flinched, bringing Vexx's steps to a screeching halt. She had not wanted this, she thought. The absolute last thing she wanted was for Jackie to flinch or recoil from her, and her stomach plummeted even as Jackie scrambled to hide her reaction.

"I'd like to go," Vexx said in a quiet voice that sounded wounded even to her own ears. She felt vulnerable and weak, and she fucking *hated* it. But even she was not immune to hurt. "Can you possibly pay for these?" she gestured to the clothing hanging outside the fitting room. "And I will give you the money once I figure out how to access my accounts in Hell?"

"Yeah," Jackie said as she stood. "I'll put it on my credit card. Don't worry about it, you can pay me back whenever." Her voice held a note of regret, the words coming out soft and slow, with none of her usual enthusiasm.

As Jackie headed to the register, Vexx got dressed back in Jackie's ex-girlfriend's clothes, and tried not to notice her reflection in the mirror, or the way she looked more disappointed than she ever had before.

10
jackie

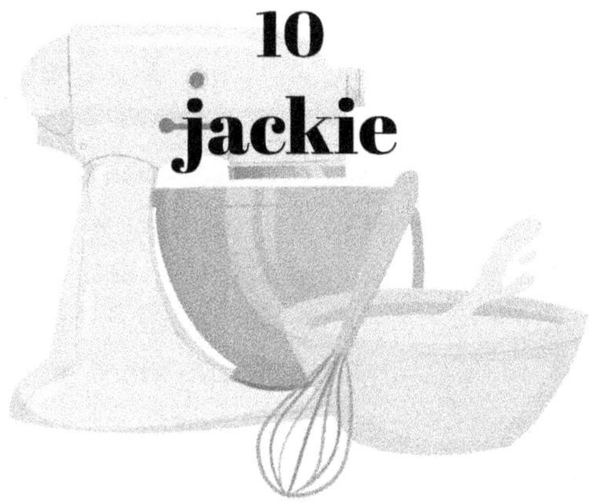

JACKIE MILLER WANTED a drink at this moment more than she had ever wanted anything in her entire life.

Nothing about the day had gone as planned, and she now not only had an additional $475 balance on her credit card, but she also had to live with the knowledge that the goddamn demon living in her apartment knew she had masturbated thinking about her.

Fuck. Fuck. Fuck.

The drive back to Jackie's apartment was nearly unbearable. Her fingers tapped against the steering wheel uncontrollably as though the tiny motion could somehow relieve some of the immense anxious pressure threatening to explode from her skin with each passing second. She cranked the air conditioning up to glacial levels, but it did nothing to cool the heat of embarrassment coursing through her. She watched the white lines snaking down the interstate as she drove, focusing on everything except Vexx's words to her. *I know what happened this morning.* Goddamnit.

Vexx remained quiet as they walked through the door to

Jackie's apartment. She carried her bags into Jackie's bedroom and shut the door behind her. Jackie walked to the kitchen, closed her eyes, and let her head fall back. As she stared at the ceiling, she heard the rustle of plastic as Vexx unpacked her new clothes.

"Where should I put all of this?" Vexx called, her voice muffled by the closed door.

Jackie cleared her throat before answering. "You can hang it in the closet," she yelled back, trying to ensure she was heard. Vexx didn't reply, and Jackie poured herself a glass of water. She heard the snick of the door opening and the soft padding of footsteps, and when she looked up, Vexx stood before her wearing only the borrowed, large t-shirt.

"Hey," Vexx said quietly.

"Hey." Jackie stared into her glass, watching her feet appear to swim from beneath the dregs of water.

"I'm—" Vexx started.

"I'm—" Jackie interrupted.

They both laughed. Jackie ran a hand through her hair while Vexx toyed with the hem of the shirt, baring another inch of her pale thigh. Jackie's eyes followed, watching her red nails fiddle with the fabric.

"I'm sorry," Jackie continued, breaking the quiet of the kitchen.

"Me too," Vexx replied, summoning a tiny whisper of fire at her fingertips. She stared down at it, making it snake in and out of her fingers. "I didn't mean to make things weird. I... I think I'm going to need some time to figure out the right and wrong things to say."

"It's not you. I'm not the greatest at communication. I was embarrassed, and instead of speaking plainly and letting you know how I felt, I shut down."

"I guess I just don't understand how things work on the surface," Vexx said, spinning the tiny flame into a ball and balancing it on a finger. "I wanted you to feel *less* embarrassed. You're attracted to me, I'm attracted to you. I don't know why that would make anyone feel any sort of shame."

Jackie wanted to reply—she really did. *She's attracted to me?* But instead of words, water sprayed from her mouth before she began to cough and choke. The glass clattered against the counter as she scrambled to set it down, and she sucked in a somewhat ragged breath as she attempted to regain her composure. She wiped her mouth with the back of her hand and looked up to see Vexx staring, wide-eyed, with her plush lips slightly parted in shock. The small flame she had been toying with winked out with the tiniest puff of smoke.

The laughter bubbled up from deep within her, beginning as a little chuckle but quickly evolving into full-blown hysterics. Jackie's eyes watered and tears streamed down her cheeks as she laughed and laughed. Vexx continued to stare, and it only made Jackie laugh more. Her stomach muscles hurt, and she wrapped her tattooed arms around her middle. "I'm… sorry…" she managed to choke out. "I… I don't know what's wrong with me."

The corners of Vexx's lips lifted, a soft smile brightening her face and making her red eyes sparkle. Jackie thought that she truly was the most beautiful woman… demon? that she had ever seen. But then she grinned, the expression positively radiant with mirth, and she began to laugh as well. *No,* Jackie thought. *Now, she is stunning.*

Jackie was the one staring now, and when Vexx noticed, her laugh shuttered abruptly. "What?" she said. "Why are you looking at me like that?"

"You are gorgeous, Vexx," Jackie said in a gentler voice than usual. "Seeing you laugh is… it's stunning. I guess I'm just…" She steeled herself, straightening her spine and allowing herself to feel bold. "I'm just astonished that *you* are attracted to *me.*"

"Is that why you laughed?" Vexx's eyebrows drew together

in an adorable, puzzled expression. "I thought you were laughing at me."

"God, no," Jackie replied. "I was laughing at myself. Spitting a mouthful of water on a demon was not on my bingo card for this year."

"Bingo…?"

Jackie shook her head with a smile. "Don't try to figure that one out. It's more to explain than it's worth. Essentially, none of this is normal, and the entire situation is so ridiculous that all I can do at this point is laugh."

"Believe me, none of this feels normal to me either." Vexx gestured toward the window. "I hadn't even seen a sky before. I've never eaten fancy chocolate desserts, or been shopping in a mall, or ridden in a car. Literally every part of this is new to me. I'm trying to figure it out too."

"I know you are." Jackie took a small step towards Vexx. "And you really are doing a great job. If anything, I should be the calm and composed one here. But I'm an anxious mess of a person, and I've had so much shit happen lately to have me on edge that this has just sort of pushed me over. I didn't expect you."

Vexx stepped forward, bringing herself within arm's reach of Jackie. She reached out, her fingers running down Jackie's bicep and curling around her elbow before dropping back to her side. "I didn't expect you either."

Jackie closed the distance between them, tipping her chin up slightly to look Vexx in the eye. This close, she was very aware of the volume of her breathing and the faint scent of smoke and cherries that clung to the silver strands of Vexx's hair. She felt Vexx's hot breath—small, nervous little bursts of air that gave away the tension that Vexx seemed to share. She allowed her hand to graze Vexx's hip, her fingertips feeling each ridge of thread in the fabric of her shirt and lifting just before they hit skin. *Am I doing this?* She thought. *Am I really touching her right now?*

Her heart pounded a frantic rhythm, and she drew her lip between her teeth to keep it from opening and spilling truth she wasn't sure she knew how to articulate. The tip of Vexx's forked tongue darted out to moisten her sinfully decadent lips, and Jackie couldn't help but want to know what it would feel like sliding against her own. She released her lip, feeling the tingle of blood rushing back to the tiny divots her teeth had made. Vexx's mouth pursed, and a shaky breath fanned across Jackie's cheek as she bent down. Her eyes never left Jackie's, not even as her graceful fingers found their way beneath Jackie's chin, tipping her head even further up toward her, as her silver hair tumbled down to frame Jackie's face.

And then someone pounded on the door.

Vexx's heavy-lidded eyes flew open, shooting to the door as her fingers dropped Jackie's chin. The movement was so sudden, so unexpected, that Jackie felt herself list forward slightly as though the invisible rope anchoring her to Vexx had been cut. The pounding came again, echoing through the apartment, and Jackie's mind seemed to shake itself off. She walked to the door, barely contained annoyance evident in the set of her shoulders, and looked through the peephole as she shouted, "What?!"

The word died in her throat, ending in a weak upturned sound that made the question sound less like a demand and more like a nervous plea. She turned back to Vexx, taking a couple steps away from the door, her expression bordering on panic.

Vexx hissed. "What? Who is it?"

Jackie's mouth opened and closed and her fingers tapped against her thighs. "It's Stella, Cam's sister."

Vexx squeaked like a baby mouse and Jackie wanted to appreciate the adorable sound, but the presence of the second-to-last person she'd like to see at her doorway kept her lips pressed together. Vexx turned, looking toward the door, the bedroom, and the kitchen in quick succession before looking at Jackie with a pained, beseeching expression. Jackie swiped a thumb over the back of Vexx's hand, rolled her shoulders, and as another thundering fistfall hit the door, she stepped away from Vexx and opened it.

Stella lurched into the apartment, the momentum of her furious knocking propelling her forward. She crashed into Jackie, yelping a disgusted sound as her chest collided with Jackie's shoulder.

"What the fuck do you want, Stella?" Jackie asked without bothering to hide the contempt in her tone.

"I'm here for Cam's shit," Stella said. Her words were clipped and sharp. "Good to see you're... busy." She looked at Vexx with a sneer. "Clearly you're heartbroken at the loss of my sister." Her sandy blonde hair was cut into a severe bob at her chin, making her look much older than she was. Paired with her designer slacks and impeccably crisp blouse, she looked like some sort of boardroom executive rather than a woman who owned a secondhand clothing store.

"Your sister is a cheating bitch, and I refuse to give her a single second more of my life." Jackie's hand settled on her ample hip, and she gestured to the bedroom with her chin. "Hope you brought a truck or something. I'm not helping and she's got a fuckload of furniture."

"You can keep it," Stella replied, walking toward the bedroom. Her thin hand lifted to grip the doorway and she looked over her shoulder. "She just wants her clothes and her shit from the bathroom. I'll be out of your hair quickly and you can go back to whoever, or—" she looked Vexx up and down, disgust contorting her angular face "—*whatever* you were about to do."

Vexx tensed, and Jackie caught the small movement of her

hands as she balled them into fists at her sides. "What, or *who* I do is none of your fucking business, Stella. Get her shit and get the fuck out of my house. I need to get to bed. Some of us have work in the morning." She turned to Vexx, whose face was frozen in an expression somewhere at the convergence of shame and anger. "Do you mind getting dressed real quick so we can get out of here? Let's walk down and get a coffee. Stella's not stupid enough to fuck with any of my stuff." She raised her voice to ensure that Stella could hear her. "She might have a sharp mouth, but if she knows what's good for her, she'll be gone before we get back and I won't have to physically remove her from my home."

Stella said nothing, just continued to toss clothes into a duffel bag set atop the bed. She didn't even look at Vexx as she maneuvered past Stella, pulling a pair of jeans and a sweater from the closet before bending to pick up her boots. She hurried into the bathroom, dressing quickly before nearly running back to the safety of the kitchen and Jackie. Stella glanced back once before kicking the door shut with one black patent heel. Jackie didn't hesitate, just reached for Vexx's hand and loosened her white-knuckled fist with her own warm fingers. Vexx turned to her before glancing down at their hands. The smallest smile tugged at the edge of her mouth, and then she nodded, intertwining her fingers with Jackie's. "I could use a coffee."

11
vexx

VEXX LET OUT an audible noise of appreciation as she stepped through the glass doors into the bustling coffeeshop. The scents of espresso and chocolate tangled with the cool bite of petrichor and humans, somehow blending into something that felt like a hug. Stella arriving had been… tense. Vexx had never felt like that before, like she should be embarrassed for just existing somewhere. Stella had looked at her like she was an insect and it made Vexx feel small and uncomfortable. *No,* she thought. *I am Vexxanthe Desmodeus Hekate Marie Morningstar, Princess of Hell, and no Chanel-clad snooty bitch is going to make me feel less than I am.*

"Well, she was a bitch," Vexx said cooly, turning to Jackie, whose hand still rested in hers. She shrugged Jackie's coat from her shoulders. She hadn't thought to grab the one she had purchased before they left, and despite the thick weave, the grey sweater she wore didn't keep out the chill. Jackie had noticed the way she curled in on herself to try and block the wind, and had literally given her the coat off her back. It was heavy wool, and it smelled like Jackie. Vexx wanted to live in it forever.

Jackie pulled down her hood and ran her other hand through her hair, making the hot pink strands curl at odd angles in a way that looked effortlessly cool. Her sweatshirt was a dark slate blue, and Vexx had the odd thought that Jackie looked like a stormy sea. "Yeah, Stella has never liked me. They wanted Cam to find someone with a fancy degree and a 401K. Instead, she ended up with a butch line cook." She let out a low chuckle. "Somehow I don't think they'd even approve now, and I have one of the most sought after positions in the city."

"Why are they like that?" Vexx asked, her brows pinching together as her nose wrinkled. "Why would they look down on you because of your career?"

"Cam's parents have always been well-off. Her dad was one of the first guys to really strike gold in Silicon Valley. He was a smart dude, developed some kind of security program that was bought out by the military or something. When he died, he left them a veritable fortune, and Cam's mom Yvette could have retired, but didn't. Their whole family views work as the center of their identity. Her sisters live and breathe their business, and even though she tries to pretend she prefers the outdoors and saving baby otters or whatever, Cam feeds on the attention she gets from her position. She's an advertising exec at a top agency, and she has campaigns all over the country to show off to her family. I make food, they don't think it's the same."

"But people actually *need* to eat," Vexx replied. "You do something creative and interesting, you work somewhere upscale, you actually *work*, not just sit behind a computer."

"Yeah," Jackie answered, stepping up to the counter. "But working with your hands just isn't something the Archer family thinks is good enough for them. But whatever, Cam can get fucked. Stella too."

Vexx laughed and Jackie's fingers squeezed hers tightly

before letting them go. Vexx's hand felt suddenly cold, tingling with the desire to be back against Jackie's skin.

Jackie looked up at the menu board, turning to Vexx. "Do you know what you want?"

There were so many options, so many drinks Vexx had never heard of, and a whole case of pastries with French names Vexx couldn't even hope to pronounce. "Can you order for me?" Vexx asked. "Something sweet?"

Jackie beamed, and Vexx knew at once that Jackie truly enjoyed this, being in service to others. Maybe it was a gender roles thing, and having someone super femme like Vexx made her want to take up the mantle of "knight in shining armor," or maybe Jackie just liked being needed. Vexx got the sense that it had been awhile since someone made Jackie feel appreciated. She looked at Jackie's wide, earnest face as she spoke to the barista. Her round cheeks with their faint spangling of freckles, her full mouth framed by deep-seated smile lines that spoke of a life lived for enjoyment. Jackie didn't look like someone who was worried about appearances, but she was stylish and suave and sexy all the same. Vexx didn't bother listening to any of the words Jackie rattled off to the girl behind the counter before tapping her credit card and punching in a generous tip. When Jackie pivoted to face her, Vexx had the nearly overwhelming urge to kiss her cheek. But instead, she took the hand Jackie offered her, and let herself be led to a small table near the window. The grey Seattle rain pattered against the window, rolling down the glass in crystal-clear rivulets, catching the glare of headlights in little flashes. The seats were well-worn leather, and as Vexx sat, she noticed there was a stack of board games as well as a shelf full of very used, if not slightly tattered, books beside the counter. The coffee shop felt cozy, homey.

"This place is cute," Vexx said to Jackie as she continued to take in the space, noticing small details in every somewhat cluttered corner. "Do you come here a lot?"

"I usually make my own coffee," Jackie answered. "But I do like this spot for when I need to get out of the house."

"They have so many fun little things," Vexx replied. "Games and books and are those art supplies over there?" She gestured to a desk against the far wall that was covered by bins overflowing with various paintbrushes, yarn, fabric pieces, a tabletop easel and what appeared to be a small sewing machine.

"Yeah!" Jackie's smile lit up her whole face. "The owners are quirky as hell. They wanted this shop to function as both a coffee shop, cafe, and a place where other quirky introverts could hang out. It started with the games, and then someone started bringing books, and when the desk showed up, people started bringing project scraps and equipment they didn't need anymore. They have classes here sometimes, well, 'classes' might be a generous description. They have guided art nights, I should say. I've always wanted to come to one, but I work most nights and Cam never wanted to."

Vexx's reply came out in a jumbled waterfall of quick-moving words that surprised even her. "I want to!"

For some reason Vexx didn't quite understand, Jackie's cheeks grew red and her gaze shifted to her lap where she fiddled with the hem of her sleeve. "If you're still around next time they do one, let's go."

Vexx's heart felt like a leaden weight in her chest, falling heavily and dragging her excitement with it. *Oh yeah,* she thought, *I have to go home eventually.* However, all she said was, "Absolutely. Let's do it."

A server wearing a violet-striped blazer arrived at their table, balancing their full tray on one tattooed forearm as they set down two steaming, mismatched mugs and a plate with three small pastries. "Enjoy!" they called as they headed to their next table, and Vexx looked down at the pastries with hearts in her eyes.

"I ordered you a honey halva latte," Jackie said as she pushed a mug in front of Vexx. "It has sesame, pistachio, honey and a bit of cinnamon. And I had them make it with oat milk, I think it makes it taste even more like dessert."

Vexx lifted the warm mug and took a deep breath of the curling sweet steam. She took a tentative sip and let out a long noise of appreciation. "Hells below," she said. "That might be the best coffee I have ever tasted."

Jackie tried to appear nonchalant, but she was clearly pleased with herself. She took a sip of her own drink, midnight black coffee—straight up. "I also got a couple treats." She pointed to each as she named them. "An almond croissant stuffed with marzipan and cherries, a chocolate pot de crème, and a slice of basbousa. It's like a dense almond and coconut cake. One of the owners is Egyptian, and she uses her mother's recipe. It's one of my favorites." She passed Vexx a small spoon, their fingers lightly grazing.

Each bite was more delicious than the last. Vexx learned very quickly that the croissant had to be picked up, there was no way to cut the flaky, buttery pastry with her spoon. The cherries were tart and sweet, nestled into a layer of marzipan. The chocolate dish was like a decadent little pudding, not too sweet and topped with a dusting of shaved dark chocolate. And the cake? The cake tasted like Vexx imagined a hug from a mom would feel like: warm, thick, and perfectly sweet. The sticky sauce stuck to her lips and she licked it off slowly, savoring every drop.

Jackie watched her from over her mug. Vexx felt her observing stare, and gave her a small smile when she had finished cleaning the sugar from her lower lip. "I suppose I should have gotten you some real food," Jackie said. "It's already well past dinnertime."

"This is great," Vexx said as she lifted another spoonful of chocolate to her lips. "I really like sweets."

"Yeah, but I haven't fed you any actual food whatsoever today. I have work tomorrow, so you're going to be on your own for like twelve hours. I really should have at least taken you to the grocery store. I'm not great at having houseguests I guess."

"I'll be fine," Vexx assured her. "I was thinking about it earlier, and I actually have an acquaintance in Seattle. I wouldn't call him a friend or anything, but I've known him for years. Since I'm going to be here for a few weeks, I thought maybe I would figure out how to get to his office and see if he had any work for me so I'm not just relying on your generosity until I get… home." The word felt sour on her tongue, but she continued. "He does consulting for my father, follows trends on the surface and what have you. It helps my father stay on top of the current sins, and what type of humans will be making their way down to our kingdom."

Jackie chuckled under her breath. "I never would have guessed that Hell is such a business enterprise. I never thought much about it, to be honest, what with all my atheism and whatever. But if you'd have asked me to describe Hell a month ago I'd have given a very Dante's Inferno-esque vibe with all the fire and torture and what have you."

Vexx rolled her eyes and an exasperated sigh found its way through her cherry-red lips. "Fucking Dante," she said. "That guy was such a prick."

"Wait," Jackie interjected. "You knew Dante?"

Vexx propped her elbow on the slightly wobbly tabletop and set her chin in her hand. It squished her cheek up a little, and Jackie couldn't help but find the gesture adorable, even for a literal demon. "Dante traded some portion of his afterlife for a tourist visa. They aren't given out often, as I'm sure you can imagine, but for some reason he was seen as valuable enough to Hell to barter for a tour. He stayed for like a week, and honestly, a lot of what he ended up writing wasn't too far from the truth. But he took a lot of creative license. I think the only reason they even let him visit was to scare some people on the surface into sinning a little less. It was during a population boom, and we really hadn't built the infrastructure to hold that many souls at once."

"This sounds like a sitcom," Jackie said with a laugh and a shake of her head. "I cannot imagine what the pope would say if he knew all this."

"Yeah, everyone thinks it's all fire and brimstone and eternal torture and whatever, but most of the time the real suffering and punishment comes from the monotony of doing something you despise every day for all of eternity. Sure, we torture and maim *really* fucked up people, but the vast majority of standard-level soul citizens of Hell just end up doomed to spend endless years doing something that made them miserable in life, and being deprived of anything that ever made them happy. Most of the human housekeeping staff of my father's estate were royalty on the surface, so it really chaps their asses to have to scrub floors and wear rags. The waitstaff at my favorite bar were mostly alcoholics in life, and so now they have to pour and serve alcohol to demons without ever getting to taste it again. Torture is in the little things, it's effective." She shrugs her shoulders. "But enough about Hell. I've lived there my whole life. I'm much more interested in life up here. That's why I'm going to go see Seth tomorrow. He's spent lots of time above and below, and he knows my father, so I'm pretty sure he will be glad to give me a temporary job."

"Wait," Jackie said, shifting back slightly in her seat. "Seth? As in Seth Kazon?"

Vexx's eyebrows rose in surprise. "You know Seth?"

"Vexx, everybody knows him," Jackie replied, astonishment clear on her face. "His company, Jungle is literally the biggest company in the United States, fuck, probably the world. I don't think I've even ever met someone who doesn't use Jungle.com.

Its headquarters is here, and they're the biggest employer in Seattle. If I had actually thought to take you to the store, we'd have gone to one of their grocery markets. Holy shit, Vexx."

"Honestly, I had no idea," Vexx said, laughing. "I took Human Studies, but it was mostly about war and violence. I didn't learn a whole lot about day-to-day life on the surface. So, Seth is like a celebrity then?"

"He's the wealthiest man in the US. He's probably in the top five wealthiest men on Earth. I have absolutely no idea how you're going to get to talk to him. I'm sure he's got security out the ass. A lot of people have a big problem with how Jungle has taken over and pushed small businesses into closing. Places like this—" she gestured around the coffeeshop "—can't compete with a company like Jungle. I could literally go on my phone right now and order seriously any product you could want, and it would be at my front door by the time we woke up."

"I know his assistant pretty well," Vexx answered, crossing her thin ankles and leaning back in her chair to stretch her back. "I'm pretty sure if I get to their main office I can get them to call her, and she'll call him. My father isn't exactly the kind of demon you say no to."

Jackie shook her head, smiling, and drank the last bit of her coffee. "Go get that money, girl. It's not like I can't afford to help you out while you're stuck up here, but I'm also not rich. I haven't even gotten my first check from Canid yet, so it would definitely help."

A server, this one wearing a faded KEXP hoodie and fishnets beneath torn skinny jeans stepped up to their table. "Are you folks all finished with this?" She pointed to the empty plate between them, and Jackie quickly reached over to set both of their mugs atop it.

"We sure are, thank you so much," Jackie said as the server loaded up her tray.

Vexx smiled up at her as well. "Everything was so good,

thank you! Tell whoever made that cake that they need to take their recipe to the grave. It's way too good to be sharing it!"

The girl grinned. "That would be my Teta. I'll let her know you liked it. She'd be happy to know she made someone's day!" She bustled off, picking up empty glassware and trash as she snaked through the crowded space.

Jackie stood, smoothing out her sweatshirt over her stomach. "Stella should be gone by now, and I really need to get some sleep tonight. I have to be at Canid early tomorrow. You picked a good day to be summoned to my kitchen. Canid is closed on Mondays, but I have to meet with Chef Martin before prep begins, so I need to be there by 9:30 a.m. at the very latest. Are you sure you'll be okay on your own tomorrow? I have a map of the metro, it's not super complicated to use once you get the hang of it. And I'll give you some cash to get around with tomorrow, at least until we figure out what the plan is moving forward. I'm sorry, I should have thought about all of this sooner, but getting you some clothes seemed more important at the time."

"I'll be fine," Vexx said as she pushed her chair back and rose. They stood facing each other for a beat too long, both unsure how to proceed. Jackie reached for her coat where it rested over the back of Vexx's chair, holding it up for Vexx to slide her arms back into. All at once the intoxicating scent of Jackie wrapped around her once again, all sugar and sex and a faint hint of salty sweat. It made Vexx's mouth water and she swallowed, not wanting to look as overwhelmed as she felt.

Her senses were so much more developed than that of humans, and being surrounded by scents and pheromones and residual heat that all made her think of sex was... a lot. She wasn't used to denying herself anything she wanted, and she honestly didn't know what she was supposed to do to hide the want that bloomed low in her stomach. She was, after all, the princess of lust. But Jackie held out her hand and Vexx took it carefully, holding her breath and hoping that whatever had been about to happen before Stella was still possible. Jackie opened the door for her, placing her strong, warm hand in the small of Vexx's back to guide her through it. She threaded her fingers back between Vexx's when they stepped into the cold, grey drizzle of Seattle after dark. She matched Vexx's stride, face hidden beneath her now rain-speckled hood, and when they got back to Jackie's apartment, she once again opened the door so Vexx could step into the comfortable warmth which still smelled of chocolate and the tiniest hint of brimstone. Stella was gone, praise Hell, and there was no indication she had even been there except for three empty drawers in the dresser and a cleared-off countertop in the bathroom where makeup and perfume had been arranged in precise rows. Vexx caught a faint whiff of Stella's perfume and wrinkled her nose.

It smelled like Stella had looked, pretentious and bitchy, heavy with roses and amber and shit that rich people thought smelled classy. But as Vexx turned to watch Jackie pull her hoodie off, her t-shirt lifting a little and exposing the soft-looking tattooed skin of her stomach above her jeans, she couldn't help but think that this is why so many people like Stella ended up in Hell. If Cam had been anything like her sister, Vexx felt she could safely assume that she hadn't appreciated what was right in front of her. Honesty and hard work were so much more valuable than overpriced perfume and cashmere. As she tugged her shirt back down and ran her hands through her damp hair, Jackie looked up at Vexx. Her bright turquoise eyes sparkled below her impossibly long lashes. Vexx actually felt her pupils dilate as she tasted that sugary scent of lust and desire in the air. Jackie's thumbs hooked in the belt loops of her cuffed indigo jeans, and her tattooed biceps looked strong and thick and like they should be around Vexx right this instant. Her heart raced, trapped within the cage of her ribs, and her pale, grey skin pebbled.

"What?" Jackie said, a flicker of flirtatious mischief in her smirk.

Vexx didn't reply, just bent down to unlace her boots, looking at Jackie all the while. She stepped out of the heavy leather platforms, losing a couple inches of height, but as she walked up to Jackie, she was still half a foot taller. Her fingers slid beneath Jackie's chin again, tipping her head up to look directly into Vexx's ruby-colored eyes, and as the air around them crackled and thickened with the sweet smell and electric energy of want, Vexx lowered her mouth to Jackie's, kissing her with all the restrained passion Stella had so rudely interrupted. Jackie's hands moved to Vexx's hips, pulling their bodies flush, and Vexx moved her fingers from Jackie's chin into her hair. Her nails gently scraped across Jackie's neck, and a low groan traveled on Jackie's tongue to tangle with Vexx's.

That sound seemed to release the chains binding all the desire trapped within Vexx. She threaded her fingers into the longer strands of Jackie's softly curling neon hair, gripping it tightly as she crushed Jackie's mouth against hers. Her forked tongue swirled around Jackie's, tasting a faint remnant of coffee and cake. Vexx felt molten heat roll down her body, tightening her nipples beneath her sweater, sliding down the curve of her hip, and pooling between her thighs. She knew she was impossibly wet, felt how slick her skin was where her thick legs pressed together in a vain attempt to contain the primal need she felt. When she pulled away from Jackie for just a second, sucking in a deep breath, her tongue flicked out like a serpent's, tasting sex on the air, emanating from them both. Hells below, she wanted to taste it on Jackie's skin. She wanted to part her slick flesh and press into her, wanted to swirl her tongue around within Jackie's drenched cunt and drown her senses in the desire that radiated from Jackie in hot, sugary waves. She wanted to eat Jackie for dessert until she came, crushing Vexx's cheeks between her thighs.

But she felt Jackie pull away, ever so slightly. Felt the electric energy in the air dissipate around them, felt the shuddering, reluctant sigh that escaped Jackie's chest. "Vexx…" Jackie said, her voice strained and heavy with contradiction that Vexx felt in her very bones. "We can't, not tonight, not now. Fuck, I want to. I don't think I've ever wanted anything more in my entire goddamn life, but we can't do this right now."

Vex let her fingers untangle from Jackie's hair, her hand falling back to her side. Her eyes found Jackie's, saw just how much she was fighting to maintain control, and she let her mouth curl into a soft smile. "I understand," Vexx replied. "Get some sleep, I know tomorrow is important. I won't tempt you into changing your mind, promise."

Jackie forced a breath out through her nose, eyes closing as she tried to regain some composure. "Vexx, you tempt me more than you can possibly imagine." She turned, rolling her shoulders like a boxer getting ready for a fight, and shook her head. "I'll see you in the morning?"

"Of course," Vexx replied. "I'll take the couch tonight."

12
jackie

WHEN JACKIE WALKED into Canid at 9:15 a.m. Tuesday morning, there was a spring in her step that even Chef Martin's pinched expression couldn't dampen. With a confident smile, she laid out her notebooks, her sketches and flipped through the photos and videos on her phone—showing him what she had done with his original concept. Martin was silent, his index finger held over his thin lips as he inspected her work. Jackie tried not to let her excitement boil over, doing her very best to appear every bit the collected professional she was. But this was where she shone, where her passion truly lay, and her skin seemed to vibrate with anxious energy as she waited for his assessment.

"How much of this can be prepped ahead of time?" he asked, that skinny finger tapping away at his chin as he continued to stare. "Will each of these elements hold? Can we prep twice a week?"

"Nearly every component, Chef," Jackie replied. "As long as we can store the domes in a dry area, they'll hold for at least 48 hours. The cakes can be baked and frozen, they're small enough that they won't require much, if any, thaw time. The only piece that will need to be made close to service is the sugared leaves, they'll absorb moisture too quickly to store in the fridge, and they'll start to brown if we leave them at room-temp for too long. Assembly shouldn't take much more than four to six minutes, including the smoke. I can cut that down if necessary, pare back on the garnishes, and focus on one or two rather than the five you see here."

"Can you train Everest on this or is it something you need to do exclusively yourself?"

"I can train anyone with a steady hand. The isomalt is a little finicky, but it's simple enough." Jackie's palms started to sweat. Martin's expression was still unreadable. Was it too ambitious? Did she make too many changes to his initial concept? She wiped her hands on her apron and took a few deep breaths through her nose. This is why he had hired her, she had no reason to doubt herself. She knew it was good, knew it was a plate that would look spectacular in an editorial article, and knew that Chef Martin's goal was always to be ahead of trends. Canid's reputation was built on skill, and she had skills that would elevate that reputation as long as she didn't aim too high.

"Excellent," Martin said, stepping back and clasping his hands behind his back. "Have Everest come in early tomorrow and get him trained on production as well as assembly. I would like to taste the completed dish tomorrow before dinner service begins. Is it feasible to add to the menu by Friday?"

Jackie gave a sharp nod. "Yes, Chef. Consider it done." A smile crept onto her mouth and though she tried to push it down, her pride refused to be dimmed. This had been a test, at least in her mind. Bringing this concept from page to plate was a way for Chef Martin to gauge her skill as well as her creativity, and she had crushed it. *Literally,* she thought as she glanced at the little mallet atop the worktable. Chef Valardi may have been an asshole as a general rule, but she respected him as a chef, and deep-down, she craved his approval. She wanted to be impressive, wanted to see her name printed in tiny italicized letters beneath professional editorial photographs. She wanted to be appreciated.

"Miller?" Chef Martin spoke, interrupting Jackie's cascade of thoughts. "Good work. This is the sort of work that makes Canid, Canid." Jackie swore she caught the edges of his mouth softening for a brief moment before he turned and walked away.

I did it, she thought. *I impressed Chef Martin Valardi.*

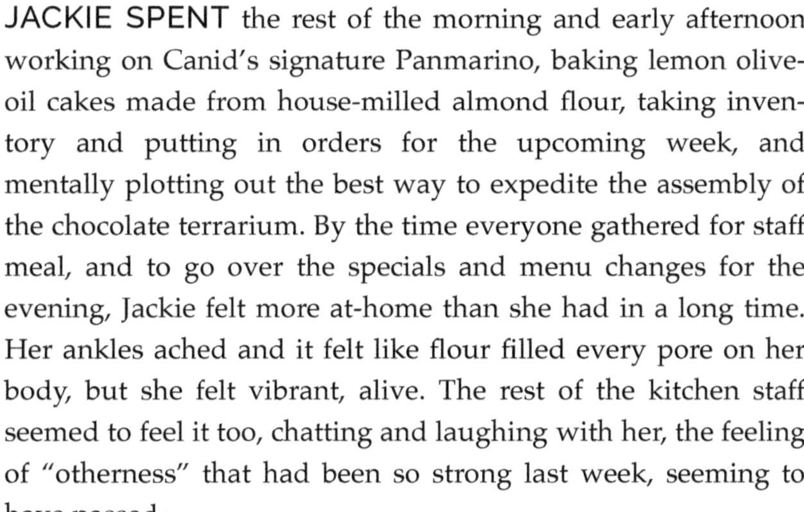

JACKIE SPENT the rest of the morning and early afternoon working on Canid's signature Panmarino, baking lemon olive-oil cakes made from house-milled almond flour, taking inventory and putting in orders for the upcoming week, and mentally plotting out the best way to expedite the assembly of the chocolate terrarium. By the time everyone gathered for staff meal, and to go over the specials and menu changes for the evening, Jackie felt more at-home than she had in a long time. Her ankles ached and it felt like flour filled every pore on her body, but she felt vibrant, alive. The rest of the kitchen staff seemed to feel it too, chatting and laughing with her, the feeling of "otherness" that had been so strong last week, seeming to have passed.

Everest, however, still stayed back from the group. As Jackie passed him, walking straight for the food, her stomach growled like a poorly trained rottweiler. He seemed to hear it, and looked up at her, shaking his head. "Traitor," he hissed, but she saw the smile lines at the corners of his eyes.

"Oh shut up," she replied. She lowered her voice. "I'm just

doing reconnaissance work, scoping out the enemy," she said in a conspiratorial whisper.

Everest rolled his eyes, and went back to whatever he had been doing on his phone. Texting Seven, no doubt.

She stepped into the throng of boys, following the scent of garlic and sauteed mushrooms. Andrew raised an eyebrow as he passed her a plate. "Good work on that showcase dessert," he said. "I wasn't sure anyone could actually turn that from an idea into reality. It's going to be really cool." Was Andrew… being nice to her?

Jackie's face split into a grin. "Thanks, man," she replied. "It's been awhile since I got to really sink my teeth into a creative project like that." She speared a couple pieces of orecchiette and a charred mushroom on her fork, swirling it in a silky, green sauce. She glanced at Everest and noticed that he also had a plate. *Maybe Andrew isn't so bad*, she thought. *Or maybe he just happened to plan a meatless meal tonight. Fuck if I know.*

"Word on the street is that not only someone from the Times, but a couple other major restaurant critics will be making the rounds this month." Andrew said as he took a bite of his own pasta. "Now that Emerald City is over, it's almost time for Seattle Restaurant Week. Chef didn't participate last year, but he's putting together a tasting course for this year's spring event, so the next couple weeks are going to be all about generating buzz for Canid's first year on the circuit."

"Oh, shit," Jackie replied, her fork clattering against her plate as she looked up in surprise. Restaurant Week meant more diners, but fixed-price menus. Last year, the most expensive tier had only been sixty-five dollars per person. With Canid's prices what they were, she was genuinely shocked that Chef Martin had decided to participate.

Andrew smirked as he replied. "It's damn good advertising, and with a fixed tasting course, it's easier on us. From what I saw a few years back at Anchor & Iron, most of the restaurant guides and magazines will be trying out hot spots in preparation. Should be a few good articles and website features about the top picks for this year. Yours is a showcase piece, and Chef is going to want to get it in front of people with influence. Who knows, maybe another star is in our future. Did he discuss a name for it with you?"

Jackie shook her head. "Nope, just gave me the original concept and told me to run with it." She felt her pulse pick up when Andrew's words really sunk in. Canid had already done the unthinkable, expanding the Michelin guide. It wasn't only California, Chicago, DC and NYC anymore. Florida had received their first stars last year, and as of this year, Canid was the only restaurant in the state to claim the honor.

Andrew looked over his shoulder to where Chef Martin stood with a handful of servers. "Chef!" he called out. "Name for Jackie's chocolate thing?"

Martin waved his hand in the air as though shooing a particularly pesky fly. "Come up with something and get it to Deandra by end of day so she can get it printed." He turned his attention back to the service staff and Andrew raised a brow at Jackie.

"Looks like it's all you, Chef."

Jackie thought for a moment, looking out the window and catching a glimpse of the cascade mountains peeking through the fog. "Amoureux de la Forêt," she said decisively. Because that, she thought, was what the dish was to her: a love letter to the forest, an acknowledgement of the region she had come to think of as home, with or without Cam. Canid was, as a whole, a restaurant built around the concept of upscale botanical. The menu was never bound by any particular culinary discipline, featuring elements from various cultures and locales, blended and developed into something entirely new. Her Amoureux de la Forêt would look like it belonged here; Jackie pictured the smoke curling over the glossy teak tabletops as guests broke into their own private little fantasy. *Jackie* felt like she belonged here, working at the best restaurant in Seattle, finally being acknowledged for her talent and drive. *Suck it, Cam.* But even as she allowed the warmth of pride to suffuse her cheeks with a rosy blush, she felt her thoughts drift to Vexx. *I wonder how her day is going.*

Throughout the evening, Jackie caught Everest giving her furtive glances. He was quieter than usual, quick to do as she asked, but with a different energy than he had last week. When she spotted him ducking into the walk-in, she followed after.

"Hey," she said. "You okay?"

Everest jumped a little, his head snapping to her in surprise. "Shit, I didn't see you come in here." He rubbed his neck, tousling his hair. "Yeah, I'm fine."

"You're acting weird, dude." Jackie watched how his weight shifted from one foot to the other. He looked like a rabbit ready to bolt. "Did I do something?"

His eyes darted to the door of the walk-in and he let out a long sigh. "Seven's position at Jungle is being eliminated. We were supposed to move in together this summer, but we can't do it on my salary, and our savings sucks. This is literally the best position I can possibly find with my work history, and it's not enough."

"Oof," Jackie huffed. "How can I help?"

"I wish there was an answer," he replied. "There's nothing anybody can do. I overheard you talking to Andrew, and I'm just hoping that restaurant week means overtime, and that I can manage to sock away some extra cash until Seven can find another job."

"What does he do? What kind of work?"

"He's an ASL interpreter," Everest replied. "He's a CODA."

"...CODA?" Jackie replied, brows furrowing.

Everest chuckled. "Sorry! It's an acronym for 'child of deaf adults.' His parents are both deaf, so English is actually his second language. Jungle has employed him as an interpreter for the last few years, but there's apparently tech now that can interpret in real time, so they don't need an actual person anymore."

"What the fuck?" Jackie said. "I can't imagine that a human being can really be replaced by a computer or whatever. Isn't there, like, nuance to language that matters?"

"Yeah." Everest reached for a Cambro of greens. "But it's business. Kazon doesn't give a fuck about people. It's all about profit." He grabbed the container and pushed open the walk-in door with a bony hip. "I'll be fine, I'm sorry I seemed sketch. Let me know if there's any extra work I can put in. I know you've got that fancy project thing going on."

Jackie nodded, the gears in her head spinning. "Totally. Come in tomorrow at nine so I can start training on that? If you work 'til close that will be a few hours overtime at least?"

"Sounds good," he said as he headed back to his station. "I appreciate you."

13
vexx

JUNGLE HEADQUARTERS WAS the largest and strangest building that Vexx could have imagined. It had taken her an hour to decipher the transit schedule Jackie had left for her, but she eventually figured it out. When she stepped off the bus in front of the trio of spherical buildings, she stood on the sidewalk, drizzle speckling her face with cool mist for at least a minute.

How the fuck do I get inside?

It didn't take long for someone to walk past her, heading toward a staggeringly high tower which loomed directly behind the rounded structures. She tried to look inconspicuous, following behind the man at what she thought was a reasonable distance, but she stood out and after a few yards, the man stopped and turned to look at her.

"I don't have any money," he said with a disgruntled expression.

"What?" Vexx replied, confused.

"You're like, some kind of busker right? I don't have anything. I'm just trying to get to work, man." He turned and walked briskly away, quickly disappearing behind the gleaming spheres.

What the fuck is a busker?

Confused and a little annoyed, Vexx headed in the direction the man had gone. The tower was huge: colorful panes of glass and gleaming steel reflecting the street below. The Jungle logo was inlaid into the street. Men and women in various levels of business attire stepped over it, entering the building through a set of triple glass doors. Vexx had the mildly uncomfortable thought that they looked like souls entering Infernius.

Vexx took a deep breath and smoothed down her pants. She had chosen an outfit that she thought looked like something a human businesswoman might wear—black pants that ended just above her ankle, black heels, and a fitted black blazer over the emerald green top. She'd done her best with the extremely limited amount of makeup she found in Jackie's bathroom, attempting to make her skintone a little closer to human. She still looked a little grey, and there wasn't anything she could do about her eyes, but she thought she didn't stick out *that* much in the city. People were weird. She could pass for a weird person, right? She had pinned her hair over her small horns into two small buns, and glancing around at the people on the street, she thought she'd done a pretty good job.

She followed the stream of people into the building, wracking her brain to try and recall the name of Seth's assistant. She had met the woman a handful of times, and they'd hit it off fairly well. *Melinda? Maritza? Matilda?* It was warm inside the building. Colorful couches and funky, modern-styled chairs were scattered about the lobby. The walls were video screens, playing advertisements and infographics about Jungle, and the many services it offered. She looked around for some sort of front desk and spotted a pair of bored looking twenty-somethings sitting behind a red and yellow modular unit that looked like stacked rectangles.

As she stepped up to the desk, her mind finally found the name she'd been looking for. The man who looked up at her had a pierced lip and wore a navy blue polo with the Jungle logo embroidered on the breast pocket. "Hi," Vexx greeted him with what she hoped was a warm smile. "I'm here to see Melissa Avilez."

The man quirked an eyebrow. "Do you have an appointment? Are you with a publication?"

"No," Vexx answered, trying to suppress the nervous quiver she felt slipping into her voice. "She's a friend of the family and I'm visiting from out of town. I was just hoping I'd be able to say hello while I was in the city."

"Ms. Avilez is… a family friend?" The incredulous look on his face told Vexx all she needed to know. He was not going to call her. *Fuck,* she thought. *I really wish I could just call my father.*

"Can you get a message to her?" Vexx said. "Surely you have some sort of in-house email system. She will want to see me. I'm happy to wait in the lobby." She looked around and saw a Starbucks tucked into the corner. "I can grab a coffee, I'm not in any hurry."

The man looked at the woman beside him, and she shrugged. "I don't have her direct line," he said to Vexx. "But I will see what I can do. What was your name?"

Vexx gave him a grateful smile. "I appreciate it! My name is Vexxanthe Morningstar." His mouth parted slightly and Vexx thought she could almost hear his brain trying to sort out her name. "Do you want me to spell it?" she asked. "I know, I know. Blame my dad."

The woman at the desk chuckled. "He a metalhead?"

Vexx nodded, though she had absolutely no idea what that meant. "Totally." The man looked at her expectantly, fingers poised over the keys of his laptop and she spelled her name slowly, repeating it for good measure.

"What's your number?" he asked. "So I can have someone call you if she's available."

Vexx made a show of patting her pockets before looking around and smacking her palm against her forehead. "Ugh, I must have left my phone on the bus. Hell!"

The woman gave her a sympathetic smile. "Girl, I've been there." She elbowed her coworker. "Send up a message and tell Rick that there's a woman here to meet with Ms. Avilez waiting in room six." He shrugged and typed out the message. The woman rose from her seat, which Vexx was baffled to see was actually a large ball. The woman chuckled. "It's ergonomic or something. Supposed to be good for posture. Let me take you to room six. Can I get you a coffee or anything? My name is Amy, by the way."

"That would be great!" Vexx followed Amy through the lobby. As they turned a corner, Vexx stared up at the glass elevators and chrome beams that made up this part of the building. The spheres were visible through huge tinted windows, and Vexx got the impression that the people outside couldn't see in. Mirrored glass maybe? They made another turn and Vexx was suddenly very grateful for Amy. This building was the most complicated place she had ever been. Buildings in Hell weren't like this. Infernius favored gothic simplicity over this sort of shiny modern maze. She would be hopelessly lost the minute Amy left.

They stepped through a sliding door into an airy room lined with plants. It was lit by hanging globe lights that shone on the surfaces of frosted glass conference tables. Amy gestured to one of the leather chairs tucked underneath the closest table. "Have a seat, and I'll have coffee sent in. I'm sure you know that Ms. Avilez is a busy woman. It's rare that anyone comes to this building to find her, so it might take some time to sort out. Mr. Kazon's private offices are in another building, but I'll work on it, okay?" She tapped a button, and the top of the conference table lit up. "I'm sorry about your phone, but you can fiddle with this while you wait. It's pretty rad. It's a touchscreen, just swipe to change screens. There's books and you can browse movies or whatever. It's new tech we get to test out here at headquarters, perks, you know?"

Vexx nodded, not sure what to reply. This was *so* outside of what she knew, and she felt suddenly very overwhelmed by the sheer magnitude of differences between Hell and the surface. She had thought this would be easy, pop on over and chat with Seth. Maybe get a temporary job for a few weeks. Now, sitting in this space filled with cutting-edge technology, Vexx realized just how unprepared she was. Human studies had *not* prepared her for this. Amy smiled warmly and patted Vexx on the shoulder. "Hang tight!"

Amy's shoes squeaked on the tile as she headed out of the conference room and Vexx let out a breath through pursed lips. She wasn't sure how to use the tabletop screen, but she gave it a shot and managed to find a digital magazine to read. She flipped through the pages, reading about architecture and design. After a few minutes of clicking on related articles, she ended up on an article about the evolution of fashion and its parallels to music. She spotted some familiar faces, momentarily missing her favorite bar back home. Fashion had always interested her, as had music. Fortunately, lust was a vice for a great deal of human musicians, and she had grown up knowing some *seriously* talented people. It was a pity, she thought, that humans lost their ability to speak in Hell. What she wouldn't give to have heard some of them sing.

She had no idea how long she sat, swiping through windows on the table, but when the door slid open she startled.

And Seth Kazon himself laughed at her.

SETH WAS AN UNREMARKABLE LOOKING MAN, but the cut of his suit and confident set of his shoulders took him from a generous four to a solid seven. He flashed a white-toothed grin at Vexx, reaching out his hand toward her as she tried, and failed, to stand gracefully. Behind him stood Amy, and a man Vexx hadn't yet seen. She had the fleeting thought that maybe he was security of some sort. Seth was, after all, rich as fuck.

"Miss Morningstar," he said, shaking her hand with a weak-wristed grasp. "You are quite possibly the last person I ever would have expected to see here." He chuckled. "Melissa texted me that there was apparently someone using your name, and I was shocked to see it was actually you."

"It is so nice to see you, Mr. Kazon—"

"Call me Seth," he interjected with a smug smile that made Vexx's skin prickle.

"Seth," she continued. "It truly is wonderful to see you. I knew you were a big deal up here—" she faltered for a second, recovering quickly with only a minor stumble to her words. "In Seattle. I am on a… business trip of my own, and have found myself stranded in the city for a few weeks."

Seth's forehead lifted in surprise. He exchanged a wordless glance with the man who stood silently in the doorway. He nodded toward Seth and left, walking down the hallway with Amy in tow. Vexx's shoulders tensed, realizing this put her alone in a room with a man she barely knew. If she had learned anything, being the Princess of Infernius, it was that being alone with human men could be dangerous. Up here, she didn't have the benefit of notoriety, and though Seth knew who she was, she wasn't sure that was enough of a threat to keep him from being a creep.

No, she thought. *Fuck that, I am Vexxanthe Desmodeus Hekate Marie Morningstar and I am not cowed by mortal men.* She summoned flame to her fingers, letting it move in graceful ribbons between her hands. Seth said nothing, but his eyes widened almost imperceptibly as they flicked down to where the fire licked at her fingertips. He cleared his throat, adjusting the lapels of his suit jacket. "Well, Miss Morningstar, how can I be of service?"

Vexx let the flame flare brightly before closing her hands around it, extinguishing it with a curling wisp of smoke. "I was hoping, Mr. Kazon," she began, "That you might be able to offer me a job."

14
jackie

JACKIE WAS SURPRISED to walk into an empty apartment. It felt strange, and a pang of loneliness that she hadn't expected twisted in her gut. Vexx had only been around for a few days, but she missed her? *What the fuck, Jax?* She knew that Vexx had planned to attempt to make her way to Jungle's headquarters. It was weird to not be able to text someone, should she get Vexx a phone?

She flipped on the lights in the living room, psst psst pssting at Mimolette, who popped up from behind the couch, stretching lazily. Jackie scratched his big orange head and poured some kibble into his bowl, kicking off her shoes and tossing her baseball cap onto the counter. She pulled off her chef coat and sweaty ass undershirt, and grabbed a clean tee from the laundry basket in the hallway. Jackie rolled her shoulders and tipped her head from side to side, trying to stretch the tense muscles of her neck. She was exhausted, but in a way that felt… good. Her workday had been busy as hell, but productive, and she felt appreciated and respected. When she had left St. Marte, she had walked away from a crew filled with friends, people who understood her dedication, who valued her input and ideas. Leaving that comfort and support for the most acclaimed restaurant on the west coast had been terrifying. She had been so blinded by the prospect of a six-figure salary and a future with Cam that she hadn't thought about what it was going to *feel* like. But now, with a budding work friendship and the respect she saw beginning to develop, Jackie thought that maybe this had been the right call after all.

The light from the fridge cast long shadows on the black and white checkerboard of the kitchen tile. God, she loved this fridge, but the retro styling did nothing to quiet the grumble of her stomach. *Goddamnit,* she thought, *I need to go grocery shopping.* She thought about ordering delivery, but it was late, and she honestly should be in bed within the hour. She glanced at her watch and felt her mouth pull to the side. It was nearly nine, where the fuck was Vexx? Her stomach did an uncomfortable flip and she chose to attribute it to hunger.

Definitely hunger and not concern for the literal fucking demon who could absolutely take care of herself. Not worry that maybe the hot as hell silver-haired vixen who had stomped into her apartment might not be back. Certainly not a flurry of terror at the prospect of maybe never pulling all six feet of that unblemished, silken skin against her again, of tasting sex and sugar on her mouth. *Fuck.*

Finding nothing worth putting in her mouth in the fridge, Jackie grabbed a bag of chips from the cupboard and leaned against the counter. She poured herself a glass of iced tea, stirring in enough sugar to essentially make it into a simple syrup rather than a beverage. The chips were stale and unsatisfying. *Much like my sex life,* she thought, but they filled the void in her stomach and gave her something to do with her hands. The disappointing crunch was just loud enough to hide the sound of the apartment door opening, and when Vexx walked into the kitchen, Jackie nearly shit herself. She dropped the bag and a puff of barbecue-flavored dust floated into the air between them. For a fraction of a second, Jackie moved to pick it up, but her eyes caught on Vexx and she stilled. Her hand moved to her glass, taking a long drink of her tea, swallowing loudly in the silence of the kitchen.

Fuck.

Vexx was breathtaking. She was dressed in black, her mile-long legs accentuated by cigarette pants and stilettos, a peek of emerald-green silk spilling from her buttoned blazer. It must have still been drizzling, because her silver hair was damp, pulled over one shoulder and curling slightly at the tips. Somehow, inexplicably, her bangs were still perfect. Her skin was dewy, flushed from the trek up the stairs, and her red eyes were bright. Jackie caught a glimpse of her crimson, heart-shaped tail flicking back and forth behind her like a cat's.

"Hey," Jackie said with all the eloquence and poise of a twelve-year old boy at a school dance. "Uh, hi. How did it go? The thing. With Jungle."

A throaty laugh tumbled from Vexx's blood-red lips and Jackie felt her face heat. "It went really well," Vexx answered. "Definitely much different than I anticipated. I know you warned me, but I was not prepared for how fucking insane that place was."

"You found it okay though? I feel like shit leaving you to figure out Seattle on your own." Jackie regained control of her limbs and knelt to pick up the nearly empty bag of old chips, scooping shards of artificially-colored potato into her palm.

Vexx stepped closer, her calf brushing against Jackie's hip. "I did just fine," she said. "And, I got a job."

Jackie looked up to Vexx and felt pride pulling up the corners of her mouth. "Hell yes! We should celebrate!" She stood slowly, acutely aware of the distance, or lack thereof, between her and Vexx. She brushed her hands off on the rough fabric of her pants, leaving faint fingerprints of orange chip dust in their wake. Her breath hitched as she felt the warmth radiating off of Vexx's still-damp skin. She didn't flinch or pull away when Vexx's hand reached out to graze her arm, but remained absolutely still.

"How would you like to celebrate?" Vexx asked, her voice sultry and rough. Her body leaned in, and Jackie's skin nearly vibrated. *God, I hope my breath doesn't smell like barbecue,* Jackie thought as she breathed in the scent of Vexx's breath—dark cherries and charred wood. Jackie licked her lips without even being aware of her own movements.

Vexx's eyes locked onto the tiny motion and the heat curling in the pit of Jackie's stomach ignited into an inferno that caused her thighs to press together involuntarily. She opened her mouth to reply, but before she could manage to drag any words out of the white-hot blaze of her thoughts, Vexx's hand was on the back of her neck, pulling their mouths together with wild abandon.

Vexx kissed Jackie like she was drowning, and Jackie's lips were her only hope of breath. Her forked tongue slid between Jackie's lips and Jackie's fingers wound their way through Vexx's silver satin hair, pulling her as close as possible. Vexx made a small sound into Jackie's mouth and it sent her heart-beat into a frantic staccato. *Is this happening? Really?* Jackie's mind raced. Thoughts of Camille momentarily knocked at the doors of Jackie's mind but she turned a key in the lock, shutting out the intrusion.

Vexx's free hand slid along the small of Jackie's back, slipping beneath her t-shirt and drifting over bare skin. Her touch was like lightning, and Jackie's body tingled as goosebumps spread from the point of contact across her body. She lifted her hand to cup Vexx's cheek, feeling the impossible heat of her skin against her palm. Vexx stepped into her, forcing her backwards until her shoulder blades hit the wall. Vexx's sharp hips pushed against her, need radiating off her in waves, and Jackie tipped her chin up, deepening the kiss even further. Vexx's hand moved from Jackie's neck and landed against the wall above her. She braced herself over Jackie, their mouths moving together seamlessly, fiercely. Vexx pulled Jackie's lower lip between her teeth, her slightly sharpened canines pricking skin as she gently bit down, and Jackie moaned at the small, sharp pain. She pressed her knee forward, pushing between Vexx's thighs and Vexx rolled her hips, grinding against her.

Vexx's fingers curled against Jackie's back and she knew she would have little crescent-shaped marks where manicured nails met soft flesh. Jackie's knee pushed against Vexx with more pressure, the inconceivable heat of her apparent even through the thick fabric of Jackie's work pants. She pulled her mouth free of the desperate kiss and panted into the miniscule space between them "My room, I need you."

Vexx moved preternaturally fast, her hand moving to grip the front of Jackie's waistband, pulling her with her as she walked backwards toward Jackie's bedroom. She kicked the door open with her black patent stiletto, and it banged against the wall as it was flung wide. Vexx spun and pushed Jackie down onto her bed, prowling over her like a cat and bracing one knee on the bed beside Jackie's wide hips. She caged Jackie in with her arms, hands curling into the duvet next to Jackie's neon hair. She moved against Jackie, pressing their bodies together with delicious friction, and Jackie's back arched as pleasure spread through her at the contact.

For the first time since she could remember, Jackie felt truly nervous. She didn't know what she was doing here, grinding against this stunning woman in her bed. Was she seriously going to fuck a demon right now? Was she supposed to make the first move? Was Vexx a top? Thoughts whipped through her head on gale force winds, but the undeniable force of desire between them snapped like a rubber band and shot her back into the present. She felt agile fingers scrabbling against the button of her pants, and reached down to assist, sliding them down her hips, leaving her in a pair of blue boxers. "I need to shower," she panted against Vexx. "I was at work all day, I'm fucking gross."

"Shut your Hellsdamned mouth," Vexx replied. "I'll taste you exactly as you are."

The words slammed into Jackie's core, sending a rush of damp heat between her thighs. *Sure,* she thought, *I'm sweaty and I probably smell like a kitchen. Totally exactly how I wanted this to go.* But she brokered no argument. Cam hadn't gone down on her for a long fucking time, be it from lack of want or laziness, and the thought of that forked tongue between her legs was more than enough to push any apprehension from her mind.

Vexx's hand moved between her legs, pressing against the wet fabric and finding her clit effortlessly. She danced over it, teasing her with barely-there pressure. Jackie's hips bucked forward, desperate for the sensation of touch, but Vexx knew what she was doing and moved along with Jackie, keeping her motions infuriatingly light. Jackie tried to reach for Vexx's pants, but her hand was slapped away with a sharp crack. The heel of Vexx's hand slid over Jackie, grinding against her roughly and pulling a hungry moan from her chest. Vexx's fingertips slipped under Jackie's boxers, nails scraping against the skin of her thighs. *Fuck,* she managed to think. *I need it.* Something hot and pointed dipped beneath her waistband, and she realized Vexx's tail had moved between them and was pulling Jackie's boxers down. She hooked her own thumbs in the fabric and helped, kicking them off into the dark room.

Vexx looked down at Jackie's bare flesh and hummed in what Jackie hoped was still desire. The heart shaped tip of her tail stroked the inside of Jackie's thighs, teasing her already dangerously aroused body to the point of pain. "Please," Jackie whispered.

"Use your words," Vexx admonished. "What do you want?"

"Touch me," she replied. "I need you to touch me."

Vexx's lips twisted into a mischievous smirk. "I am touching you. Tell me what you want."

"I want your fingers," she panted. "Fuck me with your fingers."

Vexx obliged, and Jackie thought she heard her whisper "Good girl," before her torrid fingers slid between Jackie's slick flesh and into the wet heat of her.

She moaned, the sound echoing in the silent room, and Vexx's fingers curled, somehow knowing exactly where to touch her. Her pussy tightened around her fingers and she tipped her hips up, chasing the pleasure Vexx was lavishing upon her. Her fingers plunged deeper into her before withdrawing completely, swirling against Jackie's clit, wet with her desire.

God, it felt so good.

She fucked Jackie thoroughly, the heel of her hand slamming into Jackie's over-sensitive clit with each deep thrust. Jackie's head fell back and she reached up to pinch her own nipples through her shirt and sports bra as she got closer and closer to climax. She felt it beginning to build at the base of her spine, threatening to send her tumbling over the edge at any moment, but then Vexx abruptly withdrew her fingers. Jackie's eyes flew open and she sat halfway up on her elbows, mouth open as ragged breaths moved her ribcage up and down. Vexx was grinning at her and with torturous slowness, licked both of her fingers from palm to red-tipped nail, holding Jackie's gaze.

The noise Jackie made was the shaky combination of a whine and a groan, with all the pitiful plaintiveness of a beseeching beggar.

Vexx tutted at her. "Patience, Jackie. Patience."

Jackie didn't move, just stayed perched on her elbows, knees spread wide to bare her throbbing center, still wearing a heather-grey t-shirt and sports bra. Vexx's red eyes traveled down Jackie's form, lingering on her still-clothed chest. "Take your shirt off," she said so quietly that Jackie wouldn't have heard her had she not been watching her mouth so closely. Jackie's shoulders shifted forward as she sat up in some vain attempt to hide her ample stomach. She didn't hate her body by any means, but next to Vexx's statuesque figure, she felt abundantly self conscious of the way her own well-fed physique folded and dimpled as she sat. She hesitated before reaching for the hem of her shirt, pulling it over her head and tossing it aside, following it with her sports bra. "Don't do that," Vexx said. Jackie looked up to find Vexx suddenly *very* close. Her graceful fingers gripped Jackie's round chin, pulling her face nose-to-nose with Vexx. "Don't sit like you're trying to cover yourself up. If I didn't want to see your body, I wouldn't have told you to take off your shirt."

Jackie blushed, admonished. She sat up a little straighter, but Vexx clicked her tongue and she obliged, pulling her shoulders back until a nun would have complimented her posture. She didn't feel as at-ease like this, completely nude, as she would have forty pounds ago. Her tits weren't as perky as they had been in her college days, and she had a few more tiger stripes running down her sides. Her sports bra felt like a kind of armor, holding up and in all the bits she wasn't confident in anymore, and now, there was a vulnerability she was unaccustomed to. She hadn't had a "first" in a long time. The first time she had slept with Camille had been four years ago, and she had been fresh into her thirties and still fitting into her twenties-era jeans. She had never been thin, but she had felt good about her thickness in those days.

The tingle of fingertips tracing the curve of her hip shocked Jackie out of her self-conscious thought spiral. Vexx looked down at her as though she was a slice of the most decadent chocolate cake, and Jackie liked it. She *really* liked it. *Fuck it*, she thought. *This woman wants me just as I am, who the fuck am I to deny her?* She reached up and pulled Vexx close, bringing their mouths together once again. Vexx tasted like her, and the thought sent another rush of slick desire directly between her thighs. Every muscle in her body tightened, torn between pouncing on Vexx and tearing off that goddamn sexy office lady outfit, and laying back and letting her have her way with Jackie. Vexx made the choice for her, moving an open palm to the center of Jackie's chest and pushing her back onto the bed.

Vexx knew how to tease, that was painfully clear. Jackie had the fleeting thought that maybe sexual torture was some sort of Infernius demon special ability. But as quickly as it entered her mind, it was gone, as all-encompassing bliss replaced it. Vexx had moved down Jackie's body, settling on her knees between Jackie's open thighs. Her forked tongue moved over her lips as she bent down toward Jackie, hot breath feathering over her sensitive skin. The moment that tongue slid through the crumpled satin of her pussy, Jackie's mind turned to static, and a rough "Fuuuuuuuuuck," reverberated through her chest. *Goddamn,* she thought. *She wasn't kidding about that tongue.*

The ends of it flicked over Jackie's clit, moving in opposite directions in a way she never could have imagined. It was like the best sex toy ever invented by man, but better. One drag of her tongue through Jackie's drenched flesh was almost enough to make her come right then. She let out a whimpering cry and threaded her fingers through Vexx's hair, her other hand gripping the sheets for dear life. Vexx wasted no more time, licking and sucking at the insanely sensitive spot. Just as Jackie thought she couldn't endure another second, Vexx's fingers pressed into her. Jackie had a goddamn out of body experience, eyes rolling back in her head and a garbled sound spilling from her lips. Another finger pushed into the tight center of her pussy and she stretched to accommodate. Jackie's hips rolled as Vexx fucked her, her whole body moving in rhythm. Vexx moaned, and the buzz of sound sent her over the edge.

The orgasm tore through her with a scream. Jackie's fingers tightened in Vexx's hair, pulling her hot mouth tightly against her as she came. Vexx groaned into her, the sound traveling down her tongue where it speared into Jackie along with those three fingers, and with a slight shift in angle, she was suddenly gushing into Vexx's mouth with each pulse of her climax.

Jackie had done that to women in the past, often to their surprise, but it hadn't happened to Jackie and she was shocked. She thought she'd had good sex, she thought having multiple o's had been a lot. But holy fuck, this was another thing entirely. She felt like a puddle, quaking in the sweaty, tangled cotton sheets. "Fuck," she breathed.

Vexx stood slowly, crawling onto the bed beside Jackie in long, languid movements. She laid down, eye-to-eye with Jackie and gave her a soft smile before leaning close and kissing her with a gentle brush of her lips. "You taste like sugar," Vexx whispered with a sly grin.

Jackie reached up to push her sodden hair from her forehead, chuckling. "Well, I am a pastry chef," she replied. "I think the real question is 'what does a demon taste like?'"

Vexx's pale grey cheeks darkened and Jackie realized for the first time that she had a single perfect dimple on her right cheek when she smiled. Without thinking, she ran her thumb over it, appreciating Vexx as one would appreciate a piece of fine art. "God, you're beautiful," she said, meeting Vexx's heavy-lidded red eyes with her own.

From beneath long, curled lashes Vexx gave Jackie a look that felt... serious. There were words lying just past that gaze that neither of them was ready to say or to hear. Instead, she pulled Jackie close again and kissed her deeply. She drew breath directly from Jackie's lips, and Jackie thought it felt like a claiming, as though her soul itself was pulled into Vexx's chest on the breath.

This is what this is supposed to feel like.

15

vexx

VEXX'S FORKED tongue flicked over her plush red lips, tasting the lingering sugar-sweetness of Jackie. A purr rumbled from deep within her chest, and she adjusted her legs, too aware of how wet she had become. Jackie's hand moved between them and Vexx stopped breathing for a moment, frozen in a tentative moment of desire. She felt the button of her blazer slip from its hole, felt Jackie maneuver the buttons of her blouse after. She lifted up, sliding both the blazer and emerald blouse from her shoulders and down her arms, leaving her in only a black, lace balconette bra. A rush of breath blew over her chest as Jackie took her in, her ocean eyes wide.

"Fuck," she whispered, almost to herself.

Vexx smiled and let her head fall back against the blue down pillows of Jackie's bed. Her shining hair spread around her like a puddle of mercury, and she allowed her eyes to close as she felt Jackie's confident hands run along the dip of her waist, reaching up to undo her pants in one smooth movement. She lifted her hips as Jackie tugged them off, and she heard the hushed fall of fabric as she dropped them to the ground beside the bed. Strong fingers traced lines of fire over her thighs and she heard the sharp intake of breath as Jackie's thumb brushed over her drenched center. Vexx hummed in appreciation, wiggling her hips to ask for more, but Jackie's hands moved around to her ass, kneading the curve of her backside. Jackie's lips found her collarbone, placing a gentle kiss on her heated skin, and moved down to her breasts, kissing one nipple gently through the lace. Vexx made a little sound and Jackie took the lace into her teeth, pulling on the hardened peak and licking, dampening the black fabric with her tongue.

She took her time, appreciating every detail of Vexx's body, peppering barely-there kisses over her stomach, onto her hip bone, to her lace-covered mound. She didn't mean to move, but her body and mind had long ago stopped communicating, and her hips tilted up towards Jackie's mouth with a needy whine.

Jackie gave her a low chuckle filled with mischief. "Patience, wasn't it?"

She pouted and huffed out a breath through her nose, but she lowered herself back to the bed.

Jackie kissed down her thigh, to the side of her knee, to her calf. She took Vexx's heel in her hand and lifted her pedicured foot, even pressing a small kiss to the arch of her foot. It tickled and a giggle fluttered from her lips. Moving to the other foot, she did the same before moving back up, the calf, the knee, the thigh, and finally coming to rest between Vexx's legs. The flat of her tongue dragged over the wet lace that barely covered her, and she made a faint noise of want, trying desperately to keep her hips on the bed. Jackie laughed, her breath hot on Vexx's lace-covered flesh, and then lowered her mouth once more. She sucked the lace into her mouth, her tongue rolling over Vexx's clit in a dangerous, sensuous movement. Vexx moaned in earnest, the gravelly sound seeming to trawl itself through her chest, snagging on bits and pieces of repressed need she had harbored since the day she arrived here.

Jackie's thumbs made their way beneath the thin silk strings at her hips and pulled down, her mouth not leaving Vexx's pussy until the lace that separated them had dragged over her teeth, baring Vexx to her. Her eyes were full of dark fire as she sat back slightly, pulling the scrap of panties between her lips, tasting Vexx's wetness. She groaned, closing her eyes and shaking her head. "How am I supposed to make this last when you taste so goddamn good?" Jackie said. "Smoke and salted chocolate." Her lips ticked up into a smile. "You taste like the dessert that brought you here, you wicked temptress."

Vexx narrowed her eyes. "It is my legacy, tempting you. But you are such a willing victim."

"Oh, I'm a victim all right," Jackie replied as she tossed the panties over her shoulder. "I've fallen victim to a princess of Hell. Who am I to resist?"

Vexx sat up, her abdominal muscles protesting, and grabbed Jackie by the throat. "The best way to honor a princess is to bow. On your knees, human." Her tone was sharp-edged, but her eyes were too lust-filled to be mistaken for angry.

Jackie smiled. "As you wish, milady."

Vexx released her throat and fell back onto the bed and Jackie knelt before her, lifting one foot and then the other to rest on the edge of the bed. Vexx was spread wide, her glistening center on full display, and Jackie hissed. Her fingers dragged through the wet folds of her, circling her clit before moving back down to slip one knuckle at a time into her heat. It was torture, the sensation of those fingers moving into her in a glacial slowness, and she whined.

"You want me to fuck you, princess?" Jackie asked. "You want me to stretch you wide and make you come until you can't recall your own name?"

"Yes," she panted. "Yes, I want that. Please your princess." Though she tried, the dominance in her tone faltered, shaken by the unbearable arousal racing through her body. *Fuck,* she thought. *I have never wanted anything more than I want to fuck this human woman. What is happening to me?*

Jackie's tongue parted her velvet flesh with measured precision. It felt so different from a lamia or an incubus's thin, agile tongue. It felt so *broad,* even the tip covering so much surface area within a single stroke. *Maybe this is why demons are so quick to find human lovers,* she thought. Another unhurried lick had her fingers scrabbling against the headboard, searching for some way to ground herself. She didn't know how long she could possibly last like this, pleasure tingling all the way to her scalp with every motion of Jackie's mouth against her.

And then the first two fingers slid in.

Tarantulas. Baseball. The minority leader of the United States senate.

She fought to fill her mind with the least sexy things she could imagine in an effort to stave off her climax. Jackie's fingers curled inside her, and the battle grew more fierce—a bloody war between her need to feel an orgasm cascade over her and her need to let this feeling continue.

"More, princess?" She heard Jackie say from between her thighs.

"Always," she sighed. She felt two more fingers force their way inside of her and she gasped. She had fucked an eight foot tall incubus and lived to tell the tale. The line between pain and pleasure blurred in Infernius, and she was always straddling that line. Literally. When she had been with the Gorgon, she let the vipers of her hair strike dozens of times, peppering her skin with venomous bites that left her keening in bliss. But it had been a long time, and when the knuckles of Jackie's four fingers pressed against the stretched-thin skin of her entrance, she groaned loudly at the sharp sting.

Jackie worked her fingers in and out of her, and the sound was deliciously depraved. She hooked her fingers forward, pressing against Vexx's g-spot with blinding pressure. Her tongue flicked against Vexx's clit more quickly, the pace unrelenting as she chased Vexx's finish. But Vexx continued to fight it, edging herself by pushing Jackie's face away seconds before she would have come. "More," she growled. "Give it to me."

Jackie's breath stuttered. "You want my whole hand, princess? Can you take it?"

"Yes, yes, yes," she panted, her breathing rough and stilted.

Jackie's thumb shifted from where it had pressed into the crease of her thigh, moving around to meet her palm. The tip slid in easily, but when she reached the final knuckle of her hand, her movements stopped, leaving Vexx stretched almost to the point of agony, but still teetering on absolute bliss. "Are you certain you want me to keep going?" Jackie asked. "You're doing so well, but I don't want to hurt you."

"I like when it hurts," she cried out, voice shifting to a scream as Jackie pressed further. When her hand withdrew slightly, Vexx felt suddenly empty and she whined with a pitiful sound.

"Quiet, your majesty," Jackie admonished. Vexx felt Jackie lean forward and lick the widest part of her hand. "I'm going to take care of you properly." Jackie's other hand moved up to Vexx's mouth, forcing her lips apart and thrusting fingers into her throat. Vexx sucked on them, coating them in saliva and the remnants of Jackie's release. "Good girl," Jackie said before withdrawing her hand and sliding it around her hand and Vexx's spread pussy. "I need you nice and wet."

Vexx nodded rapidly, unable to voice a response, and then Jackie's hand resumed its slow push into her core. This time, when that knuckle reached the taut skin of her entrance, Jackie rocked her hand back and forth, pushing as she did, and Vexx felt herself stretch around her.

"Breathe, princess," Jackie ordered, and she did, taking a long, shaky breath in and releasing it with a sigh.

And then she pushed past that last knuckle, Vexx crying out

in a heady mix of pain and pleasure as Jackie's hand slid wrist-deep into her. Her hand curled inside Vexx and the sound she made was nearly a scream as she felt herself be filled and stretched in a way she never had been before. Jackie turned her wrist back and forth slowly, letting Vexx's throbbing entrance adjust, and then she pulled her fist nearly free before pushing it back into Vexx with a wet sound and a moan of her own. "Fuck, Vexx," Jackie murmured. "You're fucking perfection. Look at you."

Vexx could barely move, but she lifted her shoulders from the bed just far enough to look down to where Jackie's wrist was buried inside of her. The sight made her entire body tighten with arousal, the sheer indecency of the sight sending a rush of heat and wetness between her thighs, as though she could possibly get any wetter.

Jackie lowered her mouth to Vexx's clit once more, slowly licking and sucking at her while she fucked Vexx with her fist. Vexx's hands scrabbled to grip her hot pink hair, grabbing violent handfuls and pulling Jackie's mouth against her at exactly the tempo she needed. And then she toppled over the edge, orgasm tearing through her and shredding her nerves into ribbons and tatters of pleasure. She screamed, back bowing and hips bucking against Jackie's face as wave after wave hit her. She was drowning in it, the sensation so intense that she couldn't hear. Her ears filled with buzzing and her vision went white as every single cell in her body focused its energy on coming, over and over like an endless tumble of indulgence. She felt Jackie push back against her hands and realized she probably couldn't breathe. With a breathless giggle, she let go of Jackie's hair.

"Sorry," she panted as she fought to calm her rapid heartbeat.

Jackie only smiled, and slowly unclenched her fist. As she withdrew her hand gently, Vexx whined, the largest part of her hand making her ache as it stretched her wide. Her tail thrashed back and forth. Vexx felt broken and achy and blissful and spent, and her pussy began to throb with an ache born of hedonistic pleasure.

"You good?" Jackie asked, looking at her with a bit of astonishment widening her features.

Vexx giggled again, high on post-orgasm endorphins. "Yeah," she replied. "I'm very, very good. Fuck."

"Seriously," Jackie said, blowing out a whistling breath. "That was… fuck, that was unbelievably hot."

Vexx's eyes closed as she let her head sink into the pillows. "I'm so thirsty," she murmured.

Jackie pushed a glass of water into her hand and shook her shoulder. Vexx realized she had drifted off for a second and laughed out loud. "Whoa, sorry. I guess I passed out for a second. Fuck."

Jackie smiled and leaned down, pressing a soft kiss to her lips, dry from panting and screaming for so long. "Go to sleep, princess. I'm going to shower real quick and I'll join you if that's okay?" she sounded unsure, tipping her words up at the end. What was she unsure of? *Oh*, Vexx thought. *She wants to sleep with me.*

"Of course it is, baby," she replied blearily. Come back to bed when you're done."

"Your wish is my command," Jackie replied with a smirk. "I—"

Vexx's eyes drifted shut and she didn't hear another word.

16
vexx

VEXX TAPPED her heel against the tile impatiently. The meeting was boring, and she couldn't focus on a single thing Seth was saying. Part of her felt a little guilty, knowing that tons of people would be honored to even be in the same room as Seth Kazon, but she just wanted to get home and eat cake in her pajamas, snuggled up with Jackie on the sofa.

"We'll roll out the new system slowly, offer it to only a limited number of people at first, require an invite code. It will ensure that people's competitive nature encourages them to sign up, even if they typically wouldn't. Artificial scarcity is a highly effective marketing tool." Seth's monotone voice buzzed in Vexx's ears like a persistent hornet.

Even she, princess of Hell, had come to realize just how much of a scumbag Seth was. His warehouses operated under horrific conditions, and she'd heard stories of fully-grown adults soiling themselves for fear of leaving the line. Many products were counterfeit items, and rather than crack down on it, Seth encouraged their sale. Their literary division had a total monopoly on audiobooks and paid authors poorly, which they had no choice but to accept. Vexx wished there was something she could do to rectify Jungle.com's chokehold on the global economy, but Seth had bartered a portion of his soul fair and square, and her father was nothing if not true to his deals.

A week had passed since the night she tumbled into Jackie's bed. The following morning had been a little awkward, Jackie quickly shedding her cocky dominance in the bedroom and returning to the slightly unsure woman Vexx had known. They'd slept together since then, and each time, Vexx was struck by how different Jackie was behind closed doors. She wondered if Jackie had that same unflappable confidence at work, knowing that her skills and knowledge were worthy of a bit of swagger. Vexx really wanted to visit Canid, and had called in a favor with Seth's assistant, getting a reservation for later that week, despite their lengthy waitlist. She had received her first check from Jungle.com this morning, and despite only having three days of work on it, the sum had been nearly $2000. Vexx didn't know if Seth was overpaying her because of her proximity to her father, or if a business consultant in Seattle typically made that much, but she wasn't going to look a gift horse in the mouth… even if the mouth did a lot of suggestive smirking and denigration of low income people.

Ugh, Vexx thought. *I want to do something worth doing. If I have to spend another day nodding and pretending to take notes about Seth's ideas to exploit people, I might toss myself off the Space Needle.* "Seth," she said, voice bright. "I have some ideas in regards to improving your public image, particularly in conservative areas!"

Seth's ears seemed to perk up, making him look like a doberman ready to attack. "Oh yeah? Please, *Vexxanthe,* go on."

She hated the way he said her name, like it was a dirty word said in the dark. But she cleared her throat and went on, "From the research I've done, there seems to be a fair amount of nationalism, or at least patriotism, in these areas. I know the profit margins will decrease heavily on the individual items, but I believe total sales will increase if you make the shift to American-made products—at least in these departments." She turned her laptop to face him, but rather than looking from where he stood opposite her across the conference table, he walked around, standing entirely too close to her to bend down and peer at her screen.

"Hmmm," he hummed, his body brushing up against hers in what she knew based on the scent in the air to be a lustful and calculated movement. "I'll have Melissa crunch the numbers, take it under advisement. Maybe we could talk about it over dinner sometime?"

Vexx choked on her breath, sputtering and coughing as she tried to regain her composure. "Oh, well, uh, thank you for the invite, Seth. I'll check my schedule, but I'm pretty sure I'm unavailable for the duration of my stay in Seattle."

Seth ran his fingers over the back of her chair, grazing her shoulders as he did. Sighing, he replied, "What a pity. That roommate of yours really keeps you busy, eh?"

Vexx felt her face flush and reached for her water bottle, taking a deep swig to hide her reaction. She screwed the top back onto the stainless steel bottle and set it down before answering. "Yes, we've become friends. I'll miss her when I return home."

"Maybe you'll see her again." Seth Waggled his eyebrows at her. "I know you'll be seeing me for at least a portion of my life after this one."

It took a vast amount of mental strength to suppress the grimace that threatened to pull her lip back at the implication. Jackie Miller, of all the humans Vexx had encountered here, was by far the least likely to end up in Infernius. She plastered a smile on her face. "Maybe!" Her chipper tone sounded hollow, even to her own ears, but Seth was seemingly oblivious—a man accustomed to being right all the time, and never being challenged.

"Well, miss Morningstar," Seth said, "looks like we're about done here for the day. If you have anything you need to finish up, feel free to use the conference room. Otherwise, just email Melissa your hours."

Vexx cringed internally. She was not one to typically demand being addressed by her proper title or full name, but Seth was a skeezeball and she didn't like the easy familiarity in his tone. She was not "Miss Morningstar," Hells damn it. She was her royal highness Vexxanthe Desmodeus Hekate Marie Morningstar, and though she generally forwent the formality, she wanted to see Seth grovel. Hopefully, at least once before she returned to Hell, she would.

Why does that fill me with dread? She thought. *I'm going to get to return home, to my real life. I'll see my father, get back to my routine.* But... did she want to? This past week and a half with Jackie had been, well, amazing.

The surface was nothing like what she had seen in her human studies class. Professor Azael had made it seem like the surface was a war-torn hellscape where humans dodged bullets on their way to work and lived in constant fear of conflict. In a way, he wasn't wrong. Vexx had seen the news. School shootings were a regular occurrence in the United States, there were areas where gang violence often resulted in innocent death and property damage. The citizens held protests and marches to speak out against the corrupt law enforcement system, and it seemed that their rights were being slowly stripped away by a geriatric group of people in power who should long ago had found their way down to the circles of Hell.

But there was also kindness, joy, art and music, and food that she couldn't have even imagined. She had seen giggling throngs of children racing out of the Seattle Children's Museum, couples stealing quiet kisses as they walked through Pike Place. There were news stories about people coming together to help their communities, people who rescued feral kittens, people who distributed jackets and supplies to the unhoused people of the city. There was *good* here. She saw it in the faces of the people she passed on the street, heard it in the songs she listened to in Jackie's car. Humans may have had their struggles, but they also had something that Hell didn't —hope.

And Vexxanthe Desmodeus Hekate Marie Morningstar thought that maybe she might have found a little hope as well.

VEXX DIPPED a spoon into the bubbling Dutch oven, and brought it to her lips gingerly. She didn't bother blowing on it, heat wasn't an issue for her, but she was nervous. She had never cooked before. Being a princess meant she had people who did such things for her, she had never been expected to prepare food or clean anything in her life. Every night, Jackie got home late and exhausted, and she still either found the time to cook something for Vexx, or to stop on the way home and pick up takeout. Vexx had never thought about the work required to make a meal, but seeing how much Jackie did, even after a twelve-hour shift, made her want to try. *Hells below,* she thought. *Am I being… considerate?*

She swirled the sauce around in her mouth and then laughed loudly, doing a silly little dance and pumping her fist in the air. Her tail flicked back and forth and she grinned. It wasn't disgusting! She had spent an hour scrolling through recipes on the phone Seth had given her. She wanted to make something that would impress Jackie, but she had no idea what that could be. Eventually, she found a recipe for an Indian dish that she had seen circled on a menu taped to Jackie's fridge. She hoped it was circled because Jackie liked it, and not her ex, but it would ruin the surprise to ask, so she took a chance. She video called Melissa on her laptop, and she had walked Vexx through the steps of using a grocery delivery app on her phone. She had also been nice enough to show Vexx how to use the stove. The surface, Vexx decided, was pretty rad. She was able to look up anything online, she could even watch videos of people doing the thing she was trying to do. Having infinite knowledge literally at your fingertips was unbelievable, and she wondered how humanity could still struggle so much, with so much accessible to them.

The scent of spices bubbling in the pot made Vexx's mouth water. She had scoured Jackie's cupboards thoroughly before making her grocery order, and found that Jackie already had quite an extensive spice collection. This dish, however, needed a few things Jackie didn't have. A beep sounded from behind Vexx and she jumped before realizing it was the rice maker. She turned the stove to low and replaced the heavy yellow-enameled lid on the cast-iron Dutch oven. Jackie's kitchen was so happy and bright, she couldn't help but feel sunny while cooking. It had a decidedly retro vibe, but all the appliances seemed to be new and top of the line. All her kitchenware was in coordinating pastels, and this yellow set looked adorable atop the aqua-colored stove.

Vexx opened the rice cooker and took a bite of the rice, overjoyed to find it fluffy and perfectly cooked. *Damn, I need one of these,* she thought. She untied the apron she had thrown over her clothes, hung it back on its hook, and set the new kitchen table that had been delivered earlier in the day. Vexx felt somewhat responsible for the previous table's demise, so she had ordered a new one from a local vintage reproduction store and scheduled the delivery for an hour after Jackie left for work. Nervous energy fluttered in her stomach, but she took a deep breath and looked around. She looked great; the black dress she wore fit her perfectly, ending in a pencil skirt that hit mid-calf. She wore fishnets and her boots, and had curled her hair into perfect waves. Her makeup was flawless, and she had even put on some of the cherry perfume Jackie liked. The table was set, the apartment was clean, dinner was on the stove. *I did this,* she thought with a self-satisfied smile. *I did all of this on my own.* She shook away the next thought, refusing to linger on it. *I could keep doing this.*

Vexx heard Jackie's key turn in the lock of the front door. She smoothed down her dress and tried to push down that fluttery feeling which had managed to climb up into her throat. Surprise was evident on Jackie's face; her eyes widened and her head tilted to one side as she kicked off her shoes and dropped her keys on the little table by the door. "Uhhh… Vexx?" Her voice sounded unsure and maybe a little concerned.

Vexx popped out from the kitchen, unable to repress the grin that stretched her red lips wide, showing a peek of pointed canines. "Hi! Um. Welcome home? I—uh—I made dinner." She hated how nervous she sounded, but she had never done anything like this, and she really wanted Jackie to be impressed.

Jackie blinked at her for a moment before responding. "You… *made* dinner? As in, you cooked it?"

Vexx felt heat creep up her neck to darken her cheeks and she let out a nervous giggle that was an octave higher than it should have been. Why am I so nervous? She thought. "I did. I made murgh makhani and basmati rice."

Lips parting ever-so-slightly, Jackie stared, but shook her head slightly as though to dislodge her surprise. "Wow, Vexx," she said. "I honestly cannot remember the last time someone made me dinner."

"Biang Biang Noodles makes you dinner all the time," she teased in reply.

Jackie swatted her butt with her baseball cap. "Smartass."

"Well, come on, we have to see if I used enough poison."

Her head tipped back in a hearty laugh. "If butter chicken is gonna be the thing that kills me, I've led a good life." Jackie tossed her hat onto the sofa and walked into the kitchen but stopped dead in her tracks when she saw the new table in the center of the dining room. "Holy shit, Vexx. You bought me a table?"

"I figured it was the least I could do, what with your last one breaking in half from the force of a Hell portal." Vexx shrugged. "Do you like it?"

Her eyes traced the tapered legs and the smooth curve of the square teak top. "I really, really do," Jackie replied. "It's perfect."

"Then I guess we should test it out." Vexx pulled out one of the chairs and gestured for Jackie to sit before returning to the kitchen and plating a pile of steaming rice and richly spiced chicken curry into two wide bowls. When she handed one to Jackie, she took it almost reverently, fingers brushing Vexx's in a tiny show of appreciation and affection.

Jackie bent over the bowl and breathed deeply. "This smells so fucking good." She took a forkful of the deep carmine colored dish and brought it to her mouth, chewing slowly with her eyes closed. She said nothing, just took another bite with the same long, slow movements.

"Well?!" Vexx exclaimed after what felt like an eternity. "Fuck, Jackie. You have to say something or I will quite possibly actually die." Vexx's fork still sat beside her bowl, her heel tapping against the checkerboard tile frantically.

Aqua eyes met Vexx's ruby ones. "It is perfect, Vexx. Absolutely perfect."

Vexx let loose a long rush of breath that she had clearly been holding. Then, rolling her eyes at Jackie's delayed response, she began to eat as well. Jackie's hand found her black satin clad knee below the table and stroked her thumb across Vexx's thigh. She looked up to find Jackie looking at her intently, with an intensity she couldn't interpret in her gaze.

"Thank you," Jackie said.

But Vexx wondered if maybe there was more she had wanted to say.

17
jackie

"JACKIE? HELLOOOOOOO...." Everest's voice cut through the thick fog that had settled over Jackie's thoughts.

She was rolling out shortbread, her hands going through the motions even as her mind was miles away. "I'm sorry, Everest," she replied, wincing. "My head isn't in the game right now."

Everest nodded, swapping out a full tray of shortbread for an empty one. "I get it. Shit is still up in the air with Seven's job, and my home life sucks right now. Work is actually the best escape I have; fuck, that's sad."

"Hey, just because we get paid doesn't mean we have to hate it," Jackie replied. "I got into this industry because I like cooking. This shit—" she gestured at the little squares of shortbread she positioned on the baking pan "—is meditative. I can just *do,* instead of thinking so much."

"That's valid," Everest said as he swapped trays again. I just didn't think I'd still be in this position, you know? I thought I'd be out living my best life with my partner. It might just be a bump in the road, but it sucks."

"I know that feeling well." Jackie wiped her forehead with

the back of her arm. "Cam ending things was not in my plans. And now things are… complicated."

"What's been going on?" Everest asked. "I didn't want to pry, but you've turned us down a few times now."

"I know, I'm an ass. I should've talked to you about it, I've just been chaotic as fuck. I have a long-term houseguest right now, and things are getting… Well, things are getting." Jackie laughed. "And I haven't been drinking. I got kinda out of control there for a bit, and I wanted to rein it in before it became a problem I couldn't fix."

"We don't have to drink! We can get dinner. Bring your… guest. Double date? Or, double whatever this person is to you?"

What is she to me? Jackie thought, but instead she said, "Sure! You're right. I've been making excuses. I'll do better, I promise."

Everest beamed. "I'll talk to Seven and we'll figure something out!"

Chef Martin's sharp whistle rang out through the kitchen, and everyone snapped to attention, gathering together for the evening's brief. Though Jackie paid attention, (ninety-six reservations, two birthdays and a wedding rehearsal dinner,) she couldn't help but to circle back to the question of her and Vexx. What were they? Sure, they were lovers, they had become friends, but it hadn't even been two weeks since they met. Could you have real feelings for someone you just met? Could you have real feelings for someone who wasn't human? She heard her name and forced her focus back to the present. "Yes, chef?"

"Your showpiece is on special tonight, but not until second seating. You have the menu desserts prepped?" Andrew asked.

"I do, chef. Everest and I can have everything ready by then. How many plates?"

Chef Martin held up a hand toward Andrew, silencing whatever he had been about to say. "Plan for a dozen. There are some questionable names on the books tonight, and it's likely that at least one of them will be a critic writing a piece for restaurant week. I'd like to send one to the bride, and I'm fairly certain that Tuanh Nguyen will be making an appearance."

Jackie flinched imperceptibly. Tuanh Nguyen was one of the three primary food writers for The Seattle Times, and his husband Geoff Gardner was the assistant features editor. They were a powerhouse pair in the Seattle food scene, and had been instrumental in Canid's rapid rise to the top. According to Andrew, they came in every few months and nearly every time they visited, Tuanh wrote a piece about his experience. This was her time to shine, Jackie thought. The first opportunity for *her* name to be in one of those editorial features. Her heart raced, but excited anticipation filled her, rather than nervous energy. *I can do this,* she thought. *This is where I make my mark.*

"Consider it done, chef," she replied to Chef Martin, nodding once. "We'll be ready."

"See that you are," was his only reply before he waved her off, turning to discuss entrée changes and the evening's dietary restrictions with Andrew.

She winked at Everest as he followed her back to her station.

JACKIE LOST herself in the work: crafting isomalt domes, sugaring leaves, crystallizing chocolate. Everest baked and cut and whipped meringue. The silence between them was equal parts comfortable and comforting, the two of them finding a rhythm together that Jackie was acutely appreciative of. She had no concept of the passage of time, but as she organized each group of dessert elements for efficient assembly, she felt *good.* This sense of accomplishment and pride was something she had yearned for, and had achieved to a far lesser extent at St. Marte, but now it felt like it held the correct gravitas. Jackie didn't feel like someone trying to prove herself anymore; she felt like Canid was proving itself to her—showing her that this is where she was meant to be.

By the time Jackie swapped out her sweat-heavy hat for a clean one, she realized that night had fallen fully. She looked outside, watching the faint twinkling of the few stars that shone amidst the heavy Seattle cloud cover. She took a long drink from her water, realizing that she hadn't eaten in hours, and pulled out her phone to check the time.

She had two missed calls from Vexx. *Odd,* she thought. One had come in less than an hour ago. *Maybe she's wondering when I'll be home tonight. I should have texted her.* As she opened up her messages to shoot off a quick text letting Vexx know her ETA, Andrew's head peeked around the corner.

"Miller," he said. "There is someone here for you?"

Jackie's forehead wrinkled in confusion. Who would be here for her? "A guest?"

"Yeah, she had a reservation under Avilez. Hot as hell goth girl?"

Like gasoline-soaked kindling, Jackie felt herself catch fire. It started as a tingle in her toes but spread up her body quickly, making a blazing pit stop in her core before snaking up her neck. Vexx was here?! What was she doing? Was Chef Martin going to be pissed? Was she allowed to have someone come see her?

Andrew must have seen the warring emotions on her face. He laughed under his breath. "You're fine. Martin isn't here right now, and she's a paying customer. Go say hi—I'll make sure she's taken care of and gets the full Canid experience."

She nodded erratically, still trying to figure out what Vexx was doing at Canid. "Thanks, chef," she said, shoving her hat in her back pocket and running her hands through her hair. "Am I okay to take ten?"

"Take your time," he answered, patting her on the shoulder.

"Everest can cover for you? Honestly, you can be done for the evening if you think it's handled."

"Absolutely," Jackie said with a smile. "He knows how to assemble and plate the showpiece, and everything else is good to go."

"Then you're good! Go have dinner. You haven't dined here yet, have you?" She shook her head, and he waved her forward with a smile. "Get out of here." He winked and Jackie's stomach did a somersault as she untied her apron, took a deep gulp of the warm kitchen air, and headed into the dining room.

Vexx was seated at a table near the rear of the restaurant, close to the breezeway connecting the kitchen to the dining room. Jackie paused in the breezeway and stole a glance at her from behind a cascade of foliage. Vexx was effortlessly beautiful. From the way she held her wineglass to the angle of her jaw as she looked around the dining room with an observant expression, Jackie wanted nothing more than to kiss her softly parted lips. *You're at work, Jax. Chill.*

As she stepped into the dining room, Vexx's red-eyed gaze landed on Jackie. Her hair was pulled up into two swooping spirals that hid her horns and flowed down her back. She wore a simple black silk sheath dress that came down to mid-calf, and her ankles crossed beneath the table were clad in red patent leather stilettos with a pointed toe. As always, her makeup was flawless and understated—black winged eyeliner and lipstick in the same carmine red as her shoes. The edges of her mouth lifted into a smile that was pure seduction and she looked up at Jackie from beneath a thick swoop of black lashes. Jackie's steps faltered and she nearly tripped over her boots. A server swooped in, seemingly out of nowhere, and pulled out a chair for Jackie and a nervous laugh bubbled up her throat.

"What are you doing here?" she asked before immediately correcting herself. "I mean, I'm really, *really* glad to see you, but

I didn't expect you." She sat somewhat awkwardly, knee bumping the table and jostling the glassware.

"I wanted to see where you work," Vexx replied with a shrug. "Plus, I've never been to a real human restaurant, and if I'm going to go to one, it might as well be a super fancy one with a waitlist."

"How did you swing that?" Jackie asked. "Reservations aren't even open until the first of the month."

Vexx's laugh was laced with a devious little note of mischief. "I made Seth's assistant do it. It pays off to be working for the richest man in Seattle."

"I think he's the richest man in the country, actually." Jackie looked around, taking in the room from a perspective she had never really taken the time to appreciate. "It really is a beautiful restaurant."

Vexx's eyes didn't leave hers as she replied. "Yes, it is."

Jackie gulped, trying to push down the lump in her throat, but a server stepped up to the table before she was forced to find an intelligent response.

"Tonight will feature eight dishes as well as dessert. Would you like to add wine as well? We have a pairing for each course, as well as a palate cleansing cocktail mid-meal."

"Yes, please," Vexx said, her excitement evident. She looked over at Jackie with a wide-eyed smile. "This is so fun!"

The server chuckled warmly. "Chef Miller, right?" she asked, turning to Jackie. "It's a pleasure to serve you this evening."

Jackie blushed furiously. Not only had she not known that the server knew her name, but she certainly hadn't expected the tone of deference with which she said it. "Thanks so much, I'm sorry, I didn't get your name. I should know this—"

The server held up a hand, cutting her off. "No, no. It's my fault for not introducing myself. I'm Ashley, and Trent will be assisting me this evening. Can I get you anything to drink, or would you like to wait for the wine?"

"Water is fine!" Jackie raised her glass. "Water is great." *Jesus Jackie, stop acting like you've never been anywhere nicer than an Applebee's.*

Ashley smiled and nodded once before turning and heading toward the kitchen.

The silence was deafening. Both Vexx and Jackie opened their mouths to speak, noticed the other doing the same, and promptly closed them. It was Vexx who finally broke, laughing and twisting a strand of her hair that had fallen over her shoulder.

"Why is this suddenly so awkward?" she said, her smile bashful.

Jackie rubbed the back of her neck, looking around the dining room rather than meeting Vexx's eyes. "Because this feels like a date."

"Well, is it?" Vexx asked. Jackie turned to face her, and saw the tiny line pulling between her brows.

"Do you want it to be?" Jackie replied. She wondered if Vexx could hear the pounding of her heart; it felt like a trapped creature fighting to escape the confines of her ribs.

When Vexx answered, her voice was small and thin with nerves. "Yes."

Jackie's hand slid across the tabletop and took Vexx's fingers in her own. "Good."

In what could have been a minute or ten, Jackie didn't know, Ashley reappeared with a bottle of wine, flanked by a young man. She poured a measure of a pale golden white into each of their glasses, and the man, presumably Trent, set a small plate before each of them. "Barron Point oysters from the Little Skookum Inlet, sustainably raised by the Squaxin tribe with a local salmonberry jam and toasted spruce nuts—a little taste of the Pacific Northwest. The wine is a muscadet made with grapes grown on Bainbridge island. Enjoy!"

And enjoy, they did.

Each of the next four courses was better than the last. An herbed salad dotted with foraged blackberries, local lobster with smoked brie foam and preserved rainier cherry, potato rosti topped with cured elk "ham," and the Panmarino Jackie made each day served alongside a trio of butters. The bread was soft and warm, just the right amount of crustiness, and the sweet and savory butters transformed the rosemary accented bread into something far more delicious than ordinary bread. Each dish was paired with a wine that had been selected by Canid's sommelier, and they were all divine. By the time Ashley brought the palate cleanser—vermouth with pine and pomelo—Vexx had shifted back in her chair, staring at the table in delight.

"Are you enjoying it?" Jackie asked.

"I cannot believe you work here," Vexx replied. "This is unbelievable. You made this bread? Hells below, it is the best thing I've ever eaten."

Jackie's heart bloomed with pride. "The next few courses also have stuff I make. All that was mostly Andrew and his team. Canid's whole thing is local sustainability. We work with local fisheries and tribal farms as much as possible, so we are supporting the people whose land this was before colonization."

"That's amazing!" Vexx said, scooping a tiny bit of sweet maple-miso butter onto her finger and popping it into her mouth.

Jackie's eyes lingered on Vexx's red lips as they closed around her fingertip. She saw the smallest peek of her forked, pink tongue and remembered just how good that tongue had felt. Suddenly she wanted nothing more than to leave, to go home and tear every bit of fabric from Vexx's body. Vexx's nostrils flared, and Jackie knew she could sense exactly what she had been thinking. She licked her lips and drew the lower between her teeth before shaking her head, trying to dislodge the image from her mind.

"Stop that," Vexx said in a playful command. "I'm trying to focus on my meal."

Jackie shrugged and hooked Vexx's ankle with her boot beneath the table. "Can I have you for dessert?" she said in a low, silken voice.

Jackie felt something brush her leg, and then jumped, shaking the table with her knees as Vexx's tail slid between her thighs. The heart-shaped tip of her tail scraped across the seam of her pants, sending vibrations rippling through her center. Her breath caught as the pressure increased, and for a second she wondered if Vexx's tail was pointed enough to poke through the two layers of thin fabric separating them.

Jackie pouted as Vexx stopped teasing her. "Hey—" she began.

"Be good, or you will get no dessert, real or otherwise." Vexx sounded stern, but Jackie could see tension in the thin, grey fingers that held her wine glass.

"Fiiiiiine," she acquiesced, just as Ashley returned with their next course.

The meal continued with cedar-smoked quail and hazelnut and a square of savory shortbread, sacchetti filled with Beecher's reserve cheese served atop a tangy confit tomato puree, a medley of locally foraged mushrooms including black morels, chicken of the woods and chanterelles wrapped in a thin layer of pastry with honey from Stedman's bees and nutty brown butter. The final dish was Jackie's favorite: a simply cooked local Chinook salmon filet and a strip of grass-fed wagyu, separated by blistered beans, sweet corn, and basil flowers. A cherry-whiskey reduction swirled around the beef and a wedge of smoked lemon sat alongside the salmon. Everything was perfect, the beef and salmon both were impossibly tender and rich, the fattiness cut with the acidity of their respective accompaniments. The beaujolais wine paired perfectly with both proteins, and Jackie was left feeling pleasantly full, but with just enough room left for dessert.

After the table was cleared, Vexx reached across for Jackie's hands, holding them together with a squeeze that felt almost a little desperate—like she didn't want to let go. Jackie realized then, with no room for doubt, that she didn't want Vexx to return to Hell. The thought wormed through her stomach, curdling the pleasure left by their decadent meal. None of this meant anything if Vexx were to leave. She couldn't stand the idea of returning to her empty apartment at night with only Mimolette to talk to. Cam was gone, and she was glad for it, but she didn't want to be alone. She wanted Vexx. She wanted the wide-eyed appreciation for all the normal things Jackie took for granted. She wanted the heated glances and air of tension between them that crackled when they were together. She wanted to keep having the best sex of her life. She wanted *this*.

"Vexx—" she started to say, but she was interrupted by someone stepping up to their table. When she turned, she was surprised to see Everest, wearing a clean chef coat, with a tray in his arms.

She quirked an eyebrow at him and he smiled sheepishly. "I wanted to bring it myself."

Jackie watched Vexx as Everest set the dish between them. Here, in this sumptuous dining room, her creation truly shone. It was served on a tiny pedestal atop a slice of lacquered wood. The transparent dome held a swirling tangle of smoke and green, and Everest handed them two small, golden hammers. Vexx and Jackie moved in unison, tapping the dome, and the smoke curled out, unfolding into a faint haze as the little cake was revealed. The sugared leaves glinted, the crystallized chocolate looked like loamy soil, and the scents of rosemary and cherry wood blended with the deep, rich fragrance of dark chocolate. Jackie almost didn't hear Everest as he spoke.

"Enjoy, it's a beauty Jax. See you tomorrow?"

Jackie only nodded, watching Vexx with rapt attention. It felt oddly fitting to be here, eating this dessert with her. It was the thing that had brought them together, and now they were about to share it as it had been intended. Vexx lifted a dainty gold fork, but paused before taking any of the cake.

"It's so pretty," Vexx said. "I almost don't want to eat it."

"The prettiest things taste the sweetest," Jackie replied.

Vexx's lips parted as she drew in a sharp breath. Her eyes were filled with fire, and Jackie wanted to be burned.

"Hurry up," she said. "Or I'll fuck you on this table." It was nearly a whisper, and she was surprised at herself for even letting the thought come out of her mouth. Jackie had never been shy, sexually or otherwise, but the flagrant desire she felt for Vexx was something entirely different. She had meant it. She *would* fuck Vexx on this table, and most certainly lose her well-paying and impossible to replicate job in the process. But Vexx made her wild, turned her into a woman she didn't yet know, but wanted desperately to become.

She let Vexx take the first bite, watching as her ruby eyes rolled back in appreciation. She moaned in a way that sent heat pooling between Jackie's thighs. *Fuck the cake*, she thought. *I want to make her make that sound again.* After Vex had finished, licking her lips suggestively, Jackie took an aggressive forkful of the cake, wanting to be through with it as quickly as possible. She had resigned herself to this—to this painful desire flooding her veins, and the way her still-tender heart was pulled along with the current. She wanted to fuck Vexx, she wanted to laugh with Vexx, she wanted to love Vexx. If this next week was all she would ever get, she intended to spend it wisely, and eating *cake* was not a priority.

18
vexx

VEXX STUMBLED backwards through the door, nearly tripping over Mimolette. Jackie's hands were in her hair, grasping her hips, pulling at her clothes in a desperate frenzy. She kicked off her stilettos, immediately happy to be closer to Jackie's height. She scrambled to unbutton Jackie's chef coat, her pointed nails struggling to maneuver the buttons. With an impatient growl, Jackie reached down and pulled it open, the buttons popping in quick succession. Her t-shirt was tight, showing off the curve of her waist and the swell of her hips. Vexx pulled her mouth away for just a moment, appreciating the sinful shape of Jackie's body before reaching back to unzip her dress. Jackie moved so fast, her hand untangling from Vexx's hair to swat away her hand.

Vexx made a needy sound in the back of her throat and Jackie's mouth smiled against hers. "Don't rush," Jackie whispered into her softly parted lips. "I want to take my time with you."

Vexx stomped her foot and whined, but complied. She pulled on Jackie's shirt until it was untucked, and ran her fingers up Jackie's soft stomach. She felt Jackie's body react, tensing beneath her touch as her fingers traced the dip of her waist and up over her sports bra. Jackie walked forward again and Vexx's bare feet hit the cold tile of the kitchen. Jackie's hips pressed into Vexx's, pushing her backwards until her ass hit the kitchen island. She braced her hands on either side, and pushed up on her toes. With a little jump, she was sitting on the butcher block top, moving a bowl of fruit out of the way without looking. She heard an apple roll and fall to the floor, but she didn't give a fuck as Jackie's hands moved along the inside of her thighs and pushed them apart.

The satin of Vexx's dress bunched up around her hips and Jackie *finally* reached behind her to slowly pull down the zipper. She shrugged the thin straps over her shoulders and down her arms and she lifted her hips slightly so Jackie could pull the dress from her body. Jackie threw it behind her and it landed on the couch, scaring the hell out of Mimolette in the process. Vexx giggled and looked back at Jackie who stood, staring at her totally nude body in awe.

"You came to dinner without wearing underwear," Jackie said, no hint of a question in her voice.

"I thought maybe you'd touch me under the table," Vexx replied with a wicked grin.

Jackie's mouth crashed back into hers, her hands moving over Vexx's back and down to cup her ass. "Such a bad girl," she murmured as she ran her tongue along Vexx's bottom lip.

"Are you going to punish me?" Vexx panted, feeling heat gather between her thighs.

Jackie's hand moved to Vexx's chest, guiding her body down until she laid atop the countertop. The cold wood made her skin pebble, and a small shiver skated down her body in a wave of sharp sensation. She felt hot breath on her thigh and tensed, anticipating Jackie's mouth closing over her center, but it didn't come. Instead, she felt Jackie move right over her and across her other thigh. Vexx wiggled her hips and whined but

Jackie only laughed. Strong fingers kneaded the muscles of her legs, moving slowly from her calves down to her ankles and lifting her heels to rest atop the counter. As she moved back, her shoulder bumped the fruit bowl and sent the whole thing tumbling to the floor with a clatter. Neither of them reacted beyond Jackie's booted foot kicking a wayward orange across the checkerboard tile.

Vexx was nude, knees parted, baring her slick pussy to Jackie beneath the fluorescent light of the kitchen. Knowing that Jackie was fully clothed, while she was spread out like an indecent banquet, made arousal flutter in her chest. She let her eyes drift closed, imagining a crowd of people watching the obscene display. Fuck, it made her impossibly wet, and she was struck by sudden, intense need.

"Please," Vexx moaned in a breathy, pitiful voice. "Please. I need your tongue."

Jackie nipped at the tender skin of her inner thigh and a cry escaped her lips. Again, on the other side, Jackie bit her with just enough force to make her suck in a sharp breath. She wanted to scream. She *needed* Jackie's mouth on her, *needed* to come. Jackie's lips feathered over her clit, teasing and far too gentle. The very tip of her tongue dragged across Vexx's slick entrance and Jackie hummed in appreciation. Vexx felt Jackie's hands come up, parting her delicate flesh and spreading her open. A breath of cool air moved over her, and she keened. Her skin was so hot and needy. Her hips moved of their own accord, lifting from the counter to chase Jackie's tongue, but Jackie clucked at her.

"No, no, no," she said, spreading Vexx further.

Vexx was so exposed. The cold air of the kitchen felt like an arctic wind as it drifted over her drenched center. She wanted to grab Jackie by the hair, grind against her face until she came, but the tease was addictive. There was something about the loss of control, the anticipation, the feeling of helplessness that turned Vexx into a simpering mess. And then, in one fluid moment, Jackie's tongue was inside of her.

She nearly shattered, her back arching with the blinding pleasure of it. Jackie made a soft sound and it vibrated through her tongue, Vexx's hips rolling against Jackie's mouth as she moaned. Over and over again, Jackie's tongue plunged into her. She reached down to touch herself, but Jackie snatched her wrist and held it tight. Vexx pressed forward into Jackie, desperate for friction against her throbbing clit, but Jackie moved away every time.

"Please, *please!*" Vexx cried.

"Do not move," Jackie replied. "Not one inch." She stood and disappeared into the bedroom.

Vexx's hands clenched at her sides. Her pussy quivered, feeling too empty and overly sensitive. She wanted to touch herself, feel her fingers flick over her clit until she came, but she wanted Jackie's touch more. She heard the snick of the door and shifted, pushing up on her elbows, but Jackie's voice was sharp. "I *said*, do not move." Each word was punctuated by the sound of her boots on the floor as she stalked toward Vexx. She strained to see Jackie from her position on the counter, but only caught a glimpse of black pants, a black belt.

Cool fingers slid over her, smearing something cold and slick across her. Vexx whined as her nipples became stiff, tingling points. She felt something hard press against her entrance and let her head fall back, acquiescing to whatever Jackie had in store for her. It was agonizing; Jackie slowly pushed into her, inch by inch. After what seemed like an eternity, Jackie's hips pressed against Vexx's thighs and Vexx looked up to see aqua eyes staring into hers.

"You want to be fucked, princess?" Jackie said in a low voice.

Vexx nodded, brow furrowing in a silent plea.

Jackie smiled and leaned down, pressing her lips to Vexx's.

Vexx reached up to clasp either side of Jackie's face, pulling her closer. Their tongues slid against one another, and Vexx tasted herself with a groan. She sucked Jackie's lower lip between her teeth, biting down gently, and Jackie's fingers tightened on her hips. The cold, rigid length that filled her shifted as Jackie pulled back, sliding from her. Vexx whimpered and Jackie laughed against her mouth. And in one fluid movement, Jackie slammed back into her.

Vexx cried out, hands scrabbling against the counter, nails making clicking sounds that seemed to echo through the kitchen. Again, Jackie pulled out of her before thrusting back roughly. Vexx pushed up onto her elbows and looked down. Jackie was still fully dressed, but a leather harness now wrapped around her hips. A long, thick silicone dildo was still half buried within her, and Jackie smirked as she shifted her hips back and forth. Vexx moaned and Jackie's smirk turned into a grin. "You like it, then?"

Vexx panted. "Uh huh." Jackie looked so fucking hot. Her hair was disheveled, falling into her eyes slightly. The harness cut into her hips and thighs, making her ass look unbelievable. Vexx reached forward, hooking her fingers through the straps and pulling Jackie toward her. The toy filled her deliciously, and she trembled as Jackie slowly worked it in and out of her. Jackie's hand wound around to grab a fistful of her hair and she slammed forward, rocking Vexx's entire body.

"Harder," Vexx said.

And Jackie complied.

She fucked her with increasing force, their bodies colliding in passionate rhythm. Vexx's breaths were ragged and rough. She felt her body begin to tense, tingling from her toes to her fingers. She shifted her hips so the toy hit precisely the spot she liked, and her eyes drifted closed as she let the cresting pleasure begin to build. Jackie's fingers moved between them and found her clit, moving in rapid circles against Vexx's sensitive flesh.

She broke with a loud cry, shaking and trembling as the orgasm rocked through her. For a moment, the apartment went silent. Vexx couldn't hear anything outside the rushing of her own blood in her ears. Jackie made a surprised little squeaking sound and Vexx opened her eyes to see flames dancing at the tips of her fingers.

"Whoops!" she said with a laugh, the fire winking out with a puff of smoke. "Sorry, I… lost track of myself."

Jackie took a step back and the dildo slid from Vexx. Her entire body quivered, stomach muscles tightening as her body rolled through an aftershock of the orgasm. Jackie laughed. "Sorry, baby," she said as she pulled completely free. Jackie's eyes stayed locked on Vexx's as she bent down, tongue finding her and dragging up through her slippery folds with an appreciative "*mmmm.*" Vexx pushed herself up, knees dangling over the edge of the counter, and grabbed Jackie by the hair, wrenching her face up. Her lips were glossy with Vexx, and she licked them clean without looking away from Vexx.

Vexx slid down the counter, her feet hitting the floor with a quiet thud. Her grip tightened in Jackie's hair, pulling her up until Jackie's lips were inches from her own. She lowered her head to claim Jackie's mouth. Her forked tongue traced Jackie's lower lip and she smiled. "Delicious," she said. And then she spun Jackie around, pushing her down until she was bent over the kitchen island, her perfect ass on display. Vexx smacked it, *hard*. Jackie squeaked and jerked forward, but Vexx pressed against her, hands slamming down on the counter, caging her in and holding her still.

"Did you like feeling like you were in charge?" she whispered into Jackie's ear, lips brushing against her mussed hair.

"Yes," Jackie replied, the hint of a smile in her voice.

"Aww, well, too bad." Vexx's fingers moved to Jackie's throat, applying just enough pressure on either side to make Jackie's small whine fade to silence. Her other hand reached around, undoing Jackie's belt with practiced ease. She pulled it from its loops with a sharp yank, catching the end in her hand as it swung to meet her. She released Jackie's throat, earning a ragged breath, and took a step back. Jackie shifted as though she planned to turn to face her, but Vexx drew back and brought the belt down across Jackie's wide ass with a loud *crack.*

Jackie flinched and cried out, her back arching at the sharp sting. Vexx chuckled and shifted her weight, turning her body so the next strike landed with even more force. Again, a noise tore from Jackie's chest. It was pained, but the heaving breaths that followed made it abundantly clear just how much she liked it.

"Red means stop, amber means slow down, green means you want more. Got it?" Vexx said as her hand soothed across Jackie's ass.

"Yes, ma'am," Jackie responded between breaths.

Vexx swung the belt around so it sat across Jackie's throat, the skin-warm leather resting on Jackie's shoulders. "I am not going to use any pressure, but I'm going to keep this here. Push forward if you want to use it."

"Okay," Jackie said as she shifted forward experimentally, feeling the belt dig into the skin at her neck. "Green."

"Good." Vexx licked her lips and then reached to undo Jackie's pants. She dragged the zipper down slowly, her fingers moving over the seam between Jackie's legs. She tugged, pulling the black fabric over Jackie's hips and scratching the skin of her thigh with pointed nails as she went. "Step out of them," she commanded as the pants at last fell to the floor. Jackie obeyed and Vexx pushed them away with her foot. Her knee moved between Jackie's thighs, pushing her legs apart. Vexx slipped her hand between them, running her fingers over Jackie and feeling just how much she was enjoying this..

"Are you usually a top?" Vexx asked as she circled Jackie's clit with a finger.

"Yes," Jackie answered.

"Are you comfortable submitting to me?"

Jackie's reply was quiet but clear. "Yes."

Vexx's tail took the place of her finger as she let the belt dangle for a moment and hooked her thumbs beneath Jackie's boxers, dragging them down. Jackie stepped out and Vexx's tail took the place of her hand, dragging through the slick, silky skin. Jackie shivered, rising slightly on tiptoe and rocking her hips back to give Vexx more access. Again, her tail parted Jackie's flesh and elicited a soft moan. She bent down, running her long, forked tongue from Jackie's wet pussy up to her ass. She felt Jackie tense. "Color?" she said, hot breath brushing Jackie's pebbled skin.

"Green," Jackie murmured into the wood.

Vexx wrapped the ends of the belt around one palm, holding it securely but without pulling. She pushed Jackie's legs further apart and went to her knees. Vexx pressed her mouth to Jackie, tongue swirling over Jackie's clit, and reached up to press two fingers into her. Jackie moaned and rocked back. She tasted like fucking dessert, all sugar and rich salt that made her think of cookies. When Jackie made another sweet sound and trembled beneath her touch, Vexx could only think about how she wanted to hear those fragile little noises forever.

She realized she had never felt like this, not once. Her entire life, and her scattered sexual exploits, had always been in pursuit of her own pleasures—but here, with Jackie, she just wanted to make her feel good. She smiled against Jackie's pussy as she curled her fingers, hitting her g-spot and making her knees shake.

"Green, green..." Jackie cried out before pushing forward, tightening the belt at her throat.

Vexx slowed, wanting to slow Jackie's race toward climax.

Jackie whined but she continued to work those two fingers in and out of her with agonizing slowness. Her forked tongue stroked Jackie's clit on either side, alternating pressure and changing rhythm when she heard Jackie's breaths begin to speed up. She pulled her mouth away, a thin strand of saliva connecting her to Jackie for a fraction of a second. Her tongue moved to Jackie's ass, gently moving against her in slow exploration. She tapped Jackie's hip with her free hand.

"Um… green," Jackie said in response.

Her fingers splayed open within Jackie's wet heat, stretching her open and making room for her tail. Jackie made a desperate sound and pushed forward again, chasing the heady rush of the belt at her throat. "Do you want me to choke you Jackie?" Vexx said, barely moving her mouth from Jackie's tight ass.

"Please," Jackie panted.

"I'm not going to put you in danger. You get five seconds," Vexx said, bending her wrist to pull back slightly on the leather. She felt Jackie's pussy clench around her tail. "One… two…" she counted. "Three… four… five." She relaxed her wrist, feeling Jackie quiver as blood rushed back to her face in a rush.

"Again, please?" Jackie begged.

"No," Vexx answered, moving back to lave her tongue over Jackie's ass again. Jackie whined, but didn't argue, wiggling her hips as Vexx quickened the thrusting of her tail and the flicking of her tongue. Slowly, giving Jackie adequate time to protest, she began to press her tongue into Jackie's ass. Jackie squeaked, but said nothing. Vexx felt her stiffen, body tightening at the intrusion, but she just swirled her tongue around. Jackie's hands gripped the counter, and her hips began to rock back against Vexx, meeting the press of her tail and the cautious slide of her tongue. With every movement of her tail, Vexx pushed deeper into Jackie's ass until her lips butted up against Jackie's skin. She could feel the movement of her tail, and the wicked sensation of penetrating Jackie so fully sent a rush of heat between her own legs. She knew if she were to touch herself right now she would find herself dripping, the evidence of her arousal rolling down her own bare thighs—but her hands were full.

Jackie began to lose rhythm, her hips jerking back as she started to lose control. Vexx moved her fingers to Jackie's clit and Jackie cried out. "Please don't stop, please...." Vexx drove her tongue and tail in and out of Jackie, wet sounds of flesh on flesh echoing through the kitchen, accompanied by Jackie's ragged breaths. She came with a scream, her entire body tightening around Vexx, pulsing as she rode it out, murmuring nonsense against the counter.

Vexx gave her no time to recover, grabbing Jackie's shoulders and spinning her around so her ass was against the counter. She kissed Jackie fiercely, her hands coming up to cup Jackie's flushed and sweaty cheeks. Jackie met her with the same ferocity, tongue delving into Vexx's mouth and tasting searing hot sin. Vexx looked into Jackie's ocean eyes and slowly knelt before her, lifting her knee to sit over her shoulder. Her tongue found Jackie in an instant, licking and sucking at her with no regard for the orgasm that still rocked through her body. Jackie braced her elbows on the counter, pink head falling back as she let herself be lost to sensation once again. Vexx's tail moved between them, dragging through her wetness as it moved further back. The softly pointed tip nocked itself against Jackie's ass, still slick from Vexx's tongue. She pressed, and Jackie's head shot upright. Vexx paused.

"Color?" Vexx asked.

"Um..." Jackie hummed. "Yellow? Amber? Whatever."

Vexx's mouth curled into a wicked little smile. *That wasn't a no.*

Her lips closed back around Jackie's clit, both sides of her tongue flicking back and forth rapidly, and she pushed forward ever so slightly. Jackie made a sound that sounded suspiciously like *god*, and Vexx pulled back before pressing back into her. She took her time, her mouth working Jackie's pussy as her tail slid further and further into her ass.

"Take a deep breath," Vexx commanded Jackie in a low, soft voice. As Jackie exhaled, she slipped the tip fully into Jackie's waiting body. The base was wide, and as it disappeared into Jackie she cried out at the sensation of her body pulling Vexx in, tightening around the narrow length of her tail.

"Oh fuck, oh fuck, oh fuck," Jackie panted. In reply, Vexx thrust her fingers back into Jackie's pussy. It was too much. Jackie nearly fell as she came. Loud, strangled cries fell from her lips as her hips bucked against Vexx's mouth. Vexx's skin blazed as Jackie's body tensed and pulsed around her fingers and her tail. As she withdrew her hand, she lapped at Jackie slowly, extending her climax as she gently pulled her tail free. Jackie's leg fell from her shoulder, shaking so much that Vexx was worried she might collapse.

"Yeah?" she asked.

"Yeah." Jackie's eyes were closed as she replied.

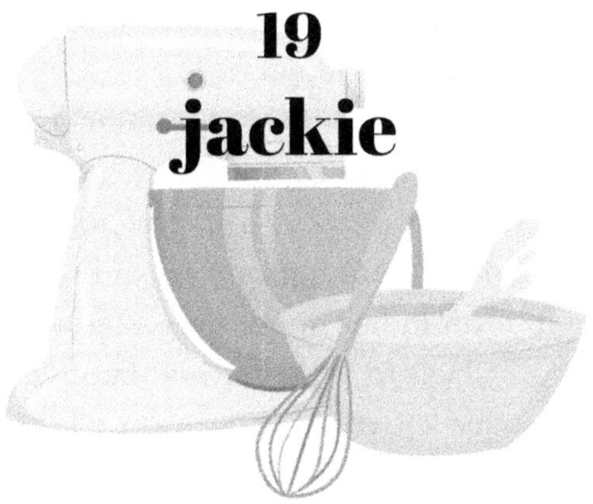

19
jackie

VEXX HAD ALREADY slunk out of bed and gone into work by the time Jackie pried her bleary eyes open at Mimolette's insistence. She was… sore. Or, Jackie supposed, her awareness of certain places was heightened to a degree she had yet to experience. She rolled over, grabbing her phone from the nightstand, and the mental images of the night before began a slow march through her mind's eye. *Fuck,* Jackie thought. *I cannot believe that happened. Any of that.* She rubbed her throat, a faint ache reminding her of just how far outside her comfort zone last night had taken her.

The floor was cool on the soles of her feet as she made her way into the kitchen to brew some coffee. It was a solid three minutes before she realized she was standing and staring at the counter. How was she supposed to just go about her day, making breakfast and taking out the trash, when all she could picture was Vexx quivering on the butcher block? A calendar hung on the wall beside the fridge and Jackie's traitorous eyes scanned the dates. Eight days. In eight short days, Vexx's father was supposed to open the portal and take her… home. It felt wrong. There were jaws gnashing and gnawing in the pit of her stomach, tearing up her insides. It hurt. *She* hurt. What could she do? It's not like she could say, "Hey, big scary demon king —I know her royal highness Vexxanthe is your daughter, and The Princess of Hell, but could she maybe stay in Seattle and work at an online retail conglomerate?"

Jackie leaned her elbows on the counter and lowered her head to her hands. Her cheeks were wet. *I must have splashed some water from the Chemex. That's it,* she told herself. But as Jackie went through the calming process of brewing her coffee, an idea began to form in her mind. Sure, she might not be able to ask The King of Hell to lend her his daughter on a permanent basis, but maybe she could show Vexx all the things worth staying for. Maybe Vexx would make that decision for herself. *Or for me.*

Jackie shot off a text message to Vexx. "Can I pick you up at 1:00 p.m.?" She stared at the little blue bubble hopefully, heart hammering in her chest. Three dots sat at the bottom of her screen, taunting her as they appeared and disappeared.

"Sure! :) I'll b there!" appeared, and Jackie's clenched hand pumped the air in involuntary excitement.

And then Jackie got to work.

An hour later, a freshly showered and caffeinated Jackie sat at her new kitchen table wearing nothing but a towel, scrolling her laptop's touchpad. Logically, she knew that booking things should be done more than five hours ahead, but goddamnit, she was thinking on the fly. It took some name dropping, sweet talking, and a shamefully femme sounding tone that Jackie would be embarrassed about tomorrow, but she did it. *Is she going to like this?* she thought, biting her already short nails and staring into the kitchen. *She will.*

Jackie's dresser was full of trash. The ugliest clothes ever made. Clearly, her wardrobe had been stolen and replaced by someone hell-bent on making her look like shit. Jackie's air-dried body paced back and forth in front of her bed. *Why am I so nervous all of a sudden?* Eventually, she put together an outfit she felt moderately good in. The slate-blue t-shirt brought out the color of her eyes, and the rolled up sleeves showed off her tattoos. Her jeans were the right amount of tight to pull in her waist and hug the curve of her ass, and her brown boots were both practical and stylish. She checked her watch—a little over an hour before she had to pick up Vexx. Perfect.

When Jackie pulled up outside Jungle headquarters, she fluffed the tissue paper in the bag sitting in the backseat. The car smelled of coffee and her perfume, and she had vacuumed the floorboards. Her palms felt sticky and her brow pinched, despite her efforts to smooth it. But as Vexx appeared, walking out into the misty grey, she took a deep breath. This felt good.

Vexx's eyes landed on Jackie's car and lit up like Christmas. She held a magazine over her head and hustled over, ducking into the car with far more grace than her height should allow for. As the damp magazine slid from Vexx's silver hair, Jackie reached over, cupping her cheek and drawing her in for a deep kiss. Vexx squeaked in surprise, but melted into Jackie.

"What was that for?" Vexx asked when at last their lips had pulled apart.

Jackie shrugged, a sly smile quirking the edge of her mouth. "Do I need a reason? I wanted to kiss you is all."

Vexx's hand found Jackie's thigh and Jackie's fingers intertwined with hers and squeezed. Warmth crept from her toes to her ears. "So what are we doing?"

Jackie reached back, retrieving the gift bag from behind the passenger seat and handed it to Vexx. "Well, I got you this."

Vexx's head cocked. "What? Why?" She looked down at the gift as though it were an alien entity.

With a chuckle, Jackie poked it, crinkling the paper. "Because I wanted to. Open it!"

Vexx withdrew the red tissue, her face brightening as she

realized it was glittery. She began to pull things from the bag, setting them on her lap and setting the empty bag beside her feet. She raised a small box but Jackie shook her head.

"Save that for last."

Vexx set it aside and instead unfolded a faded black fabric parcel. She held up a t-shirt and looked at Jackie with a smile. "Nirvana?"

"Well, it might not look like something super cool, but it's a vintage Nirvana tee. They're kind of synonymous with Seattle, and I tracked down a legit one for you instead of a reprint."

"I've heard of them!" Vexx exclaimed. "The singer died, right? He's not… you know, down there. So I haven't met him or anything, but I've heard people talk about them! This is rad, Jax! Thank you!"

"Keep going," Jackie replied, knees bouncing a little in excited anticipation.

Vexx unwound the tissue from around a small cellophane bag. "Theo…" she began.

"It's chocolate!" Jackie interjected. "You said you can't get the good stuff, and Theo is big here. There's a bunch of different flavored bars in there. I'm not sure how well they'll travel, but at least you'll have some."

Vexx didn't say anything, and her expression crumpled as she looked down at the chocolate in her hand. "Jackie, why are you giving me these things?"

Confused, Jackie touched her knee. "Hey, this is supposed to be fun, what's wrong?"

Vexx shook her head and shifted her face into a smile. "I'm being dumb—I'm sorry. This is really sweet."

"You don't have to keep going if you don't want to," Jackie's chin lifted in the direction of the final two items. "You can open them later."

"No, no, I want to." Vexx picked up another small parcel and pulled out a small blown glass pumpkin. "A… gourd?"

Laughter bubbled up from Jackie's throat. "It's blown glass. I don't know, we have a lot of it here and I thought you'd think it was cute. It doesn't do anything or anything, it's just a little decoration."

Vexx's inauthentic smile didn't change as she examined it. "It is cute, thank you."

A sick feeling began to wash over Jackie. This isn't what she wanted. The last thing she wanted to do was make Vexx sad. She reached for the small box before Vexx could take it, sliding it into her pocket. "We'll save that one for later, okay? I have some fun stuff for us to do."

Vexx nodded, not protesting Jackie's reclamation of the little gift. Jackie shoved the sick feeling down, refusing to let it bleed into her thoughts. She didn't need to spiral into an emotional place she wasn't ready for. She needed to have a fun day with Vexx, and she had worked her ass off to plan one. "Let's go," she said, pulling away from the Jungle headquarters curb and merging into the line of cars heading toward the freeway.

The drive north was quiet, and Jackie tried not to let it bother her. Vexx ran her long fingers along the lines of the glass pumpkin, clearly lost in thought. Jackie played some Nirvana and then turned the radio to KEXP, listening to some Icelandic folk rock and occasionally glancing out the window. As she pulled into the parking lot, she risked a look at Vexx. "You okay?"

Vexx nodded and rolled her shoulders. "Just tired, and thinking," she replied. "Where are we?"

Jackie got out of the car and walked around to the back of the car, pulling a comfy hoodie and her leather jacket from the trunk. She passed the hoodie to Vexx. "You're going to want this."

Vexx held it up in front of her. "Are we doing something cold?"

Jackie made a noncommittal gesture. "Maybe? Just put it on and let's go."

She led Vexx through a parking lot and around a building, stepping out to find a dock with two large boats moored beside it. A battered sign with a goofy looking painted whale looked down on them. Vexx opened her mouth and closed it again and Jackie smiled.

"Come on."

THE EXPRESSION on Vexx's face when the first whale breached the surface was a thing of indescribable beauty. It was as though an inner door opened, exposing her entire soul to light after a lifetime of shadow. Jackie supposed that in a way, it had. A couple weeks ago, Vexx had never seen the sun. She had never felt mist settle on her skin, had never seen the wide breadth of the ocean at the horizon. Jackie loved being the one to have shared these things with her, to be the person beside her as Vexx's world got a little bit bigger—one day at a time. She wanted to keep doing it.

"Oh!" Vexx exclaimed as a great grey head rose from the water, sea spray surrounding it and casting a halo of prismatic rainbows. "It's so big!"

A voice crackled over the boat's speaker, "Keep your eyes peeled for more! This is a decent-sized pod of grey whales we know pretty well. They're paying us a visit to eat their fill of local shrimp before heading north to Alaska!" A massive heart shaped plume of mist exploded only a few feet from the ship, and a whale hurled itself upward, twisting its immense body and crashing back into the ocean with a loud splash.

Vexx threw her head back and laughed. The hood slid from her silver hair and the muted, filtered sunlight caught on her horns, making them shimmer. Something about the baggy hoodie and her blatant joy made her look younger. Jackie wondered if Vexx had been able to have moments like this growing up. Did she experience such unbridled joy while among the fires of Hell? Were there things that made her heart burst like this? She tugged her jacket tighter over her chest as the brisk ocean air sent an involuntary shiver through her, and reached for Vexx's hand. She took it without even glancing at Jackie, and Jackie couldn't help but think *this feels right.*

Back on land, they ate popcorn and hot dogs as they watched the Sounders play against San Diego. Vexx was amazed at the sheer size of Lumen Field, spending more time watching the people in the stadium than the soccer game. Jackie bought her a bright green and blue scarf, which she immediately wrapped around her neck, grinning ear to ear. They jogged arm-in-arm to the metro, collapsing into the humid, smelly air with irrepressible giggles, and when they reached their stop Vexx kissed Jackie deeply before hopping off into the twinkling dark.

Jackie didn't press for conversation; she was more than happy to simply watch Vexx take in the city at night. When, legs aching and cheeks flushed, they arrived at Jackie's final planned destination, Vexx stopped dead in her tracks. Bright light in shades of hot pink and vivid blue cast over the planes of her face—her red lips looking black as they parted in astonishment. Before them, the Great Wheel spun. Its reflection danced on the water, and as the colors shifted and twirled, Jackie stepped closer to Vexx and slipped an arm around her waist. Jackie's head leaned on Vexx's shoulder and Vexx pressed a soft kiss to the top of her damp, disheveled hair.

"This was the best day," Vexx said in a quiet voice.

"I'm glad you thought so," Jackie answered. "I wanted you to experience Seattle, to get the full tourist treatment...." Her breath caught, words momentarily dissipating into the dark. "While you're still here.

Vexx said nothing in reply, and Jackie was about to speak again when she felt a tiny tremble from Vexx's shoulder. She stilled, and the tremble grew. Vexx made a muffled sound into Jackie's hair, and as Jackie tilted her face up and reached to cup Vexx's cheek in her palm, Vexx broke. It began small. One blood-red tear tumbled down Vexx's smooth grey skin, but then another and another came, and with a choked sob she folded into Jackie's waiting embrace.

20

VEXX

VEXX WASN'T sure if she could recall ever having cried, but as she stood in Jackie's arms beneath the brilliant light of the big wheel, she thought she could almost hear her heart breaking. This had been the most remarkable day of her life, and she felt as though every minute of the previous twenty-eight years had been wasted. *I didn't know*, she thought, *that I could feel like this. That there was this much* life *on the surface.* Now, as the realization settled in that she was coming to the end of her time here, she knew without a sliver of doubt that it would crush her. She would never be the same. How was she supposed to return to Infernius and carry on as though there wasn't a vibrant woman up here with a heart of blazing kindness burning Vexx's soul to cinders? How was she expected to return to her dead-end career prospects—her futile desire to pursue journalism and dismantle the Hellistocracy from within? How could she look into her father's glowing crimson eyes and pretend that she wanted to be "home?"

How could she even call it home anymore?

Home felt like the warmth of Jackie's fingers around hers.

Home was the sugar cookie scent of her skin, the taste of salted chocolate on her lips, the reverent way she worshiped Vexx's body as though she were far more than the fourteenth child of a king of Hell. Vexx had never wanted anything more for herself than this feeling, this knowledge that not only was she wanted, but she was appreciated.

Maybe even loved.

And as sanguine tears rolled down her cheeks, staining them a soft pink, she understood something within herself that felt new, fragile, fraught.

Vexxanthe Desmodeus Hekate Marie Morningstar gathered herself up, swallowing thickly and swiping at her eyes with the rain-damp sleeves of Jackie's hoodie. She drew her shoulders back and reined in her heart, caging it once again behind black iron bars. She shook herself slightly, trying to dislodge the weight of the feelings warring inside of her, and she said the only words she could manage to grasp, "Can we get a cup of coffee?"

Jackie, to her credit, rolled with it. She didn't ask what had overcome Vexx, or if she was okay. She nodded, smiled, and with a hand on the small of Vexx's back, guided her away from the still-shifting show of lights over the water.

The door to the coffeeshop jangled as they entered, and Vexx tugged her hood down more to disguise her horns and puffy, ruby eyes. "Go, sit," Jackie directed, gesturing toward a seat in the corner beside a large plate-glass window. She ordered for the two of them, and in a few minutes, she walked to the table and passed Vexx a steaming cup of slightly purple-hued coffee.

Vexx breathed in its scent, cocking her head slightly. "This smells… different. What is it?"

"Ube latte," Jackie answered, the edges of her lips softening in what could almost be called a smile. "It's sort of a type of potato?" She chuckled at Vexx's expression. "I promise, it's good. They use coconut milk and it's sweet and creamy and something a little more interesting than your regular cuppa."

Tentatively, Vexx took a small sip. She should not have been surprised that it was delicious. It was indeed sweet and velvety, with just a hint of something unique. It still tasted like coffee, and Vexx was endlessly glad of that.

"I'm sorry—" Vexx began.

But Jackie held up her hand, silencing her. "You don't need to apologize to me. You're allowed to feel things, Vexx. I know this is a lot, I'm a lot, and maybe I shouldn't have gone so crazy with packing stuff into today."

"No, no!" Vexx didn't know how to articulate what she wanted to say. "It was amazing. All of it was amazing. You're not a lot, Jax. You're the perfect amount."

Jackie's round cheeks flushed and she sipped her own coffee. "I really just wanted you to have a good day. I'm sorry for whatever happened to fuck that up."

"Jackie, today was the best day I have *ever* had," Vexx said, sitting up straighter. "That's what… made me cry." She didn't like how it felt to admit it, to share this vulnerability. "I haven't really had a lot of truly great days. My life has always been comfortable, fine, but there's not a whole lot of joy in Infernius. That's why I got Cupcakes. I wanted something to exist in my life that didn't serve some grand purpose, or answer to my father."

"I understand," Jackie said; Vexx thought that she really did. "That's sort of why I adopted Mimolette. I wanted something to love me unconditionally. People can be fickle, but cats always love you."

"I wanted a cat, growing up. My father said he was allergic, but I'm pretty sure he just doesn't like them. He's not a fan of anything that doesn't worship him, and cats don't care if you're the king," Vexx replied.

Jackie set her coffee atop the small table and chuckled.

"You're not wrong. Mimolette couldn't care less what I do for a living as long as his food bowl is full."

"He's a smart cat. I like when you feed me too," Vexx said with a smile. "But I think I get better treats than he does." She immediately felt her cheeks heat. She hadn't meant her words to sound euphemistic, but the sly twinkle in Jackie's eye told her that they had. "I didn't mean… I mean…"

Jackie reached across the table to place her hand into Vexx's upturned palm. "I know what you meant," she replied. "Do you want to go home?"

Vexx nodded, and they rose, walking into the rainy night. They returned to Jackie's car, and she started it, turning the heat on to warm up before they drove back to Jackie's apartment. Vexx played with a tiny wisp of flame, winking at Jackie as she rubbed her chilled hands together in front of the weakly blowing vent.

"Oh!" Jackie leaned over the passenger seat, her body pressing against Vexx. When she sat back up, the small box from earlier rested in her palm. "Your last present."

Vexx felt her heartbeat quicken. There was something about the open, eager expression on Jackie's face that filled her with caution. This mattered to Jackie, and after the painstakingly planned day they had shared, and the perfectly curated gifts she had received thus far, she was nervous about this last one. The box was black, not much bigger than a matchbox, and Vexx took it from Jackie with shaking fingers. She was scared. She was scared to open the box and see how much Jackie cared, because that is what it felt like—that this last, tiny gift was a little piece of Jackie's heart. Her eyes met Jackie's and she took a deep breath as she lifted the lid.

Nestled within the box was a tiny silver pendant shaped like a branch of some kind. Jackie stared at Vexx expectantly, and she lifted the pendant from the soft lining of the box. "It's beautiful," Vexx said. "What is it?"

Jackie beamed. "It's a cedar bough. It's from an Indigenous-owned company here in Seattle. It's owned by the Snoqualmie Tribe. We live on stolen land, and I wanted you to have something beautiful created by the communities that have always been here."

"I read a bit about that in my human studies class," Vexx replied. "The colonization of North America. It was horrific."

"It was," Jackie agreed. "And it still is. So I guess the very least I could do was to support local indigenous artisans. Martin works closely to source our seafood and a lot of our produce from the indigenous community as well. He's no saint, but I do appreciate that about him. He's not all bad."

Vexx gave Jackie a shy smile. "Can you put it on for me?"

Jackie took the necklace from Vexx, their fingers barely grazing, and leaned over to secure the tiny clasp. She moved Vexx's silver hair to the side and Vexx let out a soft sigh. Jackie leaned farther across the seat and pressed a gentle kiss to the long, exposed column of Vexx's neck. Vexx turned her face to meet Jackie's and pressed her lips against the corner of Jackie's mouth. She felt as though electricity had set her blood aflame. Her skin tingled with it, and when Jackie pushed her fingers through Vexx's hair to kiss her deeply, Vexx allowed herself to be lost in it entirely. If she was going to burn, this was where she wanted to be.

Vexx shifted in her seat, trying to maneuver onto Jackie's lap, but her height and Jackie's full stomach made it impossible. She made a little frustrated sound and Jackie smiled against her lips. "I can take us home, baby."

"Please," Vexx said breathlessly. "Please, I want to be close to you."

They held hands the whole ride home, fingers intertwined atop Jackie's thigh as she drove. The lights from the surrounding traffic glinted off the raindrops collecting on the windshield and cast scattered color across Jackie's face from behind the glass. Vexx couldn't help but stare. Jackie was so beautiful it hurt. Her long lashes and bright eyes, the curve of her strong shoulders and her skilled hands draped across the steering wheel, every tiny detail tugged at something deep within Vexx. She felt tethered to this woman, to this place, to this moment in time, and she wanted nothing more than to keep that tether tied forever. But she had to go home in less than a week.

Didn't she?

When they pulled up to Jackie's apartment, Vexx pulled the hood back over her hair. Jackie grabbed her damp leather jacket from the backseat and tossed it over her shoulders without putting her arms through the sleeves. "Do you need me to help you carry anything?" Jackie asked, reaching for Vexx's bag.

"No," Vexx replied, heart still racing. "I've got it. Just get me inside."

Jackie laughed quietly. "Yes, princess. Your wish is my command." When they reached the door, Jackie unlocked it quickly, opening the door to usher Vexx into the warmth of her dark apartment.

Vexx didn't bother turning on the lights. She grabbed Jackie by the front of her jacket and pulled her close. The kiss was crushing. Her teeth clicked against Jackie's with the force of it, and with a shrug of her shoulders, the jacket fell to the floor with a muted clink as the zipper hit the tile. Vexx pushed her up against the wall, hands racing beneath Jackie's shirt to move across her warm, soft skin. Jackie whispered, "God, your hands are always so warm," as her own much colder fingers pulled Vexx's sweatshirt over her head along with the shirt she wore underneath.

Vexx's grey skin pebbled, standing before Jackie in only a black balconette bra. Jackie let out a whistle of appreciation and ran her thumb from the side of Vexx's breast down the curve of her waist. "You're so perfect," she said, looking into Vexx's carmine eyes. "I can't get enough of you, Vexx."

Vexx whined, the sound full of need and emotion she wasn't yet ready to face. She grabbed at Jackie's shirt, trying to pull it off but only succeeding in tangling Jackie up in the soft cotton. "Take it *off*," she pleaded.

"Impatient," Jackie replied, even as she tore the shirt off and dropped it beside her.

Vexx bent, her lips tracing a line of gentle kisses over Jackie's collarbone. "Always." She licked the edge of the tattoo at Jackie's shoulder and nipped at the soft skin just beneath the strap of her sports bra.

"Fuck, Vexx..." Jackie panted. She shifted her knee between Vexx's long legs, knocking them apart. "How do I always want you so badly?"

"I don't know," Vexx answered as she continued to kiss her way across Jackie's chest. "But I want you just as much."

Jackie grabbed Vexx's elbows, pinning her arms to her sides, and walked her down the hallway. As Vexx stepped backward cautiously, she lowered her gaze to Jackie's. She saw only raw desire looking back at her—the distillation of all their time together, the tension that had built and crested between them. It washed over them now, a wave of heat that settled between them. Vexx lifted a foot to kick the bedroom door open and Mimolette ran out, clearly not wanting to be a part of whatever was about to happen. Jackie pushed Vexx toward the bed, but Vexx spun, taking her place and forcing Jackie down onto the plush duvet. She climbed atop Jackie, her knees resting on either side of Jackie's ample hips. When she rolled her body against Jackie's, they both moaned in unison.

"Why are you still wearing pants?" Jackie asked, voice coarse.

Vexx didn't reply, but she slowly moved her hands to the waistband of her jeans, unbuttoning them with teasing leisure.

When her zipper was fully undone, Jackie grabbed them and yanked them down. Vexx lifted up slightly, letting the denim slide over her ass, and she stood, looking down at Jackie. Jackie's gaze didn't leave hers as she slowly worked the tight jeans down each of Vexx's long, long legs, and finally to the floor where Vexx could step out of them. Her panties were black lace, high-waisted and cut high, allowing Jackie to see even more of her thighs. Jackie's calloused palms ran down the expanse of flesh, sending goosebumps racing over Vexx's skin.

"Goddamn," Jackie breathed. "You look so fucking good right now. Like a fucking goddess. I wish I could see this forever."

Vexx ignored the way the words yanked on her heart, pushing it down and allowing her lust to fill the space instead. "Me, too," she replied. Vexx got an idea, and reached for Jackie's back pocket where she knew she would find Jackie's phone. She handed it to her. "Take a picture," she said. "Then you can."

Jackie bit her lower lip, breathing heavily. "Yes, ma'am." She turned on the camera, quickly adjusting the flash, and snapped a series of photos. As Vexx moved back over her, Jackie kept going, capturing snapshots of Vexx's body stretching over hers. Her hands fell back above her head, dropping the phone to her pillow, as Vexx's fingers slid over the seam of her pants.

"If you take these off," Vexx whispered. "You can keep taking photos of me. Hell, you can record us."

"Oh, fuck." Jackie clumsily pulled at her pants, sliding them over her ass and kicking them off roughly. "God, yes."

21

jackie

JACKIE'S HANDS could barely hold the phone. The sight of Vexx's body climbing atop her, slowly moving until her lace-trapped, perfect tits were inches from Jackie's waiting mouth. Jackie set the phone to record, and set it on the bed, propped up on a pillow to face them. When her lips brushed Vexx's nipple through the fabric of her bra, Vexx's back arched and she shifted forward to press into Jackie's face. She teased—teeth grazing and tongue flicking against the thin barrier, until at last she reached up to unclasp Vexx's bra. The moment it slid from her shoulders, Jackie's fingers dug into the soft flesh, mouth closing over Vexx's peaked nipples with near-painful force. Vexx hissed, and it turned into a deep moan as Jackie's teeth bit down.

"Yes, fuck, Jax. Yes." Vexx murmured into Jackie's hair.

Jackie continued her assault, leaving crescent-shaped bite marks across Vexx's perfect, unblemished skin. She glanced at the phone screen, and though she didn't exactly love the way she looked from this angle, Vexx looked divine. Her hands moved from Vexx's chest down the delicious dip of her waist and down her hips, sliding beneath the waistband of her underwear. She pulled them down and Vexx lifted each knee, making quick work of it. As her left hand dropped the panties, her right slipped between Vexx's thighs, running her fingertips through the slick flesh. Vexx's breath caught and she leaned down to lick Jackie's lower lip. The resulting kiss was slow, intentional. Jackie's chin tipped up and she felt her chest tighten. Kissing Vexx was everything.

I don't want to ever kiss another woman, she thought. A tiny blade of fear sliced through her, a quick razor-sharp slash that stung, but she refused to give it attention. She would have a long time ahead of her to heal those wounds.

Her fingers once again dragged through Vexx's center, feeling just how much Vexx wanted her. *Fuck.* She used two fingers to spread her apart, glimpsing at the phone to ensure it was capturing every explicit inch of her.

She planned to use this video for the rest of her goddamn life.

Keeping her spread, she pushed two fingers into Vexx's luscious heat and groaned as she felt Vexx's body tighten around them. Curling her fingers, she pressed against the swollen little patch that made Vexx lose control, smiling when Vexx's hips bucked against her. She swirled her thumb over the wet entrance, and moved it to Vexx's clit. The pad of Jackie's thumb moved over Vexx in a rapid rhythm, flicking her clit as she pumped her fingers in and out of her slick pussy. Vexx's hips began to rock against her, riding her fingers as they moved, and Jackie slid a third finger into her, bending her knuckles ever so slightly to give Vexx the stretch she knew she craved. It was the exact thing Vexx needed, and with a strangled cry, she came. Her pussy pulsed around Jackie's hand, hips jerking chaotically as her body lost all sense of propriety.

Jackie pulled her fingers from Vexx and used both hands to cup her ass, pulling her up. Vexx made a squeak of protest, but

Jackie ignored her, smiling as she felt Vexx's hands land on her headboard to help pull herself forward. Her knee knocked into the phone, and Vexx reached for it, but Jackie snatched it from her hand and moved it to the center of her chest.

"Jackie…" Vexx began.

"I want to watch you," she replied as she pulled Vexx the last few inches, positioning her directly over Jackie's face. "I want to watch you come again while you ride my fucking face."

Vexx closed her eyes, but didn't argue, and lowered her hips. Jackie lifted her chin, claiming Vexx with her tongue. Her hands pulled Vexx's ass apart, opening her pussy wide so she could delve into her deeply, tasting every bit of her. Vexx moaned loudly, rolling against Jackie's lips as her tongue moved deep inside Vexx's pussy. Jackie guided her, helping Vexx ride her mouth as she alternated between fucking her with her tongue and licking her overly-sensitive clit. Jackie could feel her own arousal soaking her underwear. Knowing that her phone was recording the sight of Vexx's spread pussy grinding against Jackie's mouth, somehow made her even hotter. God, she was going to come the instant Vexx touched her. She didn't care.

Jackie knew Vexx was close, heard the fast, hard breaths she panted against the headboard, and she pulled her down onto her face hard. She couldn't breathe, Vexx's wet center slid over her mouth, her nose, her chin as she fucked herself on Jackie's face. Jackie reached up, the angle awkward as hell, to shove two fingers into Vexx, curling them roughly until Vexx came, a torrid surge of salt and smoke gushing over her tongue.

"Oh, fuck, I'm sorry, fuck—" Vexx yelped, even as she lifted herself just enough for Jackie to breathe. She continued to climax, each pulse of her pussy sending more heat dripping down Jackie's chin.

Jackie's thin control shattered, and she reached down,

pressing her fingers against her soaked boxers to grind over her own clit until she was also coming. Her tongue plunged back into Vexx as she did, tasting her own fingers—still deep inside Vexx. Neither of them moved for what felt like an hour, but in what was probably less than a minute, Vexx fell to the side, narrowly missing kneeing Jackie in the face as she collapsed on the bed. Jackie lazily reached for her phone and stopped recording, leaving a smeared fingerprint on the screen.

"Fuck," Jackie said, not knowing if she was speaking to Vexx or herself.

They both lay on the bed, panting heavily, and Jackie's arm reached to pull Vexx close to her. Her skin tingled; beneath her tongue was rubbed raw from where it had slid over her bottom teeth, and her wrist was a little sore from the uncomfortable angle required to fuck Vexx properly—but she had never felt better in her life. Not once.

"Well, that was new," Vexx said into the sweat-damp skin of Jackie's shoulder.

"Squirting?" Jackie asked.

Vexx smacked her arm. "Stop! Hells. I don't wanna talk about it." She covered her face with her forearm, but Jackie could still see the pink flush of her cheeks.

"Uh, why? It was so fucking hot. I literally couldn't help but make myself come watching you. It took like zero-point-two seconds."

"Excuse me?" Vexx replied, laughing and moving her arm to peek at Jackie. "You got yourself off?"

"I didn't even have to actually touch myself," Jackie answered with a scoff. "I still have my underwear on."

Vexx pushed up onto her elbows, looking down at Jackie's body and smiling. "That doesn't seem very fair. I didn't even get to touch you." Her fingers walked across the coverlet toward Jackie, but Jackie reached over to stop her.

"No," she sighed. "No more." Jackie laughed. "I can't. I need a break."

Vexx laid back down and curled around Jackie. Her long arm snaked around Jackie's soft middle, and Jackie turned her face to breathe in the scent of Vexx's disheveled hair. She whispered soundlessly into the silver tangle, saying the words she knew she couldn't say. Her eyes closed as she let Vexx hold her tight, images of a future she knew she couldn't have racing across her mind as she allowed herself this moment in Vexx's arms.

22
vexx

VEXX WRAPPED a towel around her freshly-washed hair and stepped into a knee-length black satin nightgown. Jackie had already gone to bed, passing out almost immediately after she showered. Vexx walked to the living room, sitting on the edge of the couch and staring down at the floor. The scent of brimstone caught her attention, and her head snapped up. An orange glow lit the kitchen, and her heart thundered in her chest as she stood and walked to the small portal which had opened amidst the checkered tile.

"Vexxanthe," Bozuran's voice boomed. "I am glad to see you well." He squinted. "Are you wearing a towel?"

"I just got out of the shower," she replied. "It's late here." She glanced at the clock on the wall. "Hells, it's nearly three a.m."

"Are you safe?" his impossibly deep voice asked. "Have the humans been appropriately accommodating?"

"Yeah," she said, tucking a stray strand of damp silver hair behind her ear. "The human I've been staying with has been very kind."

"Good. I shall spare them, then. I had intended to incinerate the person who trapped you on that repulsive sphere, but if you believe they deserve leniency I will grant it."

"Hells, father!" Vexx replied. "Please don't cremate anyone. Everything is fine, I've been fine. I've been working for Seth in my spare time, and exploring the surface. It's nothing like I thought it would be."

"I apologize for not being able to retrieve you sooner, I cannot imagine." Bozuran's face twisted.

"No, father. It's actually really nice up here."

Bozuran barked out a cruel laugh. "Nice? You have seen what eternity looks like for humans, Vexxanthe."

"Yeah," Vexx said. "And now I've met the kind of people who *don't* end up in Hell. They're pretty great. The human studies curriculum needs updating."

"Bah," Bozuran spat, shaking his massive, horned head. "It is none of your concern. I will be able to open a portal capable of retrieving you in six days' time. I require little of you. Can you provide me with the blood of the one who summoned you?"

Vexx balked. "No? I am not going to harm Jackie."

"I am not requesting that you slit her throat, Vexxanthe," Bozuran sighed, rubbing his temple with a clawed hand. "A few drops will suffice."

"Yeah, sure, probably." Vexx felt like she was going to throw up. She didn't want to do this. A plea clawed at her throat, begging to escape. "Father—"

Bozuran interrupted, "Here—" a small vial tumbled up through the portal "—this will allow you to open another communication portal from your side. It took some time to work out. Plan to be here in six days, once darkness has fallen fully. But should you require me in the interim, you will have the ability."

Vexx picked up the tiny bottle and rolled it in her fingers. "Alright, father," she sighed.

"Do not be distressed, child. You will not be forced to remain on the surface much longer. When you return, perhaps you can begin your career with a piece on your stay. It seemed to be effective for Dante on the other side."

Vexx didn't look up. The liquid in the vial glowed faintly, and she watched as it tipped back and forth in her hands. "Maybe. Sure, that's a good idea."

A crackling sound interrupted her thoughts, and Vexx saw the edges of the portal begin to flicker. "I apologize, this is not a long-lasting magic," Bozuran said through the shrinking portal. "I have missed you daughter, and I look forward to your return home."

Before Vexx could reply, the portal snapped shut—a tendril of curling smoke rising in the kitchen the only sign it had existed.

And Vexx slid to the floor, not even feeling the cold bite of the tile on her thighs as a steaming-hot blood tear rolled down her cheek silently.

***

VEXXANTHE DESMODEUS HEKATE MARIE MORNINGSTAR strode into Jungle headquarters ten minutes before ten, coffee in hand. Melissa was already in her office, wearing a sharp tan pantsuit with a pink button-up. "Ms. Morningstar," she greeted Vexx with a warm smile. "I wanted to touch base with you this morning. How much longer will you be in Seattle?"

The coffee in Vexx's mouth went cold at the question. She knew the answer, but she couldn't bring herself to say it. "I'm not certain," she answered. It was a safe, noncommittal answer. "Is there something you needed me to do?"

Melissa looked around, her normally composed expression slipping for the briefest of seconds. "It is possible that a permanent position will be opening up, one I wanted to offer you."

"Oh," Vexx began. "I'm not sure I will continue to work with Jungle—"

Melissa held up a hand and gestured for Vexx to come closer. "This position would not be with Jungle. It's not something I can—" she looked up at the camera in the office "—discuss at this time." Her voice was barely above a whisper. "Would you be available for coffee or a cocktail later?"

Vexx raised a brow. "I could likely manage that," she answered quietly.

"Meet me at Rickhouse at nine? It's a whiskey bar nearby."

"Okay," Vexx replied, confused but curious. "I can do that."

"Good," Melissa smiled in a way Vexx hadn't seen before. She had a dimple in her left cheek that seemed to appear from nowhere. "I'll see you then." she raised her voice back to normal volume. "Can you work on these acquisition contracts this morning? Mr. Kazon needs the terms reviewed before he signs."

Vexx took the folder, "Of course." And Melissa Avilez walked out of the office without a second glance.

After hours of poring over legal jargon, Vexx was pretty sure her brain had started to short-circuit. Had that line mentioned an acquittal or an actuary? She shook her head. She had done enough. All but one of the contracts had been annotated with her suggestions, and she handed the folder to Seth's secretary on her way out of the office. "Can you see that Mr. Kazon receives these this evening?" she asked.

The secretary nodded frantically. "Of course, Ms. Morningstar, it will be my pleasure. Is there anything else I can do for you?"

Vexx felt bad that she didn't know the man's name. He seemed nice, and had always been quick to help. "No, thank you so much," she replied. "That will be all for the night."

The man stood clumsily and... bowed? Slightly at the waist. "Yes, ma'am, thank you," he said before hurrying off. Vexx felt a twinge of guilt. This felt too much like Hell. she didn't want people simpering and bowing to her. She hated it. And this position at Jungle seemed to be in close enough proximity to Seth that people thought she was important. She didn't want to be important, not here. With a sinking feeling she realized that she didn't want to be sinful. She didn't want to be tied to immoral places and people. She had spent her entire life trying to figure out how to navigate Hell and its politics, and this was it—the real problem. She didn't want to be sinful.

Hells, father would shit coal, she thought. *If he knew that I was more like my mother than him....*

She glanced at her phone. It was just after eight. She requested a rideshare and took the elevator down to the lobby, nodding at Amy as she walked outside into the cool evening.

The ride was quiet and calm, the driver didn't try to talk to Vexx and she could sit with her thoughts, but it didn't make them clear. What was she going to do, truly? Could she tell her father that she...

She didn't even know what she'd say.

"Hey, daddy-o, I'm gay and I'm madly in..."

A headache began at the base of her skull, and the dull throb pulsed in time with the music which softly played. It seemed to grow more insistent as she stepped from the car and hurried into the bar and out of the drizzle. Melissa was seated at the bar and waved when she noticed Vexx. She took her seat, and the bartender sauntered over to take her order.

"Boulevardier?" she asked the diminutive woman, liking the way the strands of grey in her hair caught the moody light of the Edison bulbs overhead.

The bartender smiled. "Excellent choice," she replied. "Any preference on bourbon?"

"Something sweet," Vexx answered, thinking of Jackie. The bartender set about crafting her cocktail, and Vexx turned to Melissa. "So, why the secrecy? What is this job you wanted to ask me about?"

"I'm quitting," Melissa replied. "I can't keep working for the devil's right-hand man. "My mother would be turning over in her grave if she knew I was selling my soul to a man like Seth Kazon." The bartender placed Vexx's drink on a small, black napkin and Vexx took a sip. She reached for her purse, but Melissa waved her hand. "It's on me. Lord knows he pays me enough."

"Not that I'm disagreeing," Vexx said. "But why now? What led to you quitting? And are you offering me *your* job? I'm still confused."

"Seth is a piece of shit," she answered, shrugging. "This month alone, he's firing close to two thousand people nation-wide and replacing them with tech. My parents immigrated here and made a good life for themselves. I want to be able to tell my kids I did the same. I'm starting my own company, and I want you to work for me."

Vexx's forehead wrinkled. "You barely know me."

"But I know what a lot of people don't. I know what you are; I know where you're from, and I know that you see what I see."

"I'm surprised you see all that as a positive," Vexx replied with a wince. "You know who my father is, and you still think I'm a better person than Seth?"

"That's precisely why. I've seen your notes and Seth told me about your idea to slowly transition to American-made prod-ucts, and how you framed it. It's brilliant. Wanting Seth to think you were trying to make him look better, while also making more jobs and supporting American small businesses? Absolutely inspired. That's what I want. I want innovation and drive. I want someone who has seen the worst of humanity, and wants to make it better."

Vexx didn't say anything for a moment, taking a contemplative sip of her drink. "I'm supposed to be going back… home, next week."

Melissa's lips tipped into a smile. "And I can see that you don't want to. Don't. Stay here."

"I don't know how," Vexx answered, biting her lip to contain the quiver that threatened to warp her words.

"You do. There are things you can do to fit in better—I've seen them. You're not the first, um, downstairs visitor we've had at Jungle. There are… illusory means."

"Yeah, there's glamours we can use. But I'm not just anyone. I'm the fourteenth heir, my father is an actual king. I can't just tell him I want to stay."

"Why?" Melissa looked genuine. "You just said there are thirteen people ahead of you. Do you have a career down there? Do you have friends and family that you couldn't be away from? It's not like you could never visit. You have opportunities here, and I think you'd be happy if you took them."

"I'm my father's only daughter. Because of me, he lost the love of his life. He treasures me, I remind him of her."

"I'm my father's only daughter too. He lives in El Paso, and I see him once or twice a year. He knows I wasn't happy there, and when I got the chance to move to the west coast? He was happy to see me go. Because parents want their children to be happy. Vexx, don't you think your father wants you to be happy too?"

Vexx thought about her life—her father's frustration with her desire to change Hell, his annoyance at her refusal to fit into the image of 'Princess of Hell,' but also the genuine concern in the glow of his eyes when he spoke to her last night. "I don't know."

A familiar laugh caught Vexx's attention, and she turned, seeing the very last thing she expected: Jackie, clearly intoxicated, with another woman.

23
jackie

THE BOOKS at Canid had been full, but somehow, service ended an hour earlier than Jackie had anticipated. She knew she should go home, that Vexx would be back and she could slide beneath her blankets and lose herself in silver smoked cherries, but the clock that ticked deep within her chest refused to relent. She only knew of one way to quiet it.

Ashley, the server, stopped Jackie as she made her way to the parking garage. "Hey! Chef Miller! Do you have any plans tonight?"

"I don't!" Jackie replied, swallowing. "How 'bout you?"

"I need a drink, want to come along?"

Jackie knew the "right" answer. She knew it had been weeks since she had a drink, weeks that felt steady and grounded. But on and on, that clock ticked. She wanted to drown it out.

Ashley drove, her old Miata feeling *far* too tight for Jackie's taste, but they found parking quickly and sat at a small table in the back. "Do you come to this place a lot?" Jackie asked as Ashley smiled at the woman behind the bar.

"I do," she replied. "And that's sort of why I asked you to come?"

Jackie's head cocked to the side quizzically. "I'm not following."

"I don't have… well… a lot, or any, experience with women. The bartender here, Imani?" Ashley let out a dramatic sigh. "How do I talk to her?"

Jackie laughed. "I should have known." She dragged her hand through her hair and down her neck, rubbing the tight muscle where it met her shoulder. "I'm always the woman women ask."

"I'm sorry," Ashley replied, eyes widening. "I feel like a bitch. I didn't mean to assume you'd be cool with this, I don't know. I really have no clue what the fuck I'm doing."

"How old are you?" Jackie asked.

Ashley chuckled. "That obvious? I'm twenty-two."

Jackie nodded. "And how about Imani?"

"I don't know, forty? But god, Jackie. She's the most beautiful woman I've ever seen. I've never dated a woman; I have no idea how to flirt. She'll probably think I'm an idiot kid."

"Well, you can start by getting us another drink and saying hello. Does she know your name yet?"

"She does. I come here more than I should. I don't even like whiskey." Ashley grinned, cheeks flushing.

"Alright. Grab me a double and I'll share my years of wisdom."

They drank for hours. Jackie had four cocktails in her by the time Imani started delivering their drinks to the table. And she smiled to herself when she saw the bartender's fingers graze Ashley's as she handed back an empty highball glass. She had no idea what time it was, and when she pulled out her phone, the screen swam in her vision. *Fuck.* She knew she had made a mistake.

Jackie straightened her shoulders and asked Imani for a

water. She couldn't drink her way out of this. There wasn't a way that this ended well for her unless she sobered up and got herself home, where Vexx undoubtedly waited. *Vexx,* she thought. *Who is leaving far too soon.* Whiskey rose in her throat at the thought. She didn't want to go back to a life without Vexx in it. What was she supposed to do? Call Cam? Pet Mimolette and watch gay pirate shows on TV? Jackie Miller had it all—right now. She had the career of her dreams, burgeoning friendships with other queers, a place that finally felt like a home. But none of that felt like enough to make it matter.

She wanted to come home to silver waves and ruby eyes. She wanted to bake cakes that elicited genuine amazement and true appreciation. She wanted to keep showing Vexx the world. She knew she wasn't much; she would never have a Ferrari or tailored bespoke suits. She wasn't the kind of woman to go to the opera or adopt a bunch of kids just because she could afford to. She didn't want the world—she wanted Vexx. She wanted someone whose eyes lit up when she saw a whale, who wanted to go to grungy punk shows and drink warm beer from plastic cups, she wanted a woman who would curl her hair and slip into something slinky so they could spend hundreds of dollars on dinner and then go home to fuck like teenagers. She wanted someone who could take charge sometimes, but who wanted to be worshiped and adored in equal measure. She wanted Vexxanthe Desmodeus Hekate Marie Morningstar, and she didn't know how to say goodbye.

Ashley slipped back into her seat, grinning ear-to-ear. "I got her number!" she scream-whispered to Jackie, and Jackie couldn't help but laugh at the unbridled mirth on Ashley's face. "She said she would love to go to dinner sometime, and passed me her number. That's a date, right? She knows I want to take her on a date?"

"Oh, she knows," Jackie chuckled. "You eye fucked her for

the last two hours. Hell, even a stranger could tell you want to take her out."

Ashley pumped both her fists, just a little, close to her chest. "God, thank you Jackie. I'm buying tonight, okay? Thank you so much."

"I didn't do anything," she replied, patting Ashley's shoulder as she literally buzzed with excitement. "You did all that yourself."

Someone cleared their throat, and Ashley turned to look before Jackie. Her mouth fell open in a surprised 'o' and Jackie's attention drunkenly drifted to whomever had elicited such a reaction.

Maybe there is a God, she thought. *I at least know there's a Hell. And its princess is standing right there.*

JACKIE DIDN'T KNOW MUCH at that moment, but she knew, without a doubt, that Vexx was pissed. She had never seen Vexx's eyebrows drawn together like that, or the down-turned angle of her perfectly pouty lips. "Baby—" she began, but Vexx cut her off.

"What are you doing, Jackie?" Vexx interjected, voice low and measured.

"Ashley, the server, you met Ashley!" she gestured with a weak wrist. "She invited me for a drink and I drank." Jackie's voice wasn't quite slurred, but the consonants were a little too long.

Vexx seemed to look at Jackie's companion for the first time. Recognition smoothed her features, but the clear annoyance still remained. "Let's go," she said, reaching down for Jackie's hand.

"O-kay," she answered, placing her fingers in Vexx's. "I'm

sorry."

"We can talk about it later," Vexx murmured in reply. "Ashley, it's nice to see you again." The woman looked chastised, but only smiled in response.

Jackie was happy to see Ashley move to a seat at the bar as Vexx led her out.

"You didn't drive, did you?" she asked.

"No, Ashley drove," Jackie said. "I can get an Uber."

Vexx pulled out her phone, not letting go of Jackie's hand. "I've got it."

"You're mad," Jackie said. It wasn't a question. "I shouldn't have come—I know. I'm just… I'm trying to work through some stuff. I'm not good at this."

Vexx raised Jackie's hand to her lips and kissed her knuckles gently. "We can talk when we get home, okay? I'm not mad. I was just surprised."

The ride home was not as uncomfortable as Jackie would have expected. They were quiet, but the silence wasn't heavy. Vexx's hand on the small of her back guided Jackie in the door and together they walked inside and sat on the couch. Jackie didn't expect the prickling in her eyes, or the way that the room swam. She hadn't thought this conversation would even happen, let alone that she would break down and cry in front of Vexx. But as she sat beside her and looked up into a face that looked as sad as she felt, she buckled.

"I don't want you to leave," she said, a tear rolling down her cheek. "I know you have to, I know this wasn't ever supposed to be permanent. Hell, I know it's only been a couple of weeks and we still barely know each other. But I don't want this to end." Vexx looked away, staring at the wall instead of at Jackie. It hurt. Jackie knew that Vexx didn't feel the same; for fucks' sake, she was probably excited to go home. She was literally royalty. Sharing a one-bedroom apartment with a thirty-five year old pastry chef was no comparison to living in…

what? A palace? Jackie didn't even know. The whiskey swirled in her stomach like a stormy sea, threatening to rise with each anxious thought that raced through her mind.

"I know," Vexx said, so quietly that Jackie almost didn't hear her. "I don't want it to end either."

Jackie's heart beat frantically. "Don't go, Vexx. I don't know how it would work; I don't have answers, but please don't go."

Vexx shook her head and stood. "I need to get some air. I'm sorry. I can't—I can't talk about this right now."

The whiskey waves broke, and Jackie retched, barely able to swallow it back down. She watched Vexx walk out the door, closing it softly behind her, and ran to the bathroom, falling to her knees hard on the tile.

As she heaved, Jackie let all the shame and guilt she felt come up alongside the bourbon and vermouth. This, she thought, was something she would not do again. She had known it before she agreed to go to the bar—that she shouldn't be drinking—especially when she was trying to run from something. But this was the last time. She leaned her face on the cool toilet seat, glad she had just cleaned the bathroom, and thought about Vexx.

It's for the best, she thought. *There's nothing for her here. No, Jax, you are not enough for someone to give up their entire life.* She thought about Cam, and how they had moved here together with a hopeful vision in their plans. *Well, hope doesn't always pan out. That's why it's called hope, and not promise.*

But she wanted to promise Vexx a life worth taking the risk. She wanted to give Vexx a future where she would be happy. She wanted to be happy.

Jackie Miller climbed into the cold sheets of her empty bed and cried herself to sleep.

24

VEXX

VEXX DIDN'T KNOW how long she'd been walking. She hadn't paid any attention to where she was headed, just walked out the door and followed the streets blindly, trying to escape the ache that trailed her. Her feet hurt; her boots felt tight on her ankles, but she saw some sort of park up ahead, and walked toward it. She walked down a narrow sidewalk, passing a mirror-black pool, until she came upon a building made entirely from glass. It was a greenhouse, she realized, with white panels and large sheets of glass making up the walls and the ceiling. It was beautiful. Pale, yellow light illuminated the plants inside, and the front of the building was flanked by massive, sprawling plants with leaves twice the size of her head. The windows were fogged, and she couldn't see inside clearly, but she saw rows of green spotted with bursts of color every few feet. There was so much *life* inside the building—more plants than grew in the entirety of Infernius.

It was beautiful.

Vexx saw her own face reflected in the glass, as though she stood among the rows of foliage. She didn't realize she was crying until she saw her tears tracing thin, red lines down her cheeks in her reflection.

"Please don't go."

Jackie's strained voice wouldn't leave her thoughts. Over, and over she heard those words. Each time, she replied. *I don't want to. I want to stay. I want to be here with you. I want this chance more than I've ever wanted anything.* But she hadn't said any of that. She had run, leaving an emotionally vulnerable Jackie alone in her apartment. Hells, she was a piece of shit. She had never been brave enough to chase her dreams in Infernius, and it seemed that she wasn't brave enough to do it here, either. She turned, unable to look at herself another moment. Jackie deserved better. She deserved someone who was strong enough to choose her, someone who was confident and bold and ready to take a stand for the woman she….

Vexx let out a scream of frustration. A rustling in the trees behind her had her whirling around. She wasn't alone out here, and she hadn't thought to bring anything with her to defend herself. She had fire, she supposed, if it came to that. But it wasn't a human, who emerged from the trees. A deer, heavily pregnant if her stomach was any indication, stepped out in front of Vexx. She froze. She had only ever seen deer in books, and they had not looked this big. They stood and stared at one another, the doe's wide eyes shining in the faint glow of the moon. There, Vexx thought, was an animal in nature—doing what it was supposed to do. It didn't question things, didn't wonder if it was making a mistake, it didn't worry about disappointing others or itself. It just… lived. The deer blinked, its long lashes fanning over its cheeks, and then walked calmly back into the trees.

Vexx knew what she had to do.

VEXX SAT on the damp ground, not caring that her clothes soaked up the rain and the dirt, sticking to her thighs. She crossed her legs and withdrew the tiny vial from her pocket. She wasn't *completely* sure how to use it, but she thought that the main thing was just pouring it out onto the ground. The sharp stink of brimstone and charred earth filled the air as she uncorked the bottle and tipped its contents onto the mossy ground. The trees stirred with a faint phantom breeze, and she felt her skin prickle as the magic seeped into the soil and the air surrounding her. A crack formed in the ground. Hair-thin at first, it spread and stretched into a small chasm before yawning into an oblong portal with glowing, crackling edges. It looked like an eye opening, peering into the fiery sky of Infernius.

"Father?" Vexx said in the loudest whisper she could manage. She felt like she shouldn't be yelling, here in the quiet night, but she didn't know how the portal operated or if her father would even hear her.

His massive, horned head appeared a second later. "Vexxanthe, I am not due to retrieve you for a few days yet, is all well?"

Vexx took a deep, shaky breath. "Yes, everything is fine. It's just…" She gulped in another lungful of air, hands quivering where they sat in her lap. "Father, I'd like to stay here."

Bozuran laughed, a great, booming sound that echoed through the empty park. "Vexxanthe, you have never been one for jests. What is the actual reason you are contacting me? These portals are short-lived, and we do not have much time. Do you need me to summon you earlier? I can likely do it tomorrow with minimal lives lost."

"I'm serious," Vexx said, trying to lend confidence to her voice. "I want to stay on the surface. I know there are glamours to hide my horns and tail and to disguise my skin. If you are opening another portal in a few days, I would like that to be the reason. I'm not coming back. At least, not now. Maybe I can visit—I don't know how it all works, but I can't leave, daddy."

Bozuran's glowing eyes widened, his menacing mouth opening slightly at the address. Vexx hadn't called him daddy since she was a young child. It was seen as impertinent, and she had an image to uphold as Bozuran's heir—albeit one far removed from the possibility of rule. "You are serious," he replied. He said it as a statement, but the disbelief in his tone carried through the deep vibrations of his bass toned voice.

"I am. I have… well, I have feelings for the woman whom I have been staying with. I know it hasn't been long, and I'm sure you'll say it's foolish, but I can't leave without giving it a chance." Though she tried to infuse her words with steady conviction, she saw the portal through a pink haze as a sheen of emotion glossed over her eyes.

"You wish to abandon your place here to chase an unknown future with a human you hardly know—"

"Father, I"

"No, Vexxanthe, let me finish," Bozuran said. "I understand." Vexx's shock was apparent, and Bozuran chuckled gently. "When I met Raeleth, my own father told me I was a fool. 'A succubus is not worthy of a throne,' he told me, and he tried his damndest to convince me to find a companion elsewhere. Succubi can only bear thirteen children because they are not truly high demons," he went on. "They are typically mistresses, broodmares, the demons we seek out when our own wives are unable to bear a proper heir. My father wanted me to marry Lilith." Bozuran laughed. "As though that would have been a suitable match for either of us. Anyway, I refused. I told him that if I were to become king, I would do it on my own terms. Raeleth was the best thing to ever happen to me. She did not simply give me my children, she gave me my life." Bozuran shook his colossal head. "I know you have never known me to be an outwardly affectionate or loving parent. It is not in me to give—" his lip curled "—hugs and kisses and the like. And I admit that for a time, it hurt me to see you—to see you growing and changing and becoming your mother's daughter. I miss her every day of my life. But the same way she chose you, I chose you. She decided that you were worth an eternity away from me. She was right."

Vexx let out a choked sob. She had never heard her father be emotional; he rarely spoke about her mother and she had spent so much of her life thinking he resented her.

"So when you tell me that you want to take a chance on someone, that you think this person is worth leaving your life behind for? I believe you. I have only ever wanted you to be happy, Vexxanthe, truly. If staying on the surface is where you find that, I will not question that choice."

Vexx couldn't answer. The emotion overwhelmed her, drawing hiccuping spasms from her chest and spattering the damp ground with steaming, blood tears. She wished she could hug her father, wished that he wasn't so far away and unreachable. She wanted him to *feel* how much this meant to her.

A goliath hand rose from the portal, fingers barely breaching its boundaries. She leapt upon it, wrapping it in her own small fingers and leaning her forehead against it as she cried. "Thank you," she whispered into the searing heat of his skin. "You don't know what this means to me."

The hand withdrew, and her fingers lingered as long as they could before it sunk back into the now-narrowing portal. "I do, and I hope it is everything you wish it to be, Vexxanthe," her father said. "I will consult with those more familiar with situations such as these, and will attempt to have a glamour or some sort of solution ready for you when I open the portal. It will be a more secure conduit, and I should be able to hold it open long enough to get you what you need."

"Thank you," Vexx said, sniffling slightly. "I will be ready, and I will do whatever I need to."

"I do love you, Vexxanthe," Bozuran said. "I hope you always know that."

And as the portal closed, Vexx whispered back, "I do."

VEXX HAD GOTTEN herself hopelessly lost, so she took an Uber back to the apartment. Her legs shook the entire ride, knees bouncing up and down uncontrollably. It was unbelievably late, and she knew Jackie would be asleep, but she *needed* to tell Jackie she felt the same. She had never dreamed of a future where her father supported this decision, but she had found it and she wasn't going to squander one more minute.

Jackie hadn't bothered to lock the door, so Vexx slipped in without issue, glancing at her purse on the table as she headed for the bedroom. Jackie was turned toward the wall, huddled in on herself and looking devastatingly fragile. She felt like absolute garbage knowing she had hurt Jackie. Literally the last thing on earth she ever wanted to do was to cause Jackie harm, but she'd fucked up. Vexx silently slipped out of her damp clothes, tossing them directly in the washer to avoid tainting Jackie's hamper with the stench of brimstone, and pulled on one of Jackie's old t-shirts. She slid into bed beside Jackie's slumbering form, curling her body to fit Jackie's and wrapping her arms around her soft warmth. Jackie stirred, momentarily roused, but her head sank back down into the pillows a moment later. Vexx turned her gently, so their foreheads were nearly touching, and kissed Jackie's cheek. She tasted salt, saw the way Jackie's eyes were still red and puffy, and her heart crumpled.

"I'm so sorry," she whispered into Jackie's hair. "I never meant to make you feel like this."

Jackie's eyes fluttered open, looking blearily into Vexx's. "Oh," she said. "You're back."

"I'm back," Vexx replied, kissing her other cheek. "Jax, I'm so, so sorry."

"Isokay," Jackie said in a sleepy, slurred jumble. "You're here now."

Vexx bent in, kissing Jackie more insistently. After a breath, Jackie kissed her back—slowly at first, but quickly taking Vexx's face in her hands and deepening it into something more. Vexx felt something warm and wet on her cheek and pulled away to see that Jackie was crying again.

She thought this kiss was the beginning of a goodbye.

Vexx's thumb brushed the tears from Jackie's face and tipped her chin up so their eyes were level. "Hey," she said, "none of that."

Jackie shook her head. "I'm sorry—I'm tired and I'm just in my feelings about you leaving. It's not your fault, it's just really hard."

Vexx's chest expanded with a deep, centering breath. "And if I told you that I wasn't?"

Aqua eyes shot open, staring into Vexx's with sudden alertness. "What?"

"If I told you that I wasn't leaving, that I wanted to stay."

"Are you?" Jackie said, sitting up and looking down at Vexx. "Are you telling me you're staying?"

Vexx looked down, away from Jackie's intense, earnest gaze. She felt Jackie's thumb and forefinger on her chin, turning her face back upward. Her own eyes filled with hot, crimson tears.

"If you're going to say it, look at me," Jackie said, the line between her brows deep.

Vexx's chest felt like it was going to implode. She was hopeful, nervous, terrified. What if Jackie told her she'd changed her mind? That she couldn't put her faith in someone who left her to cry alone in bed? What if she had risked everything and it all failed? Her lower lip trembled as she took shaky breaths, trying to figure out the words. *You only get to do this once,* she thought. *Don't fuck it up.*

"Jackie…" Panic seized her tongue, and she grappled to push it down, to say what she needed to say. "I… I…" Jackie's eyes bore into her, shimmering beneath long, curling lashes, dotted with tears. Vexx felt Jackie's hand find hers, interlacing their fingers together and holding on—like if she let go, she might never get Vexx back. It was a lifeline, a rope tossed from ship to sea, and Vexx clung to it, heaving herself back from the brink of drowning in her own fear. Her voice steadied, the words emerging with none of the trembling uncertainty she had felt mere moments ago.

"Jackie, I love you."

25
jackie

THIS WAS A DREAM, it had to be. Jackie had fallen asleep beneath a heavy blanket of defeat. Vexx had walked out the door when she'd told her to stay. And yet, she was looking down at a face she'd grown to treasure more than anything else. She'd heard the words she'd pleaded with the universe to hear. Her mouth fell open, starting and stopping twice before she was able to reply.

"Vexx… I love you too."

Vexx's shoulders sagged as though the weight of worlds had been lifted from them. A nervous little giggle broke from her lips, and she began to cry, laughing all the while.

Jackie reached down, gathering her up in her arms and pulling Vexx against her chest. They clung to one another, both crying and neither letting go until Jackie's tears had begun to cease falling. She drew back, her fingers weaving through the silken silver of Vexx's hair as she met her eyes. "I wanted to tell you; Hell, I wanted to tell you at Canid. I almost did at the great wheel. God, Vexx, I love you so much it hurts. I couldn't stand the thought that you were going to leave just when I'd found you."

"I just couldn't," Vexx replied. "I couldn't leave, knowing you would be here and I'd have to go back to a life without you in it. I don't want that life. I want to be here, whatever that means."

Jackie kissed her again. It was messy and their tear-slick cheeks stuck together slightly as they both tried to imbue as much love as possible into one, single kiss. It felt like home.

"How?" Jackie murmured against Vexx's lips. "How are you staying here?"

Vexx laughed, her smile feeling like summer sun against Jackie's mouth. "I talked to my father. I told him everything. I thought he would tell me I was making a mistake, that the surface is no place for someone like me." Her voice broke, and Jackie reached down to take Vexx's small, shaking grey hands in her own. "He didn't. In fact, he completely understood. Hells, Jax, he never speaks about my mother—but he talked about her. He told me he knows what it's like to want to take a chance on someone."

"You want to take a chance on me?" Jackie asked. "You're sure?" She looked around. "This place isn't a castle. I'm not royalty or anyone special, I'm just a pastry chef with a little apartment and a lot of love I'd really like to give you."

"That's all I want," Vexx answered, kissing Jackie lightly. "You are special. You have no idea how much. I've never gone after anything in my life, Jackie. I've been letting myself just go along with everything since I was a child. There was never anything I felt strongly enough about to actually *do* something. You're the first thing I've ever fought for."

"Vexxanthe Desmodeus Hekate Marie Morningstar," Jackie said, grinning. "Did I get it all?"

Vexx laughed, nodding.

"Okay, Vexxanthe Desmodeus Hekate Marie Morningstar, I

will fight for you every day. I will work to give you what you deserve. I won't always be perfect, and I'll make mistakes and I'm sure I'll piss you off a few times. But I will choose to keep trying. I'll choose you every single day. If you're willing to give up your entire life to be with me, I will spend my entire life proving to you that it was worth it."

Vexx wiped her eyes with the back of her hand, grinning. "You don't have to prove anything to me. I don't need a palace or a title or recognition. I just want to keep waking up and feeling like this." She leaned in, taking Jackie's face in both her hands. "I just need to know you want to give this a chance too."

Jackie kissed her, arms wrapping around Vexx's waist and holding her tightly. "I have never wanted anything more."

JACKIE PACED. She had never had the best of luck when meeting her partners' parents. She was likable, sure, but *something* always happened to make things awkward. Now, not only was she going to be meeting Vexx's father (officially) for the first time, but he was a literal king, and a demon at that.

"Baby," Vexx said, sighing. "You're making *me* nervous. Can you please just sit down?"

Jackie's eyebrows nearly met in the middle, their furrow so deep, but she complied—taking a seat on the sofa. Her legs were jittery and her hands wouldn't stay still, but she was sitting as requested. "What if he hates me?" she blurted out. "What if he decides he doesn't want you staying on the surface because I'm not good enough?"

Vexx turned her head to face Jackie, staying seated on the floor. "I'm not worried about it. He wants me to be happy, and he is well aware that I need to make my own decisions."

"I wish I had a drink," Jackie mumbled and Vexx slapped her knee.

"Cut it out," she chided. "It's fine, you're fine, and when we are finished we can order takeout."

"Okay, but I want dim sum." Jackie's voice was surly, but a smile tugged at the corner of her mouth. She was nervous because this mattered to her. She wanted Bozuran to like her. *Oh god,* she thought, *what am I supposed to call him? Your majesty? Your highness? Your royal evilness?* She occupied her mind by going through recipes—recalling the weights of each ingredient, the order in which to mix them, the required oven temperature. By the time a sharp and somewhat eggy smell caught her attention, she had mentally baked and assembled three cakes and a chicken pot pie.

It looked as though orange lightning snaked across the kitchen tile. The cupboards rattled and noxious smoke began to curl into the air from the rapidly widening opening. A deep, menacing laugh echoed from what sounded like fathoms below, and every hair on Jackie's body stood on end. Sheer panic gripped her, grabbing at her guts and nearly causing her to puke on the sofa.

"Father!" Vexx snapped. "Stop that. You aren't being funny in the slightest."

As the orange crack stretched from a line to a large, dark emptiness, Jackie heard a surprisingly jovial—though terrifyingly deep—chuckle. "I apologize, Vexxanthe," the voice bellowed. "I do not often get the opportunity to interact with the living."

"You're scaring my girlfriend and she looks like she's going to barf," Vexx scolded.

Despite the all-encompassing horror that felt as though it were cracking her very bones, Jackie felt a warm flush of love. *That's the first time she's ever called me her girlfriend.*

Just as Jackie's fear began to abate, a head the size of a Volkswagen appeared from within the gaping portal, and the ceiling swam as Jackie's mind shut off completely.

"Jax," the voice from the great beyond whispered. "Jax, wake up." Her shoulders were moving—was she laughing? No, strong fingers pressed into her flesh, shaking her.

Jackie's eyes snapped open and she sat up so fast her head spun. "Jesus!" she said. "Did I pass out?"

Bozuran made a noise of disgust in the back of his throat, drawing Jackie's attention back to the unfathomably large head staring directly at her with eyes that glowed like embers smoldering in coal.

"Oh god, I mean—fuck," Jackie sputtered. "Oof. I'll stop trying to talk." Her cheeks were hot enough she thought she could likely cook an egg on them. *Great start Jackie,* she thought.

Vexx laughed from beside her. "It's fine, baby. This—" she gestured to the four-foot curling horns which were set into a face so black Jackie could barely even register it as a face "—is my father, His Eternal Majesty, Bozuran of Infernius, the second kingdom of Hell. You can call him Bozuran." At that, the hulking demon made a hissing sound that nearly made Jackie faint again, but Vexx held up her hand. "No, father," she said, glaring at him. "I do not intend to make my girlfriend address you by your long-ass fancy pants title each time she speaks to you."

Jackie's eyes were so wide she thought the room looked twice as large as usual, even with the gigantic guest taking up the bulk of the kitchen. "I don't want to be rude—I'll call you whatever you want, sir."

Bozuran shook his head slightly and sighed. "There is no offense taken. Vexxanthe is correct in not expecting you to abide by the laws of my kingdom. You are human, and not subject to my rule."

Jackie tried to say "Okay," but what came out was a squeak that sounded like someone stepping on a mouse.

"It is… nice to meet you," Bozuran said. "Vexxanthe speaks highly of you, and I am honored that she saw fit to make an introduction between us."

"Okay, okay, we all are friends now," Vexx said, gesturing flippantly with her red-tipped fingers. "It isn't a pressing matter or anything, but I wanted to let you know that I'm not going to be working for Seth Kazon any longer."

Jackie looked over, surprised. It was the first she'd heard of it.

Vexx went on, "Seth is a wretched person. I can't continue to work for someone who is so exploitative and money hungry. His, well, soon to be former secretary made me a job offer, and I accepted it this morning."

"That's amazing!" Jackie grinned.

"There are lots of details to sort out, so I might be between jobs for a little while, but Seth has paid me an outrageous amount, so I can coast for a few months if need be."

Jackie and Bozuran spoke in near unison, his booming timbre and her soft, human voice saying the same words—"You don't have to worry about money."

Vexx just smiled and shook her head. "Yeah, yeah, yeah. You're both financially stable. I get it. But I will be too, from my own labor for once, and I'm excited."

"As you should be," Jackie said fondly.

"So, on that note—father, were you able to obtain any sort of glamour for me?"

Bozuran gave her a nod that spoke of pride. "Indeed, I was, and I have somewhat of a surprise for you as well, if you are able to accept it."

Vexx's nose scrunched up and Jackie wanted to kiss it, but her attention quickly returned to Bozuran. Wickedly sharp looking claws reached up from the portal, holding a hilariously small bottle balanced between them.

"Here is the glamour. It will work indefinitely, provided

your desire to remain is continuous. There is enough for two doses, should you find yourself in any sort of spat which temporarily causes its effects to waver."

Vexx took the bottle and set it on the side table. "What is the surprise?"

"Are you permitted to have... pets?" Bozuran asked, his voice sounding almost human save for the profound depth of its register.

Vexx's head snapped up, eyes opening so far that Jackie could see the whites of them all around her ruby pupils. "I mean, we are allowed to have two pets under fifty pounds," Jackie supplied. "Mimolette hasn't had much exposure to other animals, but he's pretty chill in his old age."

"Well," Bozuran continued, "I was also able to procure a second glamour—one which is... permanent. It does not work on high demons, but it would work on a lesser demon. Or, a Hellhound."

A sound somewhere between a sob and a giggle burst from Vexx's lips. "Cupcakes! Oh, Jackie, you would love him. He's the sweetest. He's so well trained and well behaved, and he would be so gentle with Mimolette as long as I told him he's not food..."

Jackie shot her a panicked look.

"No, no, I swear, he's a sweetie. He's never seen a cat, but he knows when I tell him something is a friend." She turned to face Bozuran. "What does the glamour do, precisely? He doesn't exactly look like a labrador."

"It is a concealment charm," Bozuran replied. "It is capable of changing his appearance to nearly anything you wish, as well as his size. He will remain the same—he will simply be in a changed body."

Vexx's eyes pleaded, begging Jackie wordlessly to say yes. She couldn't look at that face and deny her this. He was her... puppy. She deserved to have him as much as Jackie deserved to have Mimolette. "Of course you can," she said, squeezing Vexx's knee. "The more the merrier."

And with that, Vexxanthe Desmodeus Hekate Marie Morningstar clapped her hands like a schoolgirl and beamed like the sun.

THE PORTAL CLOSED without much fanfare. Vexx hugged her father's giant head, passing the small, squished-face dog to Jackie, and he sank back from whence he came. Cupcakes looked a lot like a black French Bulldog, but with sharply pointed ears and a long, curled tail. He was kinda cute, Jackie thought, even though he looked like he understood just a little too much for a dog. He trotted around Vexx's feet as she stared down at the space where the portal had been.

"This is it, then," she said, sounding more forlorn than Jackie liked.

"Are you okay?" Jackie asked, watching the way Vexx rolled the vial in her palm.

Vexx sighed, shoulders bowing slightly, tail sinking to nearly drag on the floor. "Yeah, I'm fine." She smiled, but her eyes remained heavy, some emotional weight pulling the skin around them taut.

Jackie stepped closer. "Hey, baby, you can talk to me. This has been a really big fucking day. I'm sure there's a billion things running through your mind. What's going on?"

Vexx's tail ticked. "I want to be here. I want to be with you. I want this life. But I feel… weird about changing who I am to do it. I was excited about the glamour, but now it's kinda sinking in that once I drink it, I won't be 'me' anymore."

Jackie pulled Vexx to her, pressing her cheek against Vexx's chest. "You don't have to."

"But I do," Vexx countered. "I have horns. My skin is not a human color. I have this—" she waved a hand toward her tail "—and I know I've managed to avoid any issues so far, but it can't last forever. It's just… this is all I have from my mom. I don't want to lose it."

Jackie placed her hands gently on Vexx's forearms. "Babe, humans are weird. No, seriously, we are. We do all sorts of body modifications and plastic surgeries and make questionable or alternative fashion choices. If there's any place on earth you can be weird and not have anyone bat an eye, it's here—or maybe Portland." She shook her head. "Regardless, nobody is going to care. If there's one thing I know about humans, it's that if you act like you know what you're doing, people believe you. So just live your life. If people give you a funny look from time to time, who cares? Don't change for the world. I want you just as you are."

Vexx pressed her eyes shut, a minute smile lifting the corners of her deep red lips. "You promise?" she asked.

"I do," Jackie said.

epilogue

"I DO," *Vexx repeated, voice laden with joy and love. A black lace veil lay over her wavy silver hair, clipped just behind her horns, and the inky silk of her gown puddled on the floor around her feet. She bent to kiss Jackie, pulling her close. Jackie's pale grey sleeves were rolled to her elbows, and she wore perfectly tailored black cigarette pants that nipped in at her waist and ended just above her ankle. A cascade of dahlias so red as to be nearly black sat between them, the only color in the room save for Jackie's shock of pink hair. Vexx took Jackie's hand, sliding a simple titanium band onto her finger, a single black stone set flush in its center. Jackie glanced at Vexx's hand where a massive ruby sat between sculpted white gold roses. As cheers erupted from the crowd, Cupcakes pranced around like an errant, preening piece of popcorn, looking dapper in his tiny silk bow tie.*

"Hello… Vexx!" Jackie shouted, and Vexx quickly closed the video.

"Sorry! I'm coming!" She tucked the phone into her back pocket and grabbed a tray of lemon-lavender cupcakes from the stainless-steel rack, hustling to the front of the bakery. Her heels clicked a jaunty staccato against the cheery yellow tile, and when she dropped the tray on the table beside her, Jackie sighed dramatically, hand pressed to her chest.

"And here I thought I was the only person working here!" Jackie said, reaching out to playfully swat Vexx's backside with a pink kitchen towel.

"Hey!" a voice called out from the back. "I resent that!" Everest's head popped out from behind the kitchen wall, grinning.

"Can I open the doors?" Seven asked, pulling and smoothing his baby blue apron down—it barely hit mid-thigh.

Jackie picked up the small cardboard circles, placing the tiny cakes on a shelf in the display case, turning each one just so. The glass case held six shelves, filled with cupcakes, chocolate domes filled with velvety mousse and raspberry coulis, square slices of salted mexican chocolate brownies and miso caramel blondies, ramekins of brown butter crème brûlée, macarons in every color, and ube pandan tartlets topped with crisped coconut rice. Atop the case sat four towering cakes, a lime chiffon cake with passionfruit curd and mango buttercream, a victoria sponge cake with strawberries and thick, luscious pastry cream, a pumpkin cake with salted maple whip and candied pecans, and a twelve layer devil's food cake with little chocolate horns on top. Jackie's hands trembled just a bit, but as she stood back and looked at the case, she nodded. "Let's do this."

Jackie had never believed this possible—opening up her own bakery. Sure, she'd never get Michelin recognition running a quirky retro bakery downtown, but she didn't need critical acclaim to be happy. She had all she needed. Her entire life, she had found joy in baking; from the first time she made a tiny, terrible cake in her hot pink and white Easy-Bake oven, she had wanted to feed people and make them smile. Things had gone well at Canid, and it's not that she had been unhappy—she just didn't want to build someone else's dream anymore. The idea had come to her shortly after she decided to propose to Vexx. The prior year had been the best year of her life—she was finally, unequivocally, happy. Vexx had said yes, they had set a date, and when she requested two weeks off, Martin denied her request. So she did what any rational adult working for the most prestigious restaurant on the West Coast would do... she quit. She and Everest had talked about it before, smoking cigarettes after work and sharing outlandish dreams. This time, however, the dream had come true.

She looked across the space to the line of people waiting outside. They were a motley group, all ages and styles. There were families with children, tattooed punk rockers, a trio of businesswomen in perfectly chic suits. Melissa's smile was wide and genuine as she motioned to her friends to wave hello to Vexx. She waved back, the pink apron over her black a-line shirtdress shifting to the side with the movement. As she adjusted it, Jackie's eyes caught on the logo embroidered on the pocket. It had been Everest's idea, brainstormed at one of their first secret meetings together in her car in the Canid garage—a two-tiered cake with small horns and a heart-tipped tail curling around it. Jackie's heart gave a fluttery little jump as Vexx walked to stand beside her. Jackie wiped her clammy palms on the front of her checkered pants and Vexx reached down to adjust the hat over her neon pink curls. Jackie took a deep, deep breath and squeezed Vexx's fingers as the doors swung open for the very first time.

"Welcome in," she said. "I'm Jackie, this is my wife, Vexxanthe, and this is our bakery—Sweet as Sin."

JACKIE'S DEVIL'S FOOD CAKE

www.booksbynix.com

Cake Ingredients:

- 1 ¼ cups hot water
- ¼ cup milk
- ¾ cup salted butter
- 2 cups white sugar
- 2 teaspoons vanilla bean paste
- 2 cups all-purpose flour
- 1 ½ teaspoons baking soda
- ½ teaspoon baking powder
- ¾ teaspoon salt
- ⅓ cup Dutch cocoa powder
- 3 large eggs

Method

- Preheat oven to 350 degrees and oil two 8" round cake pans
  Melt the butter and combine with the hot water and milk in the bowl of a stand mixer

- Sift together the dry ingredients in a large bowl

- Add the dry ingredients to the liquid mixture and mix with whisk attachment until just combined

- Add the eggs one at a time, mixing until just combined. Be careful not to over-mix

- Scrape down sides of the mixer bowl and mix once more

- Divide into 2 - 8" round cake pans and bake 30 minutes, or until a toothpick comes out clean

- Allow to cool fully

endless thanks to my own Jackie, Meg for this delectable recipe.

JACKIE'S DEVIL'S FOOD CAKE

www.booksbynix.com

Chocolate Buttercream:

- 1 ¼ cups hot water
- ¼ cup milk
- ¾ cup salted butter
- 2 cups white sugar
- 2 teaspoons vanilla bean paste
- 2 cups all-purpose flour
- 1 ½ teaspoons baking soda
- ½ teaspoon baking powder
- ¾ teaspoon salt
- ⅓ cup Dutch cocoa powder
- 3 large eggs

Method

- Preheat oven to 350 degrees and oil two 8" round cake pans
  Melt the butter and combine with the hot water and milk in the bowl of a stand mixer

- Sift together the dry ingredients in a large bowl

- Add the dry ingredients to the liquid mixture and mix with whisk attachment until just combined

- Add the eggs one at a time, mixing until just combined. Be careful not to over-mix

- Scrape down sides of the mixer bowl and mix once more

- Divide into 2 - 8" round cake pans and bake 30 minutes, or until a toothpick comes out clean

- Allow to cool fully

endless thanks to my own Jackie, Meg for this delectable recipe.

JACKIE'S DEVIL'S FOOD CAKE

www.booksbynix.com

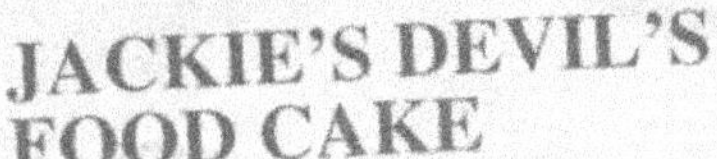

- 2 - 8" round chocolate cakes wrapped in plastic wrap and cooled overnight if possible

- prepared chocolate buttercream (see notes)

- prepared chocolate ganache

- cardboard cake circle or flat plate

Assembly

For a 4 layer cake, slice each 8" cake in half horizontally (or proceed with 2 layers!)

Place a small swipe of buttercream on your cake circle/plate and place the first layer on top

Pipe a thin line of buttercream around edges and then pipe or spread a layer of ganache inside

Repeat with other layers until cake is assembled

Frost cake with remaining buttercream and pipe remaining ganache around the top in design of your choice

Notes:
For a 4 layer cake you will need to multiply the buttercream recipe by 1.5x

If you don't have a piping bag, reinforce the corner of a food storage bag with a bit of tape and slice tip off at an angle, fill and pipe!

Want to make it authentic to the book? double the recipe and cut each cake in thirds, horizontally, giving you 12 layers! Make sure to double the buttercream and ganache as well.

Top with chocolate horns!

endless thanks to my own Jackie, Meg for this delectable recipe

acknowledgments

I know I swore I would never write a RomCom, but here we are. What can I say? I needed an emotional palate cleanser after the chaos of the Song of Gods books!

For my family, you all make me insane, but you also give me some of the greatest gifts life has to offer.

Meg, this book is definitely not about you. Totally, not at all. There are no similarities between you and Jackie. This is all a very strange coincidence. Thank you for the cake, and the pasta, and all that other stuff. Wink wink, nudge nudge. Always, always.

Rachel, you have been an unwavering support throughout this journey, and you're truly the person who makes me feel like a *writer*. Thank you for always hyping me up when I send you bizarre gibberish at 2am. Best bestie for life.

Alyson, I'm so grateful to always have you in my corner. I hope you love this one, it's a lot more sunshine.

Amber, how do I thank thee…you've made so many things possible for me. Having you at my back is a constant I don't know how I could live without. Even when you go full turtle, you're still my favorite. Even with all the ropes of seed.

Sarah, your help with this project has been invaluable. I'm so glad you took a chance on me and my lil' book. If this project brought me anything, it's a new friendship I'm immensely grateful for.

Pris, our hours of VMs say what the words I'm typing here never could, haha! Thank you so much for everything.

Olga, for continuing to encourage me to write, and being such a strong spokesperson and support. I am grateful every day to be your daughter, and I am so honored that you still believe in me.

For all my beta readers, tiktok and IG friends who continue to make me feel like a real author, I'm so grateful for you all. I can't list all of you, but IYKYK. Some of you are what keeps me going when I feel like I can't possibly write another word.

about the author

Heather Nix is the author of the Song of Gods series and the Magic and Mishaps books. Born and raised in sunny San Diego, CA she longs to return to the forest. She is the mother of two human and three cat children, and enjoys tattoos, tabletop RPGs, and creating feminist art in her limited spare time. Her favorite hobby is drinking overpriced cocktails and reading smut at her favorite nauti bar (with good company.) Heather is passionate about writing queer fantasy, and strives to create nuanced characters who resonate with underserved communities.